UNDER THE RADAR

The Spy Drone Adventure

BY

BLAINE C. READLER

DNA Press™

UNDER THE RADAR, THE SPY DRONE ADVENTURE
©2006 by Blaine C. Readler
©2006 by DNA Press, LLC. All rights reserved.

ISBN 1-933255-18-8

Printed in the United States of America on acid-free paper

Library of Congress Cataloging-in-Publication Data

Readler, Blaine C. Under the radar : the spy drone adventure / Blaine C. Readler.
   p. cm.
Summary: When Jared unwittingly steals a top-secret spy drone developed by his father's engineering department, he and his friend Russell find themself matching wits with the terrorist who was trying to steal the drone himself.
   ISBN 1-933255-18-8 (alk. paper)
   [1. Robots—Fiction. 2. Spies—Fiction. 3. Terrorists—Fiction. 4. Fathers and sons—Fiction. 5. Stepfamilies—Fiction. 6. Adventure and adventurers—Fiction. 7. Virginia—Fiction.] I. Title.
   PZ7.B23532Und 2006
   [Fic]—dc22
          2 0 0 5 0 2 6 6 3 9

DNA Press, LLC
P.O. BOX 572
Eagleville, PA 19408, USA
www.dnapress.com
editors@dnapress.com

Publisher: DNA Press, LLC
Executive Editor: Alexander Kuklin
Art Direction: Alex Nartea (www.studionvision.com)
Cover Art: Mark Stefanowicz (www.markstef.com)

To my parents, Clifford and Gladys,
for letting us goof off,
and to loml, my first reader and my only love.

A very special thanks to Rick Sexty for
his invaluable editing and advice.

Thursday afternoon, Christmas Eve

T he lab was dark, but the sounds of laughter and occasional loud shouts could be heard down the hall. Suddenly the door burst open, and banks of overhead fluorescent lights glared forth as four reveling engineers pushed in. They were all men between the ages of twenty-five and thirty. They were also all drunk. One, obviously a manager and leader of the small raiding party, crossed over to a bench at the back, carrying his wine glass high, as in tribute. He reached the bench where a small Plexiglas display box lay. A felt pad on top cradled something tiny. He turned and held up his glass for a toast.

"To our tiny friend who's been both our slave-master and our reward!"

The other three engineers raised their glasses as well and shouted drunken responses. The manager lifted his glass again. "He almost didn't make it for the Big Brass, but with just a wee little bit of help from us." Here the other engineers shouted some obscenities. "The little guy pulled through and accepted his... shall we say Endless Motivation!" The others spun in circles holding their glasses ever skyward.

"Now," continued the manager, "let us all depart, slowly and carefully, to our humble homes, secure in the thought that once again we've pulled Stelltech's metaphorical butt from the fire." He paused a moment, then added, "And deem ourselves lucky that she is so kind to continue to let us work here." This was

1

greeted with an outburst of even more enthusiastic obscenities. The manager swung on his heels and led the way to the door.

But one of the younger engineers hung back a moment, studying the display blearily. A sign sat propped on the bench shelf above the plastic box. It read simply, *TRAS*, and under it hung a small banner with an explanation of the acronym: *Tele-Robotic Actuated Servo*. After a few moments of swaying back and forth, he came to a decision and put his glass down to rummage through a bench drawer. He pushed the contents this way and that and finally pulled out a black felt marker. He ceremoniously ripped away the hanging banner and stuffed it into a trash can nearby, then took the sign and, laying it on the bench next to the display, carefully, as carefully as his drunken hand would permit, wrote something. He then placed it again in its prominent place and staggered backward to admire his achievement. He'd added the letter *H* so that the sign now read *TRASH*. When he observed his handiwork he burst out laughing. He laughed so hard he nearly fell over. Then, grabbing his glass, he made for the lab door, calling after his co-workers.

Some minutes after his exit, the automatic sensors detected no more human presence and shut off the lab's lights. The tiny display object sat unmoving in the near-darkness, oblivious to its own ignoble label.

CHAPTER ONE

Saturday afternoon, the day after Christmas

J ared rode in the passenger seat of his father's Volvo, watching the bare trees and winter-green grass of Maryland slide by. His father, Dr. Ted Martin, was going to drive him back to Northern Virginia where Jared lived with his mother and stepfather, Jack Brassard. But first his father needed to stop at the company where he directed engineering development.

Jared remembered how he had anticipated this visit with his dad. During his two weeks with his mom and stepfather he looked forward to the next weekend visit with his dad and escape from the rigors of school and homework. But then, by the end of the first day at his dad's small apartment in Baltimore, he was ready to return to his Virginia friends and the large suburban house where his bedroom waited with his computer, books, and sports gear. His dad tried to make the visits interesting with plans of outings to the Inner Harbor, or afternoon movie matinees. Inevitably, though, even though it was a weekend, his dad would get involved in his work, and then it seemed that his role towards Jared became less friend and more disciplinary parent. This had been even more the case the last month or two as some secret company project neared completion. That very afternoon his dad had scolded him for watching cartoons when he was supposed to be working on a school project. He was still sulking over it, and he and his dad hadn't talked since leaving the Baltimore apartment.

They arrived at his father's company and his dad pulled into the parking lot. The five-story office building seemed out of place among the pastures and small stands of forest. A small sign reading *Stelltech, Inc.*—easily missed until you actually pulled into the parking lot—was the sole indicator. Jared knew that his father's company developed military products and that they kept a low profile, but a sign that barely murmured its presence struck him as an odd gesture, as though determined spies would drive past without seeing it and thus take their quest elsewhere.

The parking lot was almost empty, and they were able to take a spot immediately in front of the main entrance. After he turned off the engine and patted his pocket to make sure he had his security ID card, his dad asked, "Do you want to stay here and listen to the radio?" he asked. "I shouldn't be more than maybe a half-hour." His dad's tone seemed reconciling, if not actually apologetic.

Jared considered this for a moment, since even south of Baltimore the car picked up his favorite Washington DC stations. His dad must have taken his hesitation as a snub for his tone turned brusque as he said, "Suit yourself," and walked off.

Jared had been ready to let go of their little tiff, but his dad's annoyed reaction yanked back the bitter feelings. Their arguments often seemed to go this way, each of them sensitive to any hint of belligerence from the other. What may have started as a trivial disagreement would spiral away into a seemingly endless series of defensive jabs. These drawn-out quarrels began two years ago after his dad moved out. A vague sense of abandonment haunted Jared's world, but, despite the counseling his mom had arranged at school, he resisted facing it. Admitting a feeling of abandonment was, in a sense, accepting the possibility that it might be true.

He watched his dad's back recede for a moment, then threw open the car door and ran after him. It wasn't that he wanted to be with his dad, in fact, he would rather have listened to the radio, he simply wasn't about to give in. His dad had relegated him to the car, therefore he had to go along.

He caught up at the main doors. His dad merely raised his eyebrows and held the door open for him. As they entered the

Stegorski said, "I'm not happy about it either, Ted. But I have no choice. The J-SAD monitors aren't budging. They're either going to see their demonstration next Thursday, or my boss will be getting calls from some senators."

Hearing this kind of talk about senators getting involved used to make him proud of his father. Lately, though, it just seemed to highlight the difference between his dad's world and his own—a household where rival high school football scores were often the main dinner topic. He still couldn't understand how his mom could be attracted to a high school football coach. Although Jack's enthusiasm for sports was boundless, he at least seemed to understand that, in the end, it was just a game. He just wished that his stepfather would stop trying to get him to join the football team.

"So, what happens if there's a major glitch during the demonstration?" his dad said. "How many calls will your boss get from the senators then?"

"I have to take that chance."

Jared stepped into the doorway and knocked on the door. His father sat with his back to him at a conference table. Stegorski, lean and tall, with short-cropped, white hair, was standing and looked at him with concerned surprise. "Who the hell are you?"

His father spun around. "Jared! Damn it, I told you to wait in my office!"

He felt very small and stupid. He was a teenager, but he might as well have been six. "You said you'd be thirty minutes—I was just wondering where you were," he mumbled. He listened to himself say this, and, he thought, he did indeed sound like a six year-old.

Both men appeared angry. "You left your son unattended in a secure area?" Stegorski said to his father.

His dad locked eyes with him. They spoke of an anger that only a family member can communicate: a failing of confidence. "He knows the rules." Then to Jared he said, "I'll be a few minutes yet," and dismissed him with a curt nod.

He walked back the way he'd come. He was so mad he thought he could scream. He knew the incident was his own doing, but his father was at the other end of the tugged rope, and it was easier to blame him.

As he passed the lab on the way back to his dad's office, he wondered if any of the engineers were in there working. They always seemed happy to talk to him. He decided to see. He half expected the door to be locked and was surprised when it swung open. The large room was dark, but the overhead fluorescent banks came to life when he opened the door. He knew that nobody was in here, but it appeared so inviting now, all lit up, that he walked in, letting the door swing shut behind him.

He loved coming in here. In fact, he'd have been content to spend the time here rather than the other activities his dad tried to dream up to keep him occupied. He hardly understood anything that went on, but the few times his dad brought him in, he explained as much as he was allowed—sometimes, perhaps, more than he was allowed. On a workday it was alive with engineers battling away at engineers' problems. He knew that his father's department developed servo-bots, essentially remote controlled robots. The engineers called them drones. Most were developed for the military and were used for such things as bomb removal and nuclear material handling. An operator manipulated the drone from a distance, viewing the work via one or more cameras mounted on it. Joysticks and switches controlled the early versions, but now they used a method known as waldo. The operator placed sensor devices on his arms, hands, and fingers, and by moving these he could cause a similar movement of the remote robot. The idea, and the name, of waldoes came from a science fiction story written in 1940 by Robert Heinlein. His dad had given him the beat-up copy for his birthday the previous year. He'd said that he'd read it as a teenager himself. The visual feed from the remote camera on the drone was displayed on a visor worn over the operator's head. Once rigged, the robot drone became a virtual extension of the operator.

Although most development was for the military, his dad's company had tried one version for the police. This one was about as big as a cat. In fact, it was called *The Cat,* and it could scope out dangerous situations: hostage and poisonous gas incidents, for example. Unfortunately, although police departments were interested, only those of the largest cities—LA and Chicago, in fact—could afford one, so the company had built only a few. As a birthday present, his father had given him an early prototype version that remained his prized possession. He knew from phone calls he'd overheard that they'd been working on a miniaturized version of a drone for some time.

He strolled around the lab, looking over the variety of test instruments he didn't understand, but appreciating the cool wiggles and colors of the displays. Most of the specimens under test were bare circuit boards, and he wandered along looking for some semblance of an actual drone he could recognize. He was approaching the end of his tour when he came across a nearly empty bench way at the back of the lab. A large binocular microscope sat at one end. This was equipped with a video monitor and an apparatus that he knew was a micro-manipulator, a device that allowed engineers to work at a microscopic scale, as if their fingers where shrunk a thousand times. Sitting in the center of the bench, all alone, was a clear plastic box with a cloth pad on top.

Curious, he walked over. In the middle of the cloth pad sat what looked like a large fly. He leaned over and peered closely at it. His heart skipped a beat; it looked indeed like an ever-so-tiny robot! He could make out tiny jointed legs and miniature lenses that might be part of the camera. He could hardly believe it. He wanted very badly to pick it up, but knew from long experience that this was totally taboo.

Then, for the first time, he noticed the sign hanging above it: *TRASH*. Could it be? He often saw cardboard boxes, left for the cleaning crew to remove, with just such a note attached. Had this little guy been tagged for disposal? He shook his head, as though correcting himself. He knew that prototypes were far too expensive to discard, even if they had problems. On the other hand, maybe it was an early prototype that no longer worked at all.

He'd never stolen anything, at least not since he took his cousin's miniature world globe in second grade, and then felt so bad that he'd confessed to his mom. But suddenly his urge to spite his dad seemed to overwhelm him. He reached out and carefully folded the cloth around the tiny mechanism, then slipped it into his jeans pocket. With a furtive glance around, he headed for the door. Guilt followed him through the lab, whispering its warning, but he was resolved. His dad deserved to be punished.

He opened the lab door, stepped into the hall, and ran into Tony's stomach. He gave a little yell of surprise and stepped back. His heart was racing. Did Tony know that he'd stolen the drone?

Tony stood looking at him curiously. "You okay?" he asked.

Jared puts his hands in his back pants pockets. "Jeez! I guess you got me back. You scared the daylights out of me."

"Sorry," Tony said, and smiled. "You doing some debug for us?" he asked, nodding at the lab door.

He shrugged. "I was just poking around. I thought there might be some guys working."

He stood burning with anticipation while Tony studied him a moment. "You probably don't want your dad to catch you in there alone."

"Right," Jared said. "I'd better get back to his office."

Tony nodded. "They'll be finished any minute."

Jared walked down the hall. He turned and saw Tony watching him thoughtfully.

****

He was back sitting in his father's office reading the Dilbert book again when his dad finally returned with Mr. Stegorski.

"Well," his father said to Stegorski, "we'll re-install the battery pack Monday and you can take the power source with you when you leave."

Stegorski looked at Jared and scowled. "I wish you'd be more discrete, Dr. Martin."

His dad put his hand on Jared's shoulder. "I doubt that my son constitutes a security threat."

Stegorski scowled some more and shook his head. "You know the rules—and they don't include discussions around people not involved in the work, even if they are family."

His father didn't respond to this, but simply wished Stegorski a good day and walked away towards the elevator. Jared followed, feeling the cloth bundle in his pocket. He was glad they were putting distance between them and Stegorski. He heard Tony talking down the hall somewhere ahead of them. He thought he heard his name. He thought he heard Tony say, "Jared." But Tony must have heard them coming, for he was then silent. As he and his father walked past one of the offices, he saw Tony sitting at a desk holding a phone receiver to his ear. Tony watched them as they walked by. He didn't hear Tony talk again before they were well out of earshot at the elevator.

After the elevator door closed, Jared said, "Stegorski seems like a real sour-puss."

"He's just doing his job," his father replied, then added, "He does overdo it, though."

As they walked through the inner door and back out to the large reception area, a sensor sounded with a persistent beep. Jared's heart jumped to his throat. The guard looked up in alarm, but when he saw who it was, he waved. "Dr. Martin," he said, "you're always testing the sensors with the odds and ends you carry around."

His dad looked puzzled. "Hmm, it didn't go off on the way in, and I didn't pick anything up while inside."

"Well, we know the routine," the guard said, smiling.

His father emptied his pants pockets onto the counter. There was just his keys and coins. Unlike the metal detectors at airports, Jared knew that these security sensors were looking for a substance that could be painted on objects. In this way, almost anything that wasn't supposed to leave the building could be tagged.

He took a deep breath. At the very least, his dad would arrange to have him grounded for a month. He felt a wave of panic as he imagined the jail time he'd be doing. Maybe it would be better to confess now.

"Oh wait," his dad said, and reached inside his jacket. He pulled out a piece of paper folded into quarters. He handed it to the guard who opened it up and looked at it, then flipped it over and looked at the other side.

"You wrote your shopping list on security paper?"

His father shrugged. "I didn't have a notepad; I was in the meeting with Stegorski."

The guard handed back the piece of paper, shaking his head in mock disappointment. "What are we going to do with you, Dr. Martin?"

"Get me fired—please. Then I won't have to come to work the day after Christmas."

"Sorry, no such luck. See you Monday."

"So long, Ward. Have a nice weekend."

Few words were spoken between Jared and his father on the hour ride to Virginia. This was how things usually went: his dad would fall deep into thought while Jared listened to hip-hop. This was fine with him today. He couldn't wait to get home to carefully unwrap his secret treasure in the privacy of his bedroom. He felt that conversation now would soothe the angry feelings towards his dad, and that the tiny lump in his pocket would become a huge burden of guilt.

The bare trees and winter-green grass rolled by, and Jared tapped his foot to the music, imagining the adventures he'd have with the little friend he'd saved from the trash. The friend nobody wanted anymore.

CHAPTER TWO

Saturday evening

S ara sat at her desk, focused on the paperwork in the Baltimore office of the FBI. She thought she was the only person still on her floor, and jumped in surprise when Brent knocked on her cubicle entrance.

He laughed. "Sorry. I should have telephoned from across the room to tell you I was walking over." Brent was about her age and also fairly new with the agency. They were often the last ones to leave at night.

She grinned and put down her pen. "That's quite all right. This entitles me to a stalking license."

He raised his eyebrows in question.

"You know," she said, "I get to drive up behind you when you're walking to your car some night and blast the horn."

"You'll have to be careful; my cat-like reflexes might cause me to spin around and shoot."

"You're right. I'll have to first run you over, then blow the horn."

Sara welcomed these breaks from the serious rigors of agency work. As the new kid on the block, she didn't have the rapport to joke around with the older, more seasoned agents. Besides, she had the impression that they were handling her with kid gloves.

"Hey," he said. "I heard you've been assigned to Stinky."

"Not really. I'm just the contact. The informant is his sister-in-law. They figured she'd be more comfortable talking with another woman her own age." She smirked. "I knew they'd eventually find a use for a woman agent."

Stinky was the code name for a terrorist suspect named Ahmed they were tracking. In the grand old days when J. Edgar Hoover headed the agency, cases had impressive code names like COINTELPRO, the controversial program to thwart what was seen as anti-American activities in the sixties and early seventies. Things had lightened considerably in the decades since. A few years before, an informant with a large nose and a larger habit of lying was nicknamed Pinocchio.

"At least it's a real case," Brent said. "I'd give anything to get out in the field. I'm beginning to think my duties will never extend beyond the edges of my desk. If I didn't get up to get coffee now and then, I'd probably grow roots."

"I know how you feel. It's new-guy dues. All the senior agents were in our place once, though."

Brent stood silently in her cube entrance with his hands in his pockets. She could guess what he was thinking; it was fine for her to talk about new-guy dues, but she had a leg up. Her uncle, the senator, had maneuvered her into the agency, and she was clearly marked for the fast track. At least, this is what her colleagues probably thought. It was true that Uncle Jake had pulled some strings to get her in, but she was determined to make her own path now.

"Do you want to grab some dinner?" he finally asked.

She'd guessed he'd eventually get around to this. "No thanks, Brent. I'm pooped. I'm going home to fall asleep in a hot bath. Maybe another time."

She'd been telling him maybe another time for weeks. She liked Brent, she just didn't want to complicate things at the office. She really didn't want to screw things up. She should probably tell him the truth before he decided that she didn't care for him.

Her phone rang, and she picked it up. "Hello, Sara Binsby, FBI," she said.

"*Sara?*" a female voice said. "*This is Barb.*"

She pointed at the handset and silently mouthed, "Stinky," to Brent.

Sara automatically pulled a writing pad towards her, and Brent walked away.

"Hello Barbara, what's up?" Sara said.

"*Is it okay to talk?*"

"Sure. There's nobody else here."

"*They're not recording this?*"

"No. I'd have to get your permission for that."

There was a moment of silence on the line, then the woman said, "*I think Ahmed's up to something.*"

"Like what?"

"*I'm not sure. But they had a big argument this afternoon, and Alihan won't tell me what it was about. He told me I wouldn't want to know.*"

Alihan was her husband, and Ahmed's brother. "I see. You don't have any idea what it was about?"

"*They were in the next room shouting in their own language. The only words I could make out were two names—Jared and Martin.*"

"Hmm. Does Alihan normally keep things from you?"

"*That's why I'm worried. He* never *keeps secrets.*"

"That you know of."

"*Of course, but I trust him.*"

"He may be trying to protect you, Barbara."

"*Exactly. That's why I called.*"

"Right." Sara tapped her finger on the pad. "Anything else?"

"*No, that's it....*" There was a pause, then Barbara said, "*Sara...*"

"Yes?"

"*Is Alihan in trouble?*"

"I can't know that. But we're going to try to keep him *out* of trouble if we can."

The woman sighed. "*I just hope I'm doing the right thing.*"

"Of course you are. The best thing we can do for Alihan is to stop Ahmed before he hurts anybody."

"*I know. Thanks, Sara.*"

"Okay. You have my cell number—call if you hear anything else. And Barbara, don't take any chances. I mean *any* chances, understand?"

"*I understand. And thanks again, Sara.*"

"The thanks is for you. I'm just doing my job."

"*Goodbye.*"

"Good night. Sleep well."

Sara sat for a few minutes drumming her fingers on the desk after hanging up. She then wrote, "Jared" and "Martin" on her pad. She leaned over, pulled a folder from a vertical rack near the back of her desk, ripped off the top sheet of the pad and slipped it inside with the other papers. She stuffed the whole thing into her bag and stood up to go. Before leaving her cube she looked down at the phone and said to herself, "What are you up to Stinky?"

CHAPTER THREE
Sunday afternoon

J ared kicked his bedroom door in frustration. Seconds later Jack had popped his head in to see what was the problem. Fortunately, thanks to the general mess of Jared's room, his stepfather didn't notice the fly-sized robot sitting on its felt pad on his desk. "Tough math homework problem," Jared mumbled. Twice he had to decline Jack's offer for help, the second time in irritation.

He was beginning to believe that the tiny robot he'd "saved" really was ready for the trash. No matter what he tried, he couldn't get it to respond. His only means was the waldo controls he'd gotten from his father along with the ill-fated servo Cat prototype. He'd placed the drone on his desk and donned the arm and glove controls. He'd wiggled his fingers and swung his arms, but the little guy just sat there, dead. He had vaguely hoped that it would sense the servo control transmissions and automatically activate itself. He had tried to find a power switch under a magnifying glass, but all he could see was a cube-shaped body with four attached jointed legs facing downward, two appendages in front that looked like arms with tiny claws, and two lenses, presumably for a camera. Attached to the back of the body was another featureless box. This looked different from the rest of the drone. It appeared to be made of metal, while the rest of the robot had a texture more like clay, or even that of a living insect. But he'd found nothing that looked remotely like a power switch. He'd hauled out the Cat and, after replacing the six dead C-batteries, had been able to control it just fine. In this way he convinced himself that the waldo controls themselves were working.

So, after hours of fruitless effort he decided to call for help. He picked up the phone to dial his friend, Russell. Actually, Russ was more like an ex-friend. He was a grade older than Jared and, although near the top of his class, had few friends. His mousy appearance alone was a sure strike against him, particularly in a school like theirs where sports played such a prominent role. It was his arrogance, though, that practically guaranteed his outcast status. At times he could be downright rude, apparently oblivious to the fact that he was forcing his own fate.

Although far from a star in any school sports himself, Jared fit in well. He played enough sports to join the school's main social stream, but was not so jock-minded to distance the academics. He was drawn to Russ's caustic wit. If he ignored the insults and focused on the substance of Russ's barbs, he found the guy genuinely funny. Russ's intelligence and skewed perspectives ensured a break from boredom. "Stimulation," Russ would say. "Any other characteristic is just baggage."

He sensed that Russ's suicidal social behavior was actually self-preservation. Once you were targeted for ridicule, struggle for acceptance was a slippery slope. The more you fought it, the larger a target area you presented. Russ's philosophy was that it was better to be the unpopular wise guy than the tortured whipping post.

A month before, Russ had managed to alienate even him. It was the homecoming football game, and Jared was sitting with a group of kids in his class. Three of them were on the basketball team. Two were black kids. He'd seen Russ and had called to him to join them. Russ had walked over, glanced around the group, then said, "You hanging out with the Globe Trotters now?"

Although his remark was not outright racist in itself—after all, it might be considered a compliment to be compared to the masters of basketball showmanship—coming from Russ, it could only be expected to raise some hackles. And it did. All three of his basketball friends had jumped to their feet, and it took his best diplomacy to save Russ from the proverbial "slam dunk". He'd have thought that Russ would've been thankful that he'd saved his skin, but that wasn't his way. Russ had merely told him that when he was "Ready to give up his Neanderthal friends, he'd be waiting farther down the bleachers." He'd been so mad at Russ, he'd not only snubbed him during the game, he also hadn't called him that night, even though they were supposed to hook up at the homecoming dance. Russ hadn't come to the dance, and he hadn't talked to him since.

He hesitated now before dialing Russ's number. By rights, Russ was equally at fault for letting their rift go on, but he knew that Russ would never bow for forgiveness. His walls were far too thick and high for such luxuries. Jared understood that as far as Russ was concerned, this was his cross to bear. It wasn't fair, and he resented that he was going to have to grovel, but he desperately wanted to awaken the tiny drone. He stabbed the buttons on the phone viciously.

"*Hello,*" Russ said.

"Russ, this is Jared."

There was a moment of silence, then Russ said, "*Well, well, a ghost from the past. Did you accidentally dial the wrong number?*"

He gritted his teeth. "Russ, I'm sorry for not calling sooner..., I was busy."

"*Busy? A young teenager too busy to call his friend? Have you decided to get an early start on your adult career?*"

Jared put his hand to his face. He wasn't sure he was going to be able to do this. "Look, I said I'm sorry, okay? Can you just let it go?"

"*Let it go? We'll just carry on and pretend that you haven't been snubbing me all semester.*"

"It wasn't all semester, it was only—"

"*Never mind. What's up?*"

Russ had a knack for knowing just when he'd pushed you to

within an inch of your limit. Jared took a deep breath. "I need to show you something."

"*Like what?*"

"I can't tell you on the phone. You need to come here."

"*Ooh, big secrets! What if it's something dumb?*"

Jared shook his head. He couldn't believe Russ sometimes. "Look, come on over. If you don't agree it was worth it..., I'll give you one of my Beastie Boys CDs."

"*Two.*"

"*Two* CDs? Are you nuts? No way!"

"*Okay. Nice talking to you.*"

"Okay, okay!" Jared knew Russ wasn't bluffing. "Two."

****

"They were throwing it away?" Russ said. His tone was one of disbelief. He'd arrived ten minutes before and had been immediately enthralled by the drone. He hadn't even mentioned the Beastie Boys CDs.

"Yeah," Jared replied. "There was a sign that said it was trash."

Russ took another look at the drone through the magnifying glass. "This doesn't look like trash to me. It looks like a micro-bot."

Jared peered over his shoulder. "You know about these?"

Russ straighten up and handed the magnifying glass back to him. "I read about them in Scientific American – they're suppose to use them to inspect difficult places, like inside nuclear reactor cores. They can crawl through small openings so they don't let the radiation out. Of course, after they're done, they'd be useless since they'd be radioactive themselves."

Jared nodded. He was used to Russ knowing things like this. "I think my dad's building them for the military."

"As spies."

He shrugged. "I guess."

Russ grinned. "And they were just going to throw this away ... in the trash."

"Yeah," Jared said. He felt defensive.

"Let me get this straight, Martin." Russ always called him by his last name. "They were going to let the cleaning lady carry this out and toss it in the dumpster."

"I *guess* so. I don't know! Look, there was a sign!"

"Yeah, yeah. Keep your pants on, youngster. But for the record, I disavow any involvement in its theft."

"Christ! I'm telling you I didn't steal it!"

"No cursing. You're hurting my religious sensitivities."

"Give me a break. You're about as religious as Birgy." Birgy was the family dog.

"My religious beliefs are not yours to question. You called it a drone."

"That's because that's what my dad's company makes. They're all called drones. Even my Cat."

"So, you can't get the little bugger to wake up?"

"No. I don't think the power's on."

"Or maybe the batteries are dead."

He sighed. That was a disappointing thought. He had an idea. "Hold on," he said, and went off to root through his closet. After rearranging several piles he finally found the box with the small microscope he'd received as a birthday present. He brought it to the desk, set it up, and carefully placed the drone on the specimen platform. Russ edged in and peered into the eyepiece. Jared stepped back and took a deep breath. He'd almost forgotten how much patience it took to work with Russ.

"Microscopes are meant for looking at flat objects. I can't get enough of it in focus to really see anything," Russ said without looking up from the microscope.

Jared found an objective lens with less magnification from the box. "Here, try this," he said, tapping it against Russ's shoulder.

After inserting the new lens, Russ peered for several minutes, focusing up and then down repeatedly, scanning the drone from top to bottom. "This is so wild!" he exclaimed, not taking his eye from the microscope. "It doesn't look like different pieces assembled together. It doesn't even look like it's made of metal, except for what must be the battery pack on the back."

"Yeah," Jared agreed, "it's kind of scary, huh?"

Russ finally pulled away from the microscope. "I'll bet this is MEMS."

"What's that?"

"You really don't read anything do you?" He didn't wait for an answer. "It's a way of making really small machines. They can make microscopic motors and gears."

He nodded. He knew from experience that it was best to let Russ roll once he got started.

"They make pressure sensors and compasses and build them right onto the same piece of silicon as the electronic circuits." Russ peered again into the microscope. "But I've never heard of anything so complicated and big as this."

Jared looked at him in surprise. "Big?"

Russ waved his hand. "Sure! This micro-bot seems small to us, but it's gigantic compared to integrated circuits. This thing is *way* ahead of anything else that I've read about."

Russ looked up from the microscope and gave him a hard stare. "Does *anybody* know about this?" he finally asked.

"No," Jared replied, "my mom wouldn't understand. And, the only thing Jack is interested in is sports. He'd probably take it away, especially if he knew it had anything to do with my dad."

Russ usually couldn't be bothered with your personal affairs, but sometimes he liked to play the wise psychologist. "You know, Jack is your dad too."

"He is not!" Jared said, surprised at his own anger. "He's my mom's husband, but that doesn't make him my dad."

"Hmm, that's for you to decide of course, but I think it's only natural that he's trying to get you interested in football—he just wants to share his interests with you."

"Well, I think football is dumb."

Russ sat looking at him over the tips of his fingers leaning together like a teepee. "That's curious. You love basketball, and you have friends that are on the football team. I'd offer that you only despise football *because* that's your stepfather's job."

He shook his head in annoyance. "Look, are we going to try to get the drone working, or what?"

Russ nodded his head knowingly. "Okay, mister repression." Russ slapped his knees. "So, there's no power button… at least that we can find."

He was glad to be off that uncomfortable subject. "I've tried everything except twisting the battery-pack box on the back. I was thinking that might be the switch."

Russ looked again into the microscope. "Yeah, that box on the back does look like it's a separate piece. But, let's see what else we can think of before trying that. It might be the *last* thing we try if it's not meant to be twisted."

He showed Russ how he'd been manipulating the waldo controls in an attempt to activate the drone.

"We don't even know if they use the same radio frequency," Russ observed.

He nodded in glum agreement.

"Have you tried the visor?" Russ asked.

He shrugged and shook his head. "It's worth a try," he said, and went off again to rummage through the closet. The visor had come with the Cat, but he hadn't used it since the Cat's camera had stopped working shortly after he got it. He found the visor and placed it over his head. He walked out wearing it, groping the wall a bit since he could only see straight down. It looked like a flight helmet, except that the visor didn't flip up, but was permanently positioned over the eyes. It covered the ears as well with built-in earphones.

"Well, are you getting anything?" Russ asked impatiently.

"No, nothing."

"How do you know the visor batteries are any good?"

Jared paused a moment. "They're okay – there's an LED power indicator. It automatically turns on when you put the visor over your head."

Russ was silent for a moment. "Was it designed especially for the Cat?"

"I don't think so. I've seen them use the same one on other projects."

"Then maybe it's programmable somehow. How about it?"

He shrugged his shoulders, assuming that Russ was watching him. "I dunno. I never used it after the Cat's camera broke."

He heard Russ walk over to examine the helmet.

"What's this? It looks like a cover at the back."

He felt him prying at it. "Hey! What are you doing?" he exclaimed.

"Hold your horses, I'm not going to break anything..., I think."

And with that, he heard the cover pop open.

"Bingo!" Russ said. "There's two rows of small push-buttons.

He took off the visor and turned it over. The first button was marked *PGM*, while the others were simply numbered *1* through *8*.

"P-G-M means 'program,' I'll bet," offered Russ. "Here, you put it on and I'll push the buttons."

Jared hesitated. "Ah, come on," implored Russ, "it's no good to you anyway."

He looked at Russ skeptically but put the visor back on.

"Okay," Russ said, "I'm going to push the program button."

"All right!" Jared exclaimed. He saw a display screen appear out of the darkness. "I see a menu."

The menu was similar to that of a VCR:

1. mode

2. config

3. test

4.

5.

6.

7.

8. back

He described this to Russ.

"What about four through seven?" Russ asked.

"Nothing. Just one, two, three, and eight."

"Okay", Russ said, "then two must be 'configure.' Here goes."

A new menu appeared:

1. brightness

2. contrast

3. volume

4. microphone

5. alt power

6. radio link

7. ext prog load

8. back

They decided that the fifth entry was alternative power, while the seventh was for loading new software.

Russ pushed the sixth button—radio link—and Jared saw:

1. parameters

2. bands

3.

4.

5.

6.

7.

8. back

"I say we try the bands first," Russ said. "Here goes."
The next menu appeared:

1. FM1

2. FM2 <=

3. SSB

4. 2.4G

7. enter

8. back

They decided that this must be the selection of radio bands.
"Anything else there?" Russ asked.
Jared paused, looking a moment. "Oh, wait, I almost missed

it, FM2 has an arrow next to it. Maybe this is the band we're using now?"

"Yeah, I'd say so. Okay, I'm going to try the first band. Here goes."

"The arrow went away," Jared reported, "and now FM1 has an asterisk next to it."

Russ didn't say anything for a few moments. "Okay, I think that I have to push the 'enter' button to actually activate it. Here goes."

"Uh, the asterisk turned into an arrow and a green LED in the upper right went out."

"Probably means it lost its link—not getting any reception. Okay, I'll try..., three was the next one, right?"

"Yeah. That's SSB."

Russ pushed the third button, then the seventh—'enter'.

"That green LED came back on," Jared said. "Maybe that's it?"

"We'll see. So..., I guess we now go back?"

"That was eight."

"Eight it is."

They were now back to the previous menu, the radio link choices. Russ pushed the 'back' button twice more, and the menu sequenced back through the configuration selection and the original beginning menu.

"Well," Russ said thoughtfully. "I guess the only move is another 'back'. Here goes nothing."

Jared fell back with a cry. "Holy shit!" he exclaimed. "I've got a picture!"

He turned his head back and forth, and realized that this didn't change his view.

"This is bizarre! I'm looking at..." He took off the visor and glanced around the room. "... at the wall over there," he said, pointing.

Russ was smiling. "Well, that's what I'd expect, since that's the direction the drone is pointing."

He simply stared wide-eyed at Russ, then at the drone still sitting under the microscope. The sound of Jack calling him from somewhere in the house yanked him out of his shocked state.

"Yikes!" He remembered that they were going to Jack's mom's for dinner. "We've got to get this stuff away."

They shoved the visor and waldo controls under his bed just as Jack knocked and stuck his head through the door.

"Jared—oh, hi there Russell—Jared, can you be ready in about fifteen minutes?" Jack asked pleasantly.

He shrugged his shoulders. "Yeah, I guess," he replied, not wanting to appear too cooperative.

Jack looked at him a moment. "Okay, hope you're hungry. My mom always cooks up a storm. Meet you at the front door in fifteen minutes." And he closed the door behind him.

He shook his head in disapproval. "I wish he wouldn't bug me all the time."

Russ's left eyebrow raised. "You're wacko, Martin. Sounds to me like he's just trying to get along. You have issues, my friend."

He changed the subject. "Can you come back tomorrow morning?"

"I may camp out on your front lawn tonight. I'll give you a call after breakfast."

Russ headed for the door, and Jared carefully took the drone from under the microscope and wrapped it in its felt. But before doing so, he peered at it closely one last time. "So, you really aren't dead after all," he said quietly.

CHAPTER FOUR
Monday morning

Tony Stone sat facing Bill Stegorski. They were waiting for Tony's boss, Ted Martin, in a small conference room. Stegorski was studying him, and Tony had the feeling that Stegorski was trying to look through his skull.

"You know," Stegorski finally said, "I was skeptical of the security here, but Dr. Martin assured me there'd be no problem."

Tony placed his hands, palms-down, on the tabletop. He could feel the sweat. "Let's not jump to conclusions. Perhaps he has an explanation."

"I don't need to jump to anything to see that—"

Ted opened the door. He glanced at Tony and asked Stegorski, "What's the problem?"

Stegorski looked hard at Ted, seemingly watching for a reaction. "The TRAS is missing."

Ted's eyebrows arched. "Really?"

"Yes, 'really.' This is bad, Dr. Martin. Very bad."

"Well, it certainly is—if it's really missing."

"Of *course* it's missing, it's not in the lab where we left it Friday, and nobody seems to know where it's gone. That's *missing*."

Ted turned to Tony. "You've asked all the other engineers about this?"

He lifted his hands, and saw that he'd left wet spots from his sweat. He quickly put them back down. "I've talked to Rob,

Linda, and Masahiro. Sam and Jake haven't arrived yet, but security doesn't list anybody having been in over the weekend." Tony nodded towards Stegorski. "Also, Bill doesn't want a lot of attention."

Stegorski's gaze continued to bore through Tony's head. "We need to contain the situation," he said, although really speaking to Ted.

Ted shrugged. "I'm not sure what there is to contain. We just have to track down what happened to the drone."

Stegorski's eyes were steely. "I don't really care about your drone, but it's got my career bolted to its ass."

Ted nodded at Stegorski. "And your ass is on the line."

"Of course my ass is on the line. My job was to protect the power module. I trusted your company, and now it looks like I'll have to pay for it."

"I understand," Ted said. "Hopefully this is just a miscommunication and we'll have it back soon."

Stegorski continued to stare at Ted for a moment, then said, "We've contacted everybody who's worked on it?"

Ted looked to Tony.

"The names I've mentioned are the entire development team within Stelltech—"

"Within Stelltech," Stegorski echoed. "What about the Mems Group company?"

Tony shrugged. Since being assigned to their project a month ago, Stegorski had paid little attention to the technology or the development history. Instead, he had focused single-mindedly on security. "They haven't been involved since we took over integration," Tony said. "Their expertise, of course, is MEMS technology, the actual construction of the drone. They built it according to our designs."

"I thought that nano-technology was used. That was supposed to be the hot new miracle."

Tony nodded. MEMS stands for Micro Electro/Mechanical Systems. Although the MEMS technology had been advertised as nano-technology, it was really more an extension of the existing processes for making electronic integrated circuits, using the same techniques to build tiny mechanical parts on the same die as the circuits. "MEMS Group in California has been developing their namesake technology for nearly eight years. About two years ago they picked up a small group of Stanford-based researchers who'd been specializing in true nano-technology. These Stanford guys were developing techniques to build true molecular-sized structures." Tony found this mini-lecture to be a relief. It was easier than fidgeting under Stegorski's scrutiny. "The techniques are more akin to genetic engineering than IC manufacturing," he continued. "They use molecular intermediaries to layer atomic pieces, like putting together a puzzle, one atom at time..."

Tony saw that the details were annoying Stegorski. "The MEMS Group Company," he continued, "needed funding—lots of funding—to move into full nano-technology production. Commercial applications were too far off to attract serious venture money, so they did what any self-respecting American company would do when faced with risky advanced development; they turned to the military. They'd never worked with the government before, and that's how we came into the picture."

Ted seemed content to let him carry the ball. Tony wasn't sure Stegorski was even listening to the details, though. The military intelligence agent seemed more intent on watching Tony's eyes.

Stegorski didn't say anything, so Tony continued. "The original proposal to MI for the mini-drone wasn't mini enough. In fact, that drone would have been as big as my hand. We were ready to give up on the proposal when we connected with MEMS Group. With their nano-technology we could create the complex structures of articulated legs and grasping claws. We take for granted how sophisticated an ant's leg is—it's truly a miracle what they achieved."

"A miracle we no longer possess," Stegorski said dryly.

Tony could feel that now his underarms were also wet. He decided that his best recourse was to keep talking. "We added our expertise in remote drone control and served as overall system integrator. We provide the visors and waldo controls, as well as the actual operating software of the drone itself. That's my group." Tony paused a moment, then said, "You know about the power-pack, since MI provided that."

Tony's lecture had run to completion, but Stegorski just sat there watching him. Tony drummed his fingers on the table.

Ted finally said, "And then JSAD stuck their fingers in the pie."

The newly formed Joint Services Applications Development department of the military had gotten wind of the miniaturized drone and, taking their name to heart, had pulled the whole development under their wing. The intention was to expand the role of the drone to include general use by all the service's Special Forces groups, not just the spy applications of MI.

At the mention of JSAD, Stegorski looked like he'd bitten into a sour apple. "And they'll ultimately hand the whole thing to the world on a platter."

"Yes," Tony agreed, "once these toys deploy with the troops they're pretty much out of the bag."

"We'll see photographs in the Washington Times, for Christ's sake!"

Tony nodded and shrugged.

Stegorski shook his head. "JSAD!" He fairly spat the word. "A bunch of cowboys more interested in publicity for their congressional sponsors than looking after the military's interests—"

"And keeping secrets safe," Tony finished. He'd surprised himself. As nervous as he was, he still reacted to the injustice of it.

Stegorski studied him a moment. "That's right, Mr. Stone. The military has always kept secrets to stay two steps ahead of the enemy."

Stegorski waited for Tony's response.

Tony thought, *what enemy?* Were we worried that terrorists would start manufacturing tiny drones in caves in Afghanistan? He didn't voice his thoughts, though. Instead, he turned to the white board on the wall and began erasing diagrams he'd previously drawn.

Stegorski said to Ted, "Speaking of JSAD noses, has any of our brilliant generals and admirals asked about the power-pack?"

Ted grinned at him. "Your MI group really doesn't care about line of command do they?" Stegorski only stared back without responding. "No," Ted continued, "I don't think that they know enough to even frame a question."

Stegorski gave one nod. "And we'll keep it that way."

"Safe from the world," Tony said quietly, almost to himself.

"Excuse me?" asked Stegorski.

"I said," Tony replied turning to Stegorski, "that it's important to keep all things, if possible, no matter how useful, safe from the untrustworthy hands of humanity." His heart was pounding. He knew he would regret this later.

Stegorski remained completely calm. "Your sarcasm, Mr. Stone, belies your professed duty to keep this country's secrets safe. Were you really sincere when you signed the government secrecy agreements?"

"You think that keeping a secret is all there is to patriotism?"

"Now, now," Ted said, "I think we want to stay focused on getting the drone back."

Tony composed himself. Yes, it was time to steer the game. "Before we get mired in lists of who-knows-what," he offered, "maybe we should stop and think about more obvious answers."

Both Stegorski and Ted looked at him.

"I have an idea." He headed for the door. "Let's go over to the lab," he added without waiting for a response.

When they arrived, there were only a few engineers working off to one side, and Tony, with Stegorski and Ted following, walked back to the bench where the JSAD demonstration was supposed to take place.

Tony pointed to the sign hanging above the bench. "I thought so," he said, pretending satisfaction. "See, somebody made the sign read 'trash' as a joke. I'll bet the cleaning people threw it away over the weekend, not understanding the humor."

Stegorski looked at Tony with surprise. "By God they better not have! Dr. Martin, I want every cleaning person that was here over the weekend in your office in one hour, and I want the name of the asshole who changed that sign!"

After an uncomfortable moment's silence Dr Martin replied, "Okay, Bill, I'll talk to security about pulling in the cleaning crew, even though they work nights and will probably be dragged from bed. As for punishing the person who changed the sign, I'm sure he didn't intend any harm."

"I don't care if the janitors are interrupted shitting, and there's no God-damned excuse for your engineers' childish pranks."

Ted replied calmly, "We're not the military."

"Bah!" Stegorski cried, and stormed off.

****

Tony returned to his office. He checked the hall to make sure no one was around. He dialed the phone and waited for an answer.

"*Hello,*" the familiar voice said.

"Ahmed, this is Tony."

"*Hello, Tony.*"

Just saying his name, Tony had the impression that Ahmed was being sarcastic. He wished he had some other recourse, but he couldn't do this alone. "Have you decided?"

"*Yes, I'll do it, Tony. Do you know where it is?*"

"I have the address. It's in Northern Virginia, just outside the Beltway."

"*Where will I meet you?*"

"There's a convenience store a few blocks away." Tony gave him the directions. "I'll get away from here as soon as I can, but it could be a couple of hours. I'll call you before I leave."

"*All right, ... Tony.*"

Ahmed seemed to take pleasure in saying his name. "See you later," Tony said and hung up. He sat staring at his degree on the wall. He hoped he wasn't making a mistake hooking up with a character like Ahmed. He checked his watch for the third time in five minutes. He just wanted to get all this over with.

Sara was at her desk, still working through the paperwork she'd left Saturday night, when the phone rang. It was Barbara again. "What's up?" Sara said.

"*I heard Alihan talking to Ahmed. I don't know if this is important, but I think Ahmed is going to Virginia to pick up a fax.*"

"All the way to Virginia to pick up a fax? Did Alihan go with him?"

"*Ahmed hasn't left yet. He's waiting for a call. I think he asked Alihan to go too, but he refused.*"

She could sense that Barbara had something more to tell. "Do you know why?"

There was silence for a moment, then Barbara said, "*They had an argument. Alihan was telling him not to go.*"

"I see. Do you know why?"

Silence again.

"Barbara?"

"*He thinks Ahmed will get into trouble.*"

"Okay. Anything else?"

"*No.*"

"How about the fax. Did you hear what it may be about?"

"*Not really...actually, it didn't make sense.*"

"How so?"

"*Well, Alihan called it a fear fax.*"

"A fear fax," Sara repeated, writing this down.

"*That's right.*"

"No other details—why it would cause fear?"

"*No, like I said, it didn't make much sense. I was in the next room and the door was closed. I may not have heard correctly.*"

Where would he be going to pick up a fax, Sara wondered—a postal store like Kinkos? Hardly the place to have a terrorist-related transmission sent. "Does Ahmed know anybody in Virginia?" she asked.

Barbara seemed to be thinking. "*Yes,*" she said finally, "*there's a friend that Alihan went to school with.*"

"And Ahmed knows him too?"

"*Yes, they used to all hang out together.*"

"Do you know his address?"

"*No, but I remember it was in Alexandria and the name of the street was George Mason Drive. That was over a year ago. I don't know if he's still there.*"

"Okay. Thanks, Barbara. Call if you hear any more. But, more importantly, don't take any chances. Understand?"

"*Yes. Thanks, Sara.*"

"For what?"

"*Helping to keep Alihan out of trouble.*"

"No problem. Just doing my job."

She hung up the phone and sighed. She hoped that she was indeed helping keep Barbara's husband out of jail. She'd actually lied there. Her job was really to catch him if he was doing something illegal. It was up to him to keep himself out of trouble.

She drummed her pen on the pad a minute, then stood up. She'd suggested a tap on Barbara's phone but had been turned down. She knew that court warrants were doled out like rationed coupons and that the department didn't want to waste them, particularly on a lowly junior agent like her. Well, she'd just have to make a pest of herself and try again. She really wanted to hear that phone call Ahmed was waiting for.

CHAPTER SIX

Monday morning

The morning dawned bright and sunny, a fairly typical Virginia winter day. Jared hadn't even finished his breakfast before Russ showed up.

"I'm glad to see the police haven't come to drag you away yet," Russ said, twirling a banana in the air, and then catching it.

Jared's spoon stopped halfway to his mouth. He dropped the contents back in the bowl. "You couldn't wait to ruin my day, could you?"

Russ put the banana back it the bowl and picked up the cereal box. "I could have said I *wasn't* glad to see they hadn't dragged you away... hey, look," he said, reading the back of the box, "for a dollar and three proof-of-purchases you can get a little plastic robot. You should send for one. That way when the police come, you can give that to them instead."

Jared sighed. Sometimes it was best to just not engage. He dumped his half-eaten bowl of cereal down the garbage disposal and headed off for his bedroom with Russ following. Jack had taken on a new job as assistant basketball coach, and had already left for an early practice. They had the house to themselves, at least until Jack returned to pick up Jared on the way to the airport. They were going to pick up his mom who'd flown to Boston to visit Jared's ailing grandfather.

He pulled the visor and waldo controls out from under the bed. Behind him, Russ said, "Man, I can't believe you wouldn't have already started messing with this."

"Yeah, Jack just left before you came."

"Let me try the visor this time?" Russ asked.

Jared had been waiting impatiently since the previous evening to get back under it. It was almost unbearable to be torn from it just when they'd gotten a video image. But, he didn't want to lose Russ's help, and maybe it was just fair. "Okay, but don't drool all over it."

Russ slipped the visor over his head and reported that he wasn't getting anything. Jared carefully unwrapped the covering over the drone, and as he pulled away the last flap, Russ put his hands out to steady himself and exclaimed, "Wow! I can see perfectly. This is fantastic!"

It was all he could do to resist tearing the visor from Russ. He picked up the drone, still resting on the felt cloth, and swung it slowly around in a circle.

"Whoa!" Russ cried. "Not so fast! You're making me dizzy. Also, when you move it too fast, the picture begins to break up— like Internet cams when there's a jam in the connection."

He placed the drone slowly on his desk and knelt down to look into its camera. He waved and Russ waved back laughing.

"Ha, ha! You have a huge nose, Martin! It's a wide-angle lens."

With no small amount of prodding Russ finally gave up the visor. Jared slipped it slowly over his head, and the view that greeted him reminded him of looking through his binoculars from the wrong end. The picture was crystal clear, except when they moved the drone at anything more than a snail's pace. It then got a little snowy and, as Russ had said, even broke up sometimes. Russ suggested that the radio link probably used video compression just like their Internet cameras. When the drone moved too quickly, the compression algorithm couldn't handle so much new image data. Russ's father was a computer science professor at George Mason University, and Russ always had explanations, or thought he did, for software operation.

Jared carefully felt around the desk until he came to the drone's felt cloth. He picked up the the drone and held it, controlling his own view. He found this difficult to do, for as he moved it, even a little bit, he tended to react to compensate, as though his head thought that it was doing the moving itself. It was a very disorienting experience, and before long he was thoroughly dizzy and a bit nauseous. It was actually better to let Russ control the drone's view. Jared remembered that the built-in earphones had a volume control on the side of the visor. He reached around and turned it up. The sound of the room fill his ears.

Russ moved close to the drone and said, *"Hello in there!"*

"Hey!" Jared cried, "Not so loud! It's all distorted."

Russ backed off a few feet.

"That's better," Jared said as Russ spoke again in a normal tone.

"It's odd," Jared added. "I can hear just fine, but it sounds kind of weird—like the sound effects that singers use."

"Here, let me try," Russ said taking the visor from Jared and putting it on. "Yeah, it does sound odd ... you know what it is? I'll bet the microphone of the drone is so small that it can't pick up lower frequencies. I'll bet they do a lot of processing to try to compensate, but it's not perfect and that's why we get this weird effect."

Sometimes he was genuinely impressed with his older friend. It sounded perfectly reasonable to him. After some more experimenting, Russ finally took the visor off. "We need to get the waldo working," he said.

Jared shrugged. "I tried that, remember?"

"Yeah, but you didn't have me to help you."

On the other hand, sometimes he could get genuinely annoyed at his friend.

"Okay," Jared said, "where do we start?"

Russ thought about it for a moment. "Let's go back to the visor configuration and see what we can find."

He was puzzled. "Why would the visor have anything to do with the waldo?"

"Martin," Russ said in the patronizing tone he knew meant that a lecture was beginning, "did you hear about the guy who lost a quarter and his wife found him looking for it in the bathroom?" Russ continued before he could protest. "She said, 'I thought you lost it in the living-room.' And he replied, 'Yeah, but the light's better in here.' "

Russ looked at him as though he should fill in the rest. When he only returned a dumb stare, Russ continued, "Boy, you *are* slow today. We're going back to the visor because that's the only way we've found to change setups. In other words, the light's better there."

He nodded in resignation and Russ placed the visor back on his own head. Jared took over the role of button-pusher this time. They went back through the *config* sequence again, trying the different branches, but couldn't find anything that seemed promising. They then worked back to the top menu and Russ repeated the selections.

"We have 'mode,' 'config,' and 'test' ... and 'back,' of course. I say we try 'mode' next."

Jared pushed the appropriate button, and Russ related what appeared. "Now we have 'normal,' 'multi-user,' 'PC,' and, as always, 'back.' We're already in the 'normal' mode. There's an arrow next to it. I can guess what the 'PC' mode is. It let's you use the visor in place of your computer monitor. You'd probably have to use voice recognition software instead of a keyboard. Well, that leaves just 'multi-user,' and I'll bet that's for when you have more than one visor viewing the same thing."

"Yeah," Jared replied, "I've seen that mode used at Stelltech when they're doing training classes."

"Well then, I vote we go back to the top and see what 'test' has to offer."

Jared pushed the eight button for *back* and then the three for *test*.

"Hmm," mulled Russ, "what have we here? I've got stuff I don't understand."

Jared opened his eyes wide in mock wonderment.

"I've got 'self test,' 'link test,' 'pat test,' 'protocol,' 'KGM,' and 'relay.' I can guess at a couple of these, but 'relay' sounds interesting. Hit that one, Martin—that's six."

He pushed the button, and Russ continued, "Okay ... what the heck? There's only two options—'ingress,' and 'egress.' What are they?"

He took an intuitive guess. "Ingress means 'in,' and egress means 'out'?"

"Maybe. Look it up in your dictionary."

Russ waited while he flipped though his desk reference. "Yeah, I was right."

"Don't let it go to your head, kid. So, into and out of what? The visor? Well, one way to find out—hit the 'ingress' button."

He pushed the button and Russ continued, "That's interesting. There's a blinking asterisk and the words, 'waiting connection.' Connection to what?"

Jared's face brightened. "Hold tight, Russ, I'll be right back." He grabbed the waldo controls and turned on the power switch.

"What'd you do?" Russ asked excitedly. "It found something. It says, 'connected to VisoReal 37A'."

Jared flipped the waldo controls over and looked at the model number. "Awesome Russ! That's the model of the waldo!"

"The visor must have automatically made a connection to the waldo," Russ said, explaining the obvious. "That's it, Martin! I know what this 'relay' mode is. The visor can act as a relay station between the waldo and the drone. We need to make a connection to the drone now. That must be the 'egress' option."

Russ was silent for a few moments after Jared pushed the appropriate buttons. When he finally spoke he sounded disappointed. "No luck, my friend. It just keeps blinking the word 'searching'."

Russ just sat, silent, under the visor for some time. Then, with a jerk, as though waking from a sleep, he exclaimed, "Hey! I just noticed that there's one more option still at the bottom of the view field. It says 'scan'. Hit the 'one' button, Martin."

He did as told, and within moments Russ whispered reverently, "Well, I'll be damned."

"What is it?"

"I'll be damned, damned, damned," was Russ's only reply.

"Look!" Jared said, exasperated, "tell me what you see or I'm going to disconnect you!"

"Hang on to your pants, Martin, patience is a virtue. I've got a copyright warning from ... who do you think, my young friend?"

"Stelltech?" Jared offered wonderingly.

Jared could see Russ smile under the visor. "You get a cigar."

"Holy shit!"

"Mine is, want to be baptized?"

He ignored the taunt. It didn't even register. His mind raced, thinking of the next step. "So, how do we connect the waldo to the drone?"

"Remember that virtue? We'll just have to take this a step at a time. If it can be done, ol' Russ'll figure it out."

For once he didn't mind his friend's arrogant confidence. In fact, he was counting on it.

CHAPTER SEVEN
Monday noon

Sara sat at her desk slapping the strap of her purse against the edge. She should have guessed this would happen. Her boss had given it barely a moment's consideration before saying "No." He'd told her there wasn't enough evidence to justify a phone tap warrant—it would just annoy the judge. He hadn't even looked up when he said this, as though the fact should have been obvious. She knew, though, that they'd gotten taps on much slimmer evidence before. The fact was that her boss just wasn't willing to go to bat for it. Her justification was based her intuitive sense after talking with Barbara. She was asking her boss to go out on a career limb, trusting that her intuition was sound—the new kid on the block who hadn't proved herself yet ... that had gotten the job in the first place because of a senator uncle.

She put the purse down. No use being mopey about it. She went to the file room and pulled out the bureau's collection of Virginia maps. They were substantial, and soon there were piles of them spread across the table. She pulled aside several maps of the northern counties. These comprised the southern side of the greater DC metropolitan area. In addition to Arlington, which most have heard of from its famous military cemetery, was Alexandria (technically a city), Arlington, Fairfax, and Loudoun counties as well. Alexandria was a relatively small enclave nestled at the corners of Arlington and big brother Fairfax.

Bordered on the east side by the Potomac River, and on the south by the DC Beltway, it had become an urban extension of DC.

She located the street where Ahmed's friend lived. George Mason Drive was a major thoroughfare running from the edge of Alexandria through a small corner of Fairfax County before winding through Arlington. In fact, once inside Alexandria, its names changed to Seminary Road. She guessed that either Barbara was wrong about the friend living in Alexandria, and that he actually lived in Fairfax or Arlington counties, or she didn't realize that the street name changed to Seminary Road inside Alexandria. Next to the maps was her pad where she'd doodled while talking to Barbara and wrote the word *fear*, bolded and circled, many times. She stared blindly at the maps for many minutes, waiting for some inspiration to come. Unlike her boss, she trusted her intuition. It had come to her rescue more than once in the past.

She let her mind float over the Alexandria map as a whole—Arlington at the top, the blue of the Potomac along the right, Fairfax along the left, and the Beltway cutting along the bottom. There, on the pad, was the word *fear*. Fear. Ahmed was picking up a fax that had something to do with fear. Picking it up from a friend in Alexandria.

Then, seemingly out of nowhere, her eyes were drawn to the large letters on the left side of the map: *FAIRFAX*. Fear. Fax. Fairfax.

Damn! Her mind snapped to attention, and nearly saluted. In one split instant it was clear; Barbara had misunderstood what she'd heard. She thought she'd heard two words: "fear," and "fax," when, in fact, what was said was "Fairfax." If Ahmed's friend really did live in Alexandria, then he may not be involved at all. Perhaps something was happening in Fairfax instead.

She grabbed the Fairfax and Alexandria maps and went back to her desk and dialed Barbara's number.

"*Hello,*" she heard Barbara say.

"Hi," Sara said pleasantly, "I'm calling to see if you'd like to be part of a survey on shopping habits."

"*Hello Sara. It's okay—what's up?*"

The survey was a ruse they'd agreed upon in case Barbara couldn't talk. "One question," Sara said, "are you sure that their friend lives in Alexandria. The reason I ask is that George Mason Drive changes names to Seminary Road."

"No, it was Alexandria. It's a duplex just inside the city border. I know it was Alexandria because he was happy he didn't have to pay the Fairfax county car tax. I'm not so sure, though, about the name of the street—I just know that we took George Mason from Route 66."

"Thanks, Barbara."

She hung up and opened the maps again. She knew from her visits there that, in inside the county of Fairfax, there was also the city of Fairfax, the county seat, located just outside the Beltway. She went to her Ahmed file and dug out his car license number. On a hunch—that woman's intuition again—she looked up the number to the Fairfax city police and placed a call. She asked them to watch for his car. She didn't want them to intercede, just call her if they spotted it.

She had her own college friend who lived in Vienna, only a few miles from the city of Fairfax. She hadn't seen her in a while and decided that now was a good time to pay a visit. From downtown Baltimore it was about an hour's drive, non-rush-hour. She'd let agency business take her there. She put in a call to her boss. He wasn't in, and she left a message about her plans. She then left a message with her friend in Vienna and collected her things. With one last look at the pile of maps, she folded the one for Fairfax and took it with her. She paused at the door and looked back at her desk where she spent most of the hours of her days. She was sprinting off on an impulse. She didn't know what she was after, or where it would be. All she had was one word: "Fairfax" ... and an intuitive feel about her contact, Barbara. Sara smiled and closed the door behind her.

Chapter Eight
Monday noon

Russell gave a running account of what he saw under the visor. After about ten seconds, the copyright notice had given way to an extended and severe warning about the protected nature of the drone. Basically, you were either in the military, working for the military, or in deep shit for even reading this notice. Jared had seen this type of thing before and brushed it off. He'd been feeling a low level of anxiety ever since picking up the drone, but he knew that this came from what his father's reaction would be more than some abstract military security warning. The military caution persisted longer than did the copyright notice. Presumably you were reading it over and over, memorizing it for the benefit of your country. When it finally relented, a whole new menu style appeared. Since the drone's program would have been written to operate with a variety of different control devices, the designers had limited its menu selections to just four, even though the visor had eight buttons available. A help option was available at the very top.

"The drones are designed to be used by soldiers," Jared said. "My dad says that the help menus are mainly for the officers so they don't have to ask questions and feel dumb."

The help material proved a godsend, though, for with it they were able to directly understand the control options for the drone without poking around through the various menus, which were significantly more complicated than that of the visor. They found that the drone had three basic modes of operation:

1. *Walk*, in which the four legs were manipulated. In this mode the drone's camera pointed straight ahead, and the arms and claws remained in whatever position they were left.

2. *Articulate*, in which instead of the legs, the arms and claws were controlled.

3. *Scan*, in which the camera lens continually swept back and forth, surveying an entire room every six seconds or so, apparently one of its spy features.

To their delight, the drone even interrogated the waldo directly and determined its basic control options. Thus, they were able to configure the first and second fingers of each of the waldo hands to control the drone's four legs. They were stumped at first by the *hook* option, but Russ made a shrewd guess that there was a tiny articulated piece at the end of each leg that, when bent, acted as a hook. Jared confirmed this under the microscope. They programmed the hooks to relax when their fingers were lifted, and grab when their fingers were pressed against a surface. In this way, they could walk the drone by walking their fingers across a table, the hooks engaging each time they placed their fingers on the surface.

Configuring the arms and claws was more obvious since the waldo had fairly direct analogs: arms for the arms, and opposing thumb and finger for the claws. They found that the three modes of operation, *Walk*, *Articulate*, and *Scan*, were mutually exclusive, meaning that only one mode could be used at a time. They changed modes via a chin switch built into the visor. The current mode was displayed in the lower left corner of their view. When they went from *Walk* to *Articulate*, the legs remained where last positioned, but the leg hooks automatically engaged; and when going from *Articulate* to *Walk* modes the arms and claws also remained where last positioned.

After nearly an hour and a half, the boys had mapped all the functions of the drone to their waldo and were ready to give it a go. Uncharacteristically, Russ, suggested that Jared go first.

They lay the drone in the middle of the desk, monitored by Russ through the magnifying glass, while Jared donned the waldo and visor and sat at a small table cleared for the purpose. They'd left the configuration program ready to engage normal operation by one last push of a button, and Russ, with a dramatic countdown, now engaged it.

"Okay, I've got visual," Jared said sitting motionless with his hands lying on the table. "It looks like I'm in walk mode." He tapped the chin switch. "And, now articulate," he said happily. He tapped again. "And scan. Wow, this is wild—aha! There, I can see you, Russ ... and now you're gone from view, and I'm looking the other way. Now it's coming back." He tapped the chin switch again quickly. "Whew! I'm dizzy. That'll take some getting used to. Are we ready to walk?"

"Go ahead," replied Russ, "I'm ready with the magnifying glass."

He carefully lifted his right forefinger.

"I see your right, front leg lifting," reported Russ.

He carefully moved his finger forward and placing it back down on the table, then slid the rest of his fingers forward.

"Your right leg tried to walk, but it just slid on the table-top. The drone didn't move."

He tried again. This time he stepped both his right forefinger and his left middle finger together and lifted his other fingers as he stepped forward.

"Two legs walking ... and it moved!" exclaimed Russ.

He continued to walk his hands forward, with Russ reporting similar progress by the drone. Soon his hands were stretched out in front of him as far as he could reach. "Hey, what do I do now?"

Russ laughed. "Ha, what a pickle! Well, dim wits, why don't you just lift your hands and move them back?"

"Uh, yeah," he said sheepishly, and he did just that. He could then continue to walk until the drone came close to the edge of the desk. There he stopped and they moved it back and switched places. Jared noticed that when he was in control of the drone he no longer experienced the dizziness he had the day before when it was moved around by somebody else.

Russ took off the visor, and they sat reveling in the glow of satisfaction. Jared, smiling, looked at Russ. "Let's try something adventurous."

Russ looked around the room. "How about climbing a curtain," he suggested.

They switched places again and Russ carried the drone over to the window while Jared donned the gear. Using tweezers, Russ held the drone against the curtain as Jared placed his fingers against the table, closing the leg hooks.

"I'm holding my hand under it in case it falls," Russ said. "I'm going to let go with the tweezers." A second later he continued, "The drone's just hanging there. It looks like a fly resting."

"Should I try to climb?" Jared asked.

"I've got my hand under it. Go ahead."

"This is scary," Jared said. "It looks like a mile up to the top of the curtain. If I fall, I think I'm going to have a heart-attack."

But as he lifted two legs at a time the hooks of the two remaining held firm and the drone made its way slowly up the curtain. He was ecstatic. Soon, once again, he found his arms were extended their full reach across the table. Without thinking he lifted his hands to move them back as he'd done before. As soon as he did, all the leg hooks relaxed and the drone fell away. He cried out as he saw his view swing wildly in circles.

"It fell and rolled under the bed!" Russ called. "I tried to catch it, but I wasn't fast enough!"

Jared sat paralyzed with shock. He heard Russ scrambling under the bed. He could still see a dim band of light and realized that this must be the space between the bed and the floor. But rather than horizontal, this band angled at about 45 degrees. Just then he saw, dimly, the form of Russ crawling down a steep incline off to his right. He realized that the drone itself was tilted and he felt sick realizing that it must be broken. "Over here!" he yelled.

"Yeah right," came Russ's clear reply through the earphones. "So, where is 'over here'?"

"Uh, yeah—I'm off to your right." He saw Russ turn. "More."

Russ had still not turned quite enough.

"Raise your right hand," he said.

"... to the right.

"... more.

"... a little to the left.

"... come towards me.

"... a little more to the left."

"Yeah!" Jared cried as a huge hand enveloped him.

All was now darkness as he heard Russ's grunts as he struggled out from under the bed using only one hand. Then his view washed back as Russ opened his hand. He was getting dizzy again, since everything was upside down and tilted. He could sense that Russ was right next to him at the table, and then he realized that he was seeing himself sitting there at a crazy angle. Instinctively he hadn't moved since the fall.

"It curled up into a ball." Russ said.

"Huh?"

"When it started to fall from the curtain, it curled up into a ball. It's still curled up, like a dead bug. I'll bet it does that automatically to protect itself."

"What should I do?" he asked.

"Hmm, I guess you should uncurl your legs."

With a little shrug he lifted all his fingers.

"Hold on while I get the magnifying glass."

He did indeed almost have to hold on as his view swung crazily around until Russ set him back on the felt cloth.

"Okay," he heard Russ say, "it looks like your legs came part of the way out, but they're still folded up. Try to go some more."

He thought for a moment, then lightly pressed his fingers against the table and lifted them again. As he did so his view shifted slightly.

"They moved some more. Do it again."

He repeated the maneuver. His view shook and settled into its normal horizontal orientation.

"Well," reported Russ, "it looks like your legs are completely out now. Try walking."

With a deep breath he tried the maneuver.

"He walks!" exclaimed Russ, feigning a revival preacher. "It's a miracle, folks!"

He let out his breath in a rush of relief. "I know what happened. I should have switched to *articulate* mode when I moved my hands on the table. That way the claws would have continued holding."

They switched positions and Russ suggested that they let the drone ride on Jared's shoulder. He hesitated, cautious after the curtain fall, but Russ persisted, and he finally positioned the drone carefully on his shoulder as Russ placed his fingers against the table top to set the leg hooks. He paraded around the room.

"Oooeee!" cried Russ. Jared was amused to see Russ careening as he made turns. He then walked up to Russ and leaned over so that the drone looked directly at his visored friend. Russ smiled and, without thinking, turned and lifted his hands in mock attack. He'd made the very same mistake as Jared. The drone obediently fell off his shoulder when the legs hooks disengaged as Russ lifted his fingers.

He didn't panic this time as Russ uncurled the drone's legs where it lay in a ball on the carpet and started crawling laboriously towards Jared's foot. He stood still and watched as Russ climbed his shoe and found a secure position among his shoelaces. He danced around the room accompanied by Russ's jubilant cries of alarm. Russ climbed Jared's sock, but claimed that the darkness under his pant's leg was uninteresting, so he returned to his first class seat among the shoelaces. To Jared it was an odd, tingly sensation to feel the drone work its way up and down his sock.

"Okay," Russ said finally, lifting the visor, "let's send this guy on the kind of mission he was made for. What if we were a couple of Special Forces Navy Seals and we needed to spy on other rooms in the house?"

He watched his friend suspiciously. "So, what are you thinking? We have him crawl under the door?"

Russ's grin indicated something different. "That'd be pretty obvious. He could get stepped on." Russ paused for effect. "No, he'll take the Captain Kirk route."

Jared didn't get the puzzle.

"You know," Russ continued, "almost every episode Captain Kirk ends up outflanking the creepy aliens by crawling through the Enterprise's air vents. He practically lived in there."

He shook his head. "No way! What happens if it gets stuck? We'd never get it back!"

"Have faith my lad. I'm telling you, this is what this guy was made for."

He remained unwilling.

"Look, if it gets stuck I promise to get it back. I'll crawl in myself to get it."

He was not comforted, but as so often happened with his strong-willed friend, he gave up the battle. "So help me, I'll shove you in myself if we can't get it back."

"All right! Let the games proceed!"

Russ placed the visor back over his head, and Jared took the drone from his shoe and placed it on the edge of the vent in his room. It was near the ceiling, and he had to stand on a chair to reach it. He tried to envision Russ crawling into the twelve inch-wide hole at that height in the event the drone did get trapped. He was not successful.

"To do, or die!" Russ called from under the visor. And with that, he began to walk the drone forward.

Jared watched the tiny device disappear into the darkness.

"It's getting darker," Russ reported, "but I can still see okay so far. Here comes a seam—up and over, no problem." A few seconds later he said, "It's getting darker. I can barely see now ... hmm, seems like I've come into the main duct—the one for your bedroom vent is just a branch from this. I turn to look left, ... and I only see darkness. I turn right, ... and I see some light down there. I'll go this way."

Jared visualized the layout in his head. "That'll be my mom's bedroom."

"And Jack's too."

He scowled. "Whatever."

Russ was whistling the theme song from *The Great Escape*. "Okeedokee," he said after a bit. "I'm turning right, towards the blinding light, ... and up to the giant, one hundred-foot I-beam rails that are, in reality, half-inch vent louvers, ... and, I carefully ease myself up to the edge, ... and here's a vast cavern spread out below me—a Grand Canyon filled with rock formations shaped like stupendous pieces of furniture. I dub this unexplored territory 'Mom Canyon'."

Jared rolled his eyes.

"Okay, I'm going to jump to the floor—"

"No!" Jared cried.

"Just kidding, lad. Calm down, I'm safely perched ten thousand feet above the bottom of the cavern. I'm going to proceed with my mission: spy out the enemy lair."

"I thought it was a mile-wide canyon?"

"You suffer from imagination deprivation, Martin. Our world is multi-dimensional. What is a canyon of unimaginable vastness by one perspective is simply the cozy hideaway for our surveillance subjects by another. What dirty deeds are carried out here behind closed doors?"

He didn't like the possible implication of that.

"Whoa! What have we here? Do I see the stray evidence of nocturnal naughtiness?"

The direction of Russ's ramblings irritated him. "That's enough. Come on, the battery's going to go dead."

"No, no, we have definitive evidence here: a bra slung carelessly over a chair..."

"Enough!" he cried. "Give it up, Russ!"

"Okay, okay, Mr. Prude. Mission accomplished. I'll start my retreat."

Russ worked his way easily back and Jared picked him off the edge of the vent. His anger was ebbing, but he still had a raw nerve.

"You know," Russ mused as he lifted the visor off his head, "what *about* the battery? We've been running this guy for a total of at least five hours and he doesn't show any sign of slowing down."

He shrugged. It was a depressing thought that at some point, maybe very soon, the battery would run down, and they had no way to replace or re-charge it.

Russ didn't allow him to dwell on that thought too long. "Our Special Forces operative has completed his training with flying colors. He's ready for a truly hair-raising experience."

Jared feigned mock exasperation. "And how do you intend to lose it now?"

"Ouch! Thy lack of faith doth smite me mightily. I already gave you a clue—a 'hair-raising' adventure?"

Russ walked to the bedroom door. "Birgy! Yo, Birgy! Here girl!"

He heard a thump and the scratching of claws on linoleum floor as the retriever made her way from the kitchen door where she could usually be found lying waiting for somebody, anybody, to come through. Birgy burst into the room, tail waving madly. Although Birgy was originally Jack's dog, she and Jared got along like pals.

His eyes lit up with realization. "Oh no! That's going too far. It'll drop off where we can't find it, or Birgy will bury it, ... or *eat* it!"

"Tsk tsk. Birgy won't even know it's riding on her back."

Russ took off the visor and waldo and held out his hand. Jared glowered at him for a moment, then handed over the drone and donned the gear. Russ had a difficult time mounting the drone on the dog, since every time he tried to put it on her back, the dog turned to see what was up. He had to finally keep Birgy occupied while Russ placed the drone. Even then, as soon as Birgy felt something touching her back, she spun around to investigate. Once Russ had the drone tentatively placed, Jared quickly put on the visor and began manipulating the waldo to get a claw-hold.

"Umph," he said, "this isn't as easy as the curtain. Birgy's hair is too long and smooth. Okay, I think I've got a good hold, but I can't see anything, just a bunch of dog hair. I'm going to try to get a better position."

"You're down on the left side," Russ reported. "Try moving up."

"Sure. But what's 'up'?"

"Well, how about using gravity? Grab with your arm claws only. You should then hang facing upward."

He manipulated the waldo, but couldn't tell whether he was successful or not. "This is impossible. Birgy's hair is just too long. I can't make any headway. It's like trying to walk through grass that's taller than you—and bigger around than your legs."

Russ didn't have a chance to respond, for just then they heard the front door open. He knew it was Jack arriving home when he heard him toss the keys on the stand next to the door. He then heard the klinking of Birgy's leash lifted off its hook. "Oh shit—"

"*Birgy! Here girl!*" Jack called out.

Before Jared had a chance to react, the dog dashed away out the hall. He almost ran after her but decided that it would be better to stay in control and maintain the tentative hold the drone had on her back.

"*Jared,*" Jack called, "*I'm taking Birgy to the park!*"

He didn't answer, and he heard Jack close the door behind him, probably assuming that he was out somewhere.

"Wow!" Russ whispered. "What do we do?"

He was concentrating on the drone. "I can hardly see anything. I think I'm in the back seat. I see the back of Jack's head. I can hear the radio. It's Jack's oldies station. Oh man, he's singing along to California Dreamin'."

"Can you tell where he's going?"

"I get glimpses out the windows, but it's all moving so fast it's just a blur—oh man! I think Birgy's jumping around. Uh oh!"

"What happened?"

"I think I've slipped some. I only see the roof of the car. I'm going to switch to *articulate* mode and try to get a grip with the claws."

"Maybe you should let go. It'd be better to have the drone fall into Jack's back seat than outside when they get to the park—"

"I'm losing the video! It's getting snowy!"

"Let go, Martin! Let go!"

Jared lifted his hands off the table and sat listening. "I've lost the signal altogether."

He took off the visor and the two boys stared at each other in silence.

Two cleaning staff women stood before Tony Stone in the lab. Stegorski, talking on a cell phone, eyed the women suspiciously. One of the women, a middle aged Hispanic, was twisting the handle of her purse back and forth. The other, a teenager, was looking from Stegorski to Tony for some clue. The moment of truth has arrived, Tony thought. More like the moment of un-truth. He hoped he could pull this off.

Ted came through the lab door. "Security has confirmed," he said, "that it was only these two ladies in the lab over the weekend ... at least according to the door access records."

"Is this true?" Stegorski asked the women.

The Hispanic woman looked to the teenager who replied, "Yes, we cleaned in here yesterday."

"No! I mean were you the only two?"

"You mean in this room?"

"*Yes*, damn it!"

"Bill," Ted cautioned, putting up his hand. He turned to the women. "Were you the only two who cleaned in this room over the weekend?"

"Yes," replied the teenager.

Ted smiled at her. "What's your name?"

"Patty."

"Okay, Patty. I'm Ted Martin." Then, turning to the Hispanic woman, he said, "And, your name?"

"Eh?" she replied, looking worried.

"Your name?" he repeated.

"Maria."

"Okay," he continued, "so, there was nobody else in here that you know of?"

"That's right," replied the teenager. "What's the problem?"

"I'll explain that in a minute. Does she," he said, indicating Maria, "speak English?"

"Very little. I pretty much have to translate everything for her."

"Oh? Where did you learn Spanish? In school?"

"Yeah, and I have cousins from Puerto Rico—"

"Let's get on with it!" Stegorski snapped.

Tony saw the two women jump visibly at this.

Ted gave Stegorski a stern look. "Okay," Ted continued, "could you ask Maria if she saw anybody else in here over the weekend?"

The teenager talked to the Hispanic woman who then replied, all in Spanish. The teenager then relayed, "She says 'no.'"

Ted then led them over to the bench where the drone had been set up. "Do you remember seeing anything on this bench?"

The teenager shook her head and asked the other woman. "No," came the reply.

"Okay, now, this is important—and you aren't in any trouble here—you're sure that you didn't throw anything away from this bench?"

The teenager's eyes went wide, and she replied, "No! I never take anything off the tables or benches. We were told never to do that!" She turned to the other woman, translated the question, and listened to the reply. "Maria says that she's sure she didn't throw anything away. In any case, she dusted and I collected the trash."

This wasn't going as well as Tony had hoped. "But," he broke in, "what about the sign there?" he said, pointing to the modified *TRAS* banner.

The teenager looked at it. "I never noticed it. Anyway, we were told that the only trash we throw away has to be on the floor next to the trash cans."

"So," he persisted, "even though that sign says 'trash,' you wouldn't have thrown anything away?"

"No!"

"And her?" he asked, indicating to Maria.

The women's Spanish flew back and forth, accompanied by emphatic waving of hands. "No, she says definitely not."

Tony looked at them a moment. The teenager was coming across a lot more sincere than he would have liked. "Well then, did you see anything unusual in the trash can?" he asked, pointing at the can next to the bench.

The teenager thought a moment. "I don't think so."

"Anything like a plastic box?"

"Oh!" the teenager replied, apparently remembering. "Yeah, there was a clear plastic box that somebody threw away. I remember thinking that it looked brand new."

"Ah ha!" he said, looking around to Stegorski.

Stegorski stepped forward. "But, what about the—"

"It was probably too small for her to notice," he offered.

"Patty," Ted asked, stepping forward, "do you remember seeing anything else besides the plastic box?"

She shrugged. "No."

"A small piece of cloth? A purple cloth?"

She shook her head. "No. I'm sure, because I remember looking around in the can for other pieces. The plastic box was so unusual, I was curious what it was for."

"Patty, do you remember if you lifted the plastic box out of the can, or did you pick up the can and turn it upside down to empty it?"

"I lifted the box out. There was definitely nothing else in it. Look, what's this all about, anyway?"

"Something has disappeared ... we lost something. Something very small, but important."

"I didn't take anything!" Patty exclaimed, her brow wrinkled in consternation. "I'll take a lie-detector test if you want."

She's totally credible, Tony decided unhappily.

Ted shook his head. "No, no. That won't be necessary, Patty.

Thank you very much for coming in on your day off."

Ted's calm manner seemed to reassure her. "I'm sorry if I accidentally threw something out, but I really don't think that I did. Honest."

Ted smiled. "I'm sure you didn't. It'll turn up, don't you worry any more about it. You're not in any trouble."

The two women headed off for the elevator. Once the lab door closed behind them, Tony spoke up. "Well, it seems pretty obvious that we know what happened."

"No, I don't think so," said Ted, shaking his head. "I believe that Patty remembers the events clearly enough. I don't think the drone was in the trash can."

He lifted his hands, palms up. "But, how do we know she didn't take it herself? She may have taken it and is afraid to admit it."

Ted shook his head again. "No, I don't think so. She wouldn't even know what it was. And besides, it would've tripped the sensors when she left. The guards would've caught it."

"But, it's the only reasonable explanation!" He could feel his plan slipping away from him.

Ted was staring at the empty spot on the lab bench. "Somebody filched the drone, and the cloth, and took the time to throw away the box it sat on." He looked up at Stegorski and Tony. "No, there was one other person who had access to the lab over the weekend, ... and who also has motivation to take it. Come to think of it, we actually did set off the sensor alarm when he left."

Stegorski's eyes lit up with understanding. "Your son!"

Tony knew now that the ruse had failed, but not completely. Ted thought that Jared had placed the display box in the trash. He was completely missing the fact that there was, in fact, one other person who fit his criteria; that it had been Tony himself who'd placed the box in the trash can after realizing that Jared had taken the drone.

Ted nodded in resignation. "I'm afraid so. Jared is fascinated by drone technology. I didn't think anything of it at the time because it's almost become routine, but the front entrance sensor alarm went off when we left."

"So, why didn't the guard stop you!" Stegorski snapped.

Ted looked at him a moment. "Ward trusts me, Bill. It's not his fault."

Stegorski took a deep breath. "Well?"

Ted had already pulled out his cell phone and was dialing. Tony watched nervously as Ted waited, apparently listening to a phone message greeting. "Jack, Alice," he said into the phone, "this is Ted. Listen, I can't explain on the phone, but when you get in, please don't let Jared go anywhere until I get there. I'm leaving now from Stelltech and should be there in about an hour or so. I'm sorry that I can't explain yet, but this is very important."

Ted closed his cell phone and was obviously about to leave. Tony had to think quickly. No, there wasn't even time for thinking. He just had to act, and pray it would work out. "Ted, I need to show you something."

"What?" Ted said, surprised.

"Wait here, I'll go get it."

Ted looked puzzled. "What is it, Tony? We have to hurry."

"I'll be right back. Just wait here."

He left the two men and walked to the door. As soon as it shut behind him, he sprinted to the elevator. He jabbed the button, and waited as it slowly made its way up the shaft. By the time the elevator reached him he was ready to scream. He got in, pushed the lobby button, and watched the agonizingly slow floor indicators as they fell, one by one. When the door opened, he ran to the lobby and through the main entrance door. The guard at the desk looked up in alarm as he dashed past and out into the parking lot.

This would buy him five, maybe ten minutes before they finally gave up on him and headed out themselves. He had to get to Jared's house before they did. He hoped he wouldn't get a speeding ticket; it would waste precious time.

He knew that his ploy was going to finger him. So be it. He'd made up his mind long ago. Some things were more important than freedom. He was willing to pay the consequences.

His tires squealed as he left the parking lot. He took out his cell phone, dialed, and waited for the pick-up. "Ahmed, I'm on my way."

CHAPTER TEN
Monday afternoon

J ared took off the waldo controls. They'd had the drone for barely one day. How could he feel so empty about it now that it was gone? Russ picked up the visor and placed it on his head.

"Geez!" Jared said, "What if it falls off while Birgy's running around the park?"

From inside the helmet, Russ said, "Once we get close enough we should pick up the signal again, although I'm not sure how that'd help. Maybe if the drone falls facing up we can walk around and look for ourselves looking for it."

"But what if the battery goes dead?"

Russ drew his finger across his throat under the visor. "Bye bye, drone. Hmm, what's this?"

"What's what?"

"I dunno. There's an LED blinking in the upper left corner."

Jared pondered for a moment. "Wait, I remember that. Before the Cat's camera died, that LED would blink when the signal got too weak."

Russ turned this way and that. "Interesting, ... the blinking rate changes with position." He turned back and forth a few more times in smaller arcs, and then stopped and pointed. "Wherever I'm pointing now, that's where the LED blinks the fastest. I'll bet the drone's transmitting a location beacon. Maybe it knows to start this when it loses a connection."

Russ pulled the visor off and looked where he was pointing.

"Is there a park in that direction?"

Jared looked that way and thought about it. "Yeah, that's Accotink Creek. Jack takes Birgy there sometimes."

"How far?"

"A quarter mile, maybe."

"Well, let's go!" Russ grabbed the visor and they ran outside to their bikes. Jared strapped the visor to his bike rack with bungee cords. He heard the phone ringing inside the empty house, then he heard his mom's recorded greeting, and finally he heard his father's voice. He couldn't make it all out, but he thought he heard him say that he was leaving Stelltech and that he was on his way. Uh oh! They must have figured out who took it. And now he'd lost it. He was in deep shit.

****

They stopped a couple of times along the way and donned the visor to make sure they were still on track. When they came to the park's small parking lot, Jared saw Jack's all-wheel SUV. At the entrance, he held up his hand and Russ stopped behind him. "Do you see Jack?"

"No." Russ replied. "Maybe he took Birgy for a walk."

"Okay, keep an eye out for him while I try the visor."

"Maybe you should let me do that," Russ suggested.

"No, just watch for Jack," he replied as he walked to one end of the parking lot and placed the helmet on his head. He turned back and forth until the LED flashed the fastest, then looked out from under it and noted the direction. He went to the other end of the lot and did the same.

"Triangulation," observed Russ.

"Huh?"

"That's what you're doing dim-bat; establishing two intersecting lines."

"Yeah, yeah." He was only half listening. He'd identified what he thought was the common point. It was across a small meadow bordered by the gulch of Accotink Creek. He headed in that direction and Russ followed.

Near the bank, he put the visor on again. "Wow! I've got video!" The image was indistinct, but definitely different from the snowy picture when there was no connection.

"I'll bet the drone's down near that stream," he heard Russ say next to him. "The bank was blocking the signal. The bushes down there probably brushed it off Birgy. What do you see?"

"Branches and leaves, I guess. It's kind of hard to tell. I think I can see some sky. What do we do now?"

"I've got an idea," his friend said. "You walk away until you lose the video, then come back a little until you get it again. Then, sit down and listen. Raise your hand when you hear me."

He did as instructed. After a few minutes, he heard Russ whistling through the helmet's earphones and he raised his hand. He guessed that his friend was working his way along the bank. The whistling faded and he dropped his hand and took off the helmet. Russ waved him over.

"Okay," Russ said when Jared got to the bank, "this is the middle of the area where you had your hand raised. Tell me when you see me." And with that Russ started beating his way through the thick bushes.

"Don't step on it!" Jared yelled, putting the visor back on. Even as he said it he realized that there was really nothing Russ could do about that.

Based on the curses that emanating from the gulch, he guessed that Russ was getting a lot of scratches as he thrashed about.

"I saw something move!" Jared called.

Russ shook a bush.

"Nothing," Jared directed.

Russ shook another bush.

"Yeah, I saw some movement there. Be careful!"

After a long pause Jared called out, "Your hand! I saw your hand for a second!" He waited. "There! Your hand!"

Suddenly his view changed dramatically as leaves and branches swept by, and, there was Russ's huge face grinning at him.

CHAPTER ELEVEN
Monday afternoon

Sara had made good time down Rt. 95 from Baltimore. She'd picked up the north side of the Washington Beltway and was heading west, counter-clockwise, through the Maryland suburbs of DC. The Beltway wound through curves here, following the path that the builders had found through the early Washington sprawl. This was a favorite spot for her as the glowing white towers of the Mormon Temple swung into view, like the Disney castle. The weather had held the last few days and the sun shone brightly on the bare trees and green grass. Her cell phone rang. "Sara here."

"*Sara, this is Barbara. What's that noise?*"

"It's okay, I'm driving. What's up?"

"*I have more about Ahmed.*"

"What's that?"

"*He's trying to get some military secret.*"

"I see. Why do you think this?"

"*Alihan told me.*"

"He told you?"

"*We had an argument. I was afraid he was getting himself in trouble, and I told him that I knew about the fax ... Sara, it's not about a fax.*"

"I guessed that. The argument, ... did he get—"

"*No, he didn't hit me. Alihan would never do that. We yelled a lot though. The neighbors complained.*"

"And he told you that Ahmed was after a military secret. What else?"

"Nothing, really. Just that he—Ahmed—was going to Virginia to get it, and he wanted Alihan to go along. Sara, I'm so worried. What's going to happen to Alihan if Ahmed gets in trouble?"

That was a good question. Alihan was in a tough position: either turn in his brother, or risk going to jail as an accomplice. "Listen, Barbara, this is between just you and me; if this blows up, we'll say that Alihan passed on the information on his own. We don't have to mention that it came out in an argument. We'll make him sound like he came forth himself. That should keep him clear. Okay?"

Sara heard just the crackle of the cell phone connection for a while.

"All right, Sara. I hope to God this turns out okay."

"It seems to me like you really are keeping Alihan out of jail."

"Yeah—oops! I have to go, Bye!"

"Bye," Sara said, but she could tell that the connection had already been broken.

Sara watched the pavement slide away beneath her. She hadn't lied, she thought, and it really did look like Barbara's spying was going to keep her husband free.

J ared came through the bedroom door and dropped the visor and waldo controls on the bed. Russ followed behind, and unfolded the candy wrapper in which he'd carried the drone and carefully placed the tiny device back on its felt home.

"Man," Jared said, flopping on the bed next to the gear, "that's enough adventure for one day."

"What a wimp." Russ said, picking up the visor. "You wouldn't have lasted a day in Shackleton's crew."

"Who's Shackleton?" Jared lay on the bed talking to the ceiling. "The new baseball coach?"

"That's Sheldon, dumb-ass. Shackleton was an English explorer who tried to reach the South Pole during World War I. He didn't make it. His ship was frozen in the ice and crushed, and it sank. Shackleton and his crew survived for months and months floating around on ice floes, hunting penguins and seals for food. This was during the winter below the Antarctic Circle and the sun didn't come up for months, and it was below zero all the time. They finally made it to a deserted island, but then Shackleton and three of his men had to make a five hundred-mile voyage in a rowboat through all kinds of storms to get help. It was ten months before the last men were rescued. They survived for almost a year with only water and ice and the dirty faces of their companions to look at. Not a single man died."

Jared was impressed, but didn't want to feed his friend's ego.

"Oh really? How do you know all this?"

"I just finished a book about him called *Endurance.* That was the name of their ship that sank."

"Pretty cool. Maybe next time we're walking home from school and you start complaining about the cold I'll remind you about this."

"I don't complain, I merely make observations." Russ slapped Jared's knees. "Come you lazy slug, the day's still young, and the drone's batteries seem to be holding out. We should be taking advantage."

He remembered the phone call he heard come in the answering machine. "I think my dad is sending somebody from Stelltech here to get the drone."

Russ looked at him in surprise. "How do you know that?"

"I heard my dad call and leave a message as we were leaving for the park."

Russ looked disgusted. "You really did steal it, didn't you?"

Jared's heart sank. He'd been trying to ignore the fact that his possession of the drone would have to come to an end sooner or later. He was dreading the time when he'd have to face the anger of his father. "Not intentionally." It was the first time he actually admitted that he had.

Russ shrugged. "All the more reason we should use it while we can."

With a groan he pulled himself up. "You're lucky the drone has no willpower. He's the perfect slave for your heartless ambition. Come to think of it, so am I. So what's the next step, oh Master?"

"I think we should find out its radio signal range, and maybe what kinds of barriers it can go through. How 'bout I take it down to the basement and see if you still get good reception here?"

"Nothing doing. We came too close to losing it. You stay right here with it, and *I'll* go down to the basement."

"Fair enough, weeny-heart, but Shackleton would be ashamed."

Jared pulled on the waldo controls while Russ picked up the drone and looked around for a place to position it. Jared picked up the visor, and headed for the basement. Before leaving, he took two walkie-talkies from a drawer and handed one to his friend.

When he got to the basement he cleared off his mom's laundry table and pushed the call button on the walkie-talkie. "Yo! Russ."

The walkie-talkie clicked and he heard Russ's voice: *"You're supposed to say, 'Russ, do you read me, over.'"*

He rolled his eyes. "Right, ... er, 'Roger.' I'm going to put the visor on. When I do, I won't be able to hear you on the walkie-talkie, but I should be able to hear you through the drone, ... uh, 'over.'"

"Okay, but be careful with the waldo when you put on the visor. I've got the drone in a precarious spot that you won't want to fall from."

"Geez, Russ!" he said, shaking his head in exasperation. "Give it a rest already, will ya?"

Chapter Thirteen

Sara had arrived at her friend's home and was walking up the walk to the front door when her cell phone rang.

"Sara Bigsby."

"*This is the Fairfax Police dispatch. We have a monitor sighting for you. The officer's waiting instructions.*"

That was quick! These Fairfax police are on the ball, she thought. She confirmed Ahmed's license number then asked, "What's the subject's status?"

"*I'll check.*"

After a few seconds the dispatcher came back. "*The officer reports that the vehicle is parked in residential—Southwick Street, between Kirkwood and Barkley.*"

She could feel her heart pounding. This was the real thing. "Is the officer out of sight?" she asked.

"*I'm sure he is.*"

That had probably been a dumb question. The dispatcher hadn't even bothered to check with the patrol car.

"I'm on my way. I'm about ten minutes away." She hoped that was the case. She didn't really know.

Sara spread her map on the hood of her car and worked out her route. She threw the half-folded map on the front seat and sped away without even telling her friend that she'd been there.

She was about half way there when her cell phone rang again. It was the dispatcher, calling to inform her that the officer had been pulled away from his monitor position on an emergency call.

Sara tossed the cell phone aside, gripped the steering wheel, and pressed her foot to the throttle. She was nervous as hell. Maybe sitting at a comfortable desk wasn't so bad after all.

CHAPTER FOURTEEN

"Russ, you'd better catch it if it falls," Jared said into the walkie-talkie.

"*Don't worry,*" Russ replied. "*Just be careful when you activate the controls.*"

Jared was lifting the visor to place it onto his head when something caught his eye out the basement window. Standing at the back patio sliding door were the legs of a man. He leaned over to see more and was shocked to find that the man had a crowbar and was forcing open the door. He was so surprised that he was momentarily paralyzed. This didn't happen in real life! He heard a thud and saw the man leave his view as he entered the house.

He picked up the walkie-talkie. "Russ!" he whispered loudly. He could hear the man walking around above him.

After an eternal few seconds, Russ responded, "W*hat's up 'bro?*"

"Russ! There's a burglar in the house!"

"*Yeah, right.*"

"No man! Russ, I'm tellin' ya, I saw a guy just break in the back!"

The walkie-talkie was silent a moment, then Russ responded, whispering now as well, "*You're not kidding are you, Martin?*"

"No! Russ, we 'gotta call the police!"

"*Yeah.*" Russ's voice sounded scared. "*Do you think I call 911 or the regular police number ... never mind, that's dumb.*"

And then the walkie-talkie went silent as Russ apparently put it down to place the call. Jared quickly put on the visor. A view of his bedroom instantly appeared and he saw Russ finish dialing. From his viewpoint, Jared could tell that Russ had placed the drone on the trim above the bedroom doorway. From that position he could see the whole room.

He saw Russ look up in alarm, and then the top of a man's head appeared. The man jumped at Russ, grabbing the phone from him. The man listened in the receiver a moment then hung it up. The man was dark-complexioned and appeared middle-eastern. He turned to Russ, who looked terrified. Jared heard the man say, "Where is it?"

"Where's what?" Russ replied, backing away as far as he could.

"You know what I'm talking about, Jared—the tiny robot."

"I ... I'm not Jared!"

"Don't play games with me, kid! You took it from the lab. If you just give it to me you won't get hurt. Now, where is it?"

"I'm telling you—"

Jared heard the front door slam and Jack yell out, "JARED, WE HAVE TO LEAVE FOR THE AIRPORT TO PICK UP YOUR MOM. WE'RE LATE, LET'S GO!"

He heard Jack run up the stairs, taking them two at a time. That's where his clothes closet was. Through the visor he saw the man grab Russ from behind and put his hand over his friend's mouth. The man pulled out a knife, held it in front of Russ's throat, and began dragging him to the bedroom door. He thought the man was going to cut his friend's throat right there in his bedroom. He involuntarily put his hands to his head. His view of the bedroom spun drunkenly. He cried out in confusion and tried to understand what was happening. The drone must have simply reacted to the waldo movements when he moved his hands, and had tumbled from its sentinel post above the doorway. He saw constant movement, though, and realized that he hadn't simply fallen to the floor. He recognized the kitchen, and he then got a glimpse of the top of Russ's head. He'd fallen on the man!

From the flashing views of Russ's head and the right side of the man's face, Jared decided that he'd fallen onto the man's shoulder. His view was constantly being obscured by something brown and out of focus, which Jared guessed must be the wide fur collar of the man's coat. His view slowly tilted downward, and he realized that he must be sliding down the collar. He intuitively knew that he needed to hang on. He had to stay with Russ. Placing his waldo-covered fingers on the table, he tried to grab onto the fur, but it was even smoother than Birgy's hair. No matter how he tried, he couldn't get a grip. He continued to slide slowly down the collar. He saw that he'd reached the edge. He was falling sideways over what looked like the edge of a hairy glacier. In the background was the man's hand holding the knife.

His heart pounded madly. He could now see that the material of the main coat was a coarse weave: perfect for the drone's leg hooks. With a deep breath he lifted his fingers completely, and the drone obediently began its long fall. But he immediately slammed his fingers back onto the laundry table and his view jiggled to a stop. The knife-bearing hand was still there before him. He'd caught onto the breast of the man's coat.

He let out the breath. He slowly, carefully began crawling back up the coat. In the background he could see that the man was pushing Russ into a car. He caught glimpses of a second man in the car.

"What the hell is this?" he heard the second man say.

The voice sounded familiar. The man with the knife said, "I had to bring him. The father came home!"

Jared had now climbed back up to the edge of the fur collar. The second man had apparently not noticed the black fly on the coat. He turned the drone so that he was facing downwards.

The second man said, "You idiot! This isn't Jared!"

He struggled to back his way under the collar.

"What!" the knife man said. "What do you mean?"

He saw that by applying constant backward pressure, he was slowly easing under the collar each time the man moved and his collar shifted slightly. He could hear the car engine changing gears and knew that they were driving away.

"This *isn't* Jared, you shithead!" screamed the second man. "Not only did you *not* get the TRAS, you've *kidnapped* some kid!"

And that was the last that Jared saw and heard as the view snowed out. The signal was gone.

He sat stunned in dim light of the basement. He realized as he sat there that he did indeed know the voice of the second man; it was Tony Stone from Stelltech. The terrible knowledge that he had indeed *stolen* the drone exploded as tearing fear rising up from his stomach. He *had* stolen it and he was in big, big trouble. It seemed extreme that the company would break into his house to get it back, but in the flood of adrenaline, he didn't question their means. The man with a knife was probably from MI or even the CIA. Even though his father had explained that most spying was boring work done at a desk, he'd been raised on James Bond movies. If he could just make them realize that they already had it, maybe he could contain the damage.

"JARED!" he heard Jack calling from upstairs, "ARE YOU HERE?"

He didn't even think about telling Jack what happened; he'd contain the problem, and get the drone back to Tony Stone. He dug out the dusty basement phone from underneath some boxes and dialed. He waited as the phone at the other end rang four times and his father's voice ran through its message announcement. "Dad, this is Jared," he said quietly so that Jack wouldn't hear. "Dad, I screwed up. I'm really sorry. Saturday, I took the drone from the lab, and Tony Stone and another man came to get it back, but ... it's all messed up because they took Russ, ... the man thought it was me ... anyway, I'm going to try to give them the drone back."

He paused a moment. "Dad, I'm really, really sorry." He paused again, then said simply, "Bye."

He hung up the phone and, as quietly as he could, went out to the backyard and around to where he'd left his bike. He strapped the waldo and visor to the back rack and pedaled up the street in the direction that the car had departed. After a block he stopped and put on the visor. He turned his head back and forth in ever smaller arcs, then took it off and continued on. He turned the corner and was gone.

CHAPTER FIFTEEN

Passing through the kitchen, Jack noticed the blinking light of the answering machine. He hit the play button and heard Ted's message asking him to keep Jared there.

"JARED!" he yelled even louder as he headed for Jared's bedroom. He didn't need to knock, as the door was open. His stepson wasn't there. The doorbell rang. He went to the front door and opened it, and Ted stood there before him. A shorter, dour-faced man was standing next to him.

"Ted! I just picked up your message. What's this all about?"

"Can we come in, Jack?" Ted said. "I'll try to explain."

"Of course," Jack replied, stepping aside.

Ted introduced the other man as Bill Stegorski, and said that he was with Military Intelligence, which made Stegorski scowl.

"So, what has Jared done?" Jack asked.

"He ... took something from the lab at Stelltech—possibly by accident."

Stegorski scoffed.

"This was a first working prototype," Ted continued, ignoring Stegorski, "of a very important development that involved a lot of people—"

"And of utmost importance to the government," cut in Stegorski.

"... at least to the military," added Ted.

"So, what is it?" Jack asked. He didn't think he liked this Stegorski guy.

Ted stared at his folded hands. "I can't tell you, other than that it was rather small. Jared could have carried it out in his pocket."

He looked at Ted, then at Stegorski. "That doesn't sound like Jared. He's quite a straight kid."

Ted smiled. "Yes, I know."

He could feel himself blushing. "Of course. He's not here, though. We're supposed to go to the airport to pick up Alice, and even this is unusual—that he's not ready to go." Jack glanced at his watch and frowned. "And I need to leave to pick her up now."

"Do you mind if we wait here in case he comes in?" Ted said.

"Not at all. Should I put some coffee on?"

"No thanks, we're holding you up already."

Stegorski went off to use the bathroom, and Jack started up the stairs to finish getting ready. "JACK, BILL!" Jack heard Ted yell out. He came back down the stairs and found Ted holding his cell phone. Stegorski came in from the hall zipping up his pants.

"Jared left a message for me," Ted explained to them. "He did indeed take the TRAS, but I'm not sure I understand the rest of the message. He also said that Tony Stone—that's a manager who works for me—already came with another man to get it back. What the hell? Bill, what do you make of that?"

Stegorski's eyes narrowed. "I *told* you Tony purposely delayed us. It's clear: he wanted to get here first. Can I hear the message?"

Ted dialed, waited a bit, then handed the phone to Stegorski who listened, then handed it back. "The time stamp was just ..." he looked at his watch, "ten minutes ago! He sounds upset, Dr. Martin. Also, he was attempting to not be overheard. Who's Russell?"

Ted was shaking his head in disbelief. "I think Russell is Jared's friend—Jack?"

"Yes," Jack replied, "I'd say his best friend. But what's this Traz?"

"That's Tras, T-R—"

"No need for you to know that," Stegorski cut in.

Jack was getting frustrated with this anal Stegorski fellow, but decided not to push it ... at least not yet. "So what's going on here?"

he asked instead. "Who's this Stone guy? Is Jared in any danger?"

"I'm sorry about this, Jack," Ted replied. "Jared took ... something very important. Tony Stone's a colleague of mine. He heads up the software development on my project. We don't know who this other man is. Jared said they took Russell. They apparently thought he was Jared. He didn't explain why they'd do that, but he sounded ... scared."

Jack could feel his concern firing his temper. "This thing that Jared took," he said, "you're telling me it's secret and important. I'm hearing that two men kidnapped Russell thinking that he was Jared, presumably thinking that he had this ... thing. It sure as hell sounds dangerous to me! We need to call the police—"

"NO!" Stegorski pounced. "There's no need for that yet. We don't even really have anything for the police to go on. We need to find out more about what's going on."

He looked to Ted. "And you?"

Jared's father took a deep breath. "I guess so. I find it hard to believe that Tony Stone would be mixed up in any dirty deeds. It's certainly incredible that he'd try to harm Jared, or anybody. I imagine that this is some mix-up and we'll have it cleared up soon."

He looked hard at the two men for a minute. Finally he said, "Okay, but I'm going to call the police if we don't get some answers soon."

"I agree, Jack," Ted said. "*Real* soon."

"What about your wife, Mr. Brassard?" Stegorski asked. "Don't you need to be leaving for the airport?"

He sighed. "Damn! Hold on a second." He had the feeling that Stegorski was just trying to get rid of him. He called Alice's cell phone and left a message, telling her only that he was going to be late picking her up and that she should continue checking for messages. The three of them went out the front door: Jack to look for Jared or Russell's bikes, and Ted and Stegorski to ask the neighbors if they'd seen anything.

Chapter Sixteen

Sara took a right onto Southwick Street, then watched the cross-streets until she came to Barkley. Ahmed's car had been sighted somewhere along the next block. She drove slowly down the street, but didn't see any cars matching its description. On the right, though, she did see two men watching her intently. She pulled over and got out of her car to meet them. One man was taller with glasses and seemed mild, but the other was shorter and had a stern, pinched face. The shorter man spoke up first. "What's your business here, lady?"

She looked him up and down before answering. This was a guy who was obviously used to being in charge. "I might ask the same. What's your name, sir?"

His eyes flashed as he reached into his pocket for his wallet. He took out an ID card and handed it to her. "I'm with the government and I'd like to know your business *now*," he said.

Sara looked back at him impassively as she reached into her car and extracted her FBI ID. "Well, as it turns out," she said flipping open the black leather case and holding it up to show him, "it looks like we *both* work for the government." She looked again at his name on his ID card before handing it back. "Mr. Stegorski, I'm on an investigation for the Bureau and I'd like your cooperation."

"Well, Ms. Bigsby," he said looking at her name, "I have critical matters of my own to attend to—issues of national security—and I expect *your* cooperation."

Sara grinned. "Looks like an impasse: FBI versus Military

Intelligence. Do you want to arm-wrestle?"

Stegorski scowled, but before he could reply, the tall man broke in, "Look, we're all on the same side; at least we should be. We might just all be on the same subject as well. Can I suggest that we sit down together in the house?"

Sara held out her hand indicating he should lead on. They picked up yet a third man from the driveway, and they all went back into the house. The tall, mild man introduced himself as Ted Martin and shook hands with her. He then introduced her to the other man, Jack Brassard, and explained both their relationships with Jared. Jack responded with, "I don't know, ... this is getting scarier by the minute."

After they all sat down in the living room, Sara explained that she was following up on a lead regarding one of her cases, giving no names or other specifics. She told them that her subject's car had been reported on this street.

"When was that?" asked Stegorski.

"Maybe fifteen, twenty minutes ago."

Stegorski turned to Ted Martin. "That would be too much coincidence, this has to be the other man with Mr. Stone." Then to Sara he asked, "Would your subject possibly be involved in terrorist activities?"

Sara didn't speak at first. This was all going way too fast. She really needed five minutes to absorb it all. She finally replied. "I can't give any details, but if you know of anything like that then you need to tell me."

"I'll take that as a yes," Stegorski said.

Ted shook his head. "That's preposterous! Tony wouldn't be involved in terrorism!"

"We can't make that assumption, Dr. Martin," Stegorski pressed. "The facts are speaking to us. One: your son steals government property, two: he leaves a message that Tony Stone and another man are after it, and have taken your son's friend— presumably kidnapped him—and three: an FBI agent shows up, hot on the trail of a suspected terrorist—"

"Hold on!" Sara interrupted. "What's this about a kidnapping?"

Ted explained the situation quickly, referring to the object everybody seemed to be after only as the "military project."

Jack was pacing back and forth and finally broke in, "Isn't it time to call the police?"

"No!" Stegorski said sternly. "No police yet. We're still trying to get a handle on things. Besides, we have the FBI involved, for Christ's sakes!"

Jack looked to Sara. She nodded. She wasn't going to let Stegorski intimidate her. "I'm going to call in to my office."

Stegorski seemed about to say something, but kept silent as Sara opened her cell phone and dialed. Ted Martin, the guy who developed this secret thing, seemed to be lost in thought. Sara heard him ask Jack if it would be all right for him to take a look in Jared's room. Jack nodded and Ted left. She heard her boss's phone ringing. Jack said to Stegorski, "We've got to do something. The longer we wait around here, the farther these men and the boys are getting away."

Her boss didn't answer. She heard his phone ring a second time. Stegorski looked at Jack levelly. "And, what, exactly, do you suggest we do, Mr. Brassard? Start driving around in circles hoping we'll run into them?"

She heard her boss's message announcement.

Jared's stepfather was obviously getting frustrated with Stegorski. "Well for one," he said, "the police could put out a ... what's it called, an APB?"

The message announcement finished. Stegorski was about to begin another lecture. Sara cut in. "That's an excellent suggestion, Jack—Bob," she said into the phone when she heard the message recording beep, "I'm calling from the field...." She summarized the situation and asked him to contact the police. For the benefit of the men standing around her, she tried to make it sound smooth and routine. In reality, she knew that her boss, Bob, was going to have a fit when he got this message. She could imagine him shouting that this was no place for a junior agent.

Stegorski rubbed his hand through his short, gray hair. "If this gets out of hand, I'm going to put a clamp on the whole thing."

She closed her phone. She'd had about enough of this pushy MI guy. "I'm sure you could," Sara said between tight lips. "I'm sure you could marshal your secret squads and pull down an airtight gag on us all. I took an oath when I joined the Bureau. That oath was a pledge of service to the citizens, not the military; so until I get an order from my boss to stand down, I will continue to do my job." This wasn't exactly true, but seemed appropriate at the moment. "And that job consists of, first, securing the safety of the two boys, second, pursuing my subject and, third, your 'military project' ... in that order."

Stegorski was unfazed. "Nice speech, agent Bigsby. We're all moved by your dedication, I'm sure, but I'll do what I have to do to protect our interests."

"And whos interest, exactly, do you represent?"

The heated discourse was interrupted by Ted's return. He was carrying what looked like a football with stubby legs and a camera lens.

"Jared's Cat robot?" Jack asked.

Ted was studying the underside. "Yes," he said without looking up, "Jack could you get me some tools?"

"Sure, what kind?"

"Small pliers, screwdrivers—electronic assembly tools."

"Why don't we take it to the workbench in the garage?"

They all filed out and watched silently as Ted took apart the silly looking robot. From the innards of wires and gears, he extracted a circuit card about two inches square.

"What's this about?" Stegorski finally asked.

Ted held up the circuit card to take a closer look. "This is the radio receiver. We use different reserved frequencies for these drones, mostly fairly short range. One frequency, though, has a longer range. It doesn't work well for carrying full video, but we use it for general direction beacons. The drone that the boys took—" he looked up to see Stegorski about to pounce. "Sorry, Bill. The 'thing' that the boys took will automatically transmit a direction beacon on this frequency when it loses contact with its control unit. It should have been transmitting ever since Jared took it from the lab. I may be able to use this to receive it."

He was using a pencil to make changes to tiny switches on the circuit board. Jack spoke up. "And the boys don't have a control unit?"

"No," Ted replied. He paused. "Actually, I guess the Cat's visor and waldo might be programmed to act as a controller, but the boys wouldn't have known how to do that. The ... 'thing' should be continuously transmitting."

Ted stripped the insulation from some wires and attached the Cat's battery pack containing four C-batteries. Sara saw some LEDs flashing on the board.

"Well," Ted said with satisfaction, pointing to one of the green LEDs, "if I got the switches right, that light should be indicating reception of the carrier frequency. The beacon signal is encoded, but I think we can identify it by the periodic modulation." He looked up at their questioning faces. "In other words, it should get brighter and dimmer every second or so," he explained.

Sara saw that the green LED seemed to be flashing dimly and randomly.

"No beacon yet," continued Ted, "that's just background noise. Jack, could you get a clothes hanger for me?"

Jack left and returned a few seconds later with wire hanger. Ted clipped off the hook and bent it into an oblong hoop. He then stripped the insulation from two wires hanging from the circuit card and wrapped them around the two ends of the looped hanger, holding the wraps in place with electrical tape. The evolving contraption now included three different parts, the circuit card, battery pack, and makeshift antenna—all dangling together by thin wires.

Ted pointed to the green LED as he turned the clothes hanger in one direction and then another. Sara saw that, although it continued to flash seemingly randomly, she could discern that there was an overall change in brightness every second or so. Ted experimented with the position of the clothes hanger loop, and the brightness differences peaked.

Ted placed the clothes hanger on the table and looked at the people standing around him. "The drone is either that way, or that way," he said, pointing with his arms out in two opposite directions.

"Dr. Martin!" Stegorski reprimanded.

So, Sara thought, *the mysterious object is some kind of robot.*

"Bill, look, I'm sure they understand that we're after a very small spy drone by now. Let's give up the pretense. It's just getting in the way."

Sara decided that she liked this Ted Martin, and Jack too.

Stegorski clenched his fists. Sara thought she understood what Ted was talking about. "The loop antenna can only give you an axis?" she queried, "its not completely directional?"

"Yes, that's right. But we can fix that to some extent."

Ted used a hubcap, grounded with a wire and nail to shield one side of the antenna. By then turning the loop antenna first one way, then the other, he was able to declare a final direction for the drone.

"Now that we have the general direction," he concluded, "we can use just the loop to guide us."

Jack gave him a small cardboard box to hold the wired pieces. Ted held the box in his hands and looked at the three of them. "Well, posse? Shall we track down these here varmints?"

Stegorski drove Ted's car while Ted sat in the back, working the homemade direction finder. Sara followed in her car with Jack. They slowly drove off, and Sara wondered where in the world the invisible electronic beam would lead them.

CHAPTER SEVENTEEN

It was slow going for Jared. At each street corner he stopped and donned the visor to re-establish the direction of the drone, and, hopefully, Russ. Often he had to decide between two streets, neither of which took him in the direction he needed. The suburbs of Fairfax are nestled among hills and streams, and the streets are anything but a regular grid. Jared worked from his memory of the neighborhood. Some streets led to dead-ends, others veered off, away from where he needed to go. Once, after several blocks, he realized he'd put himself on the wrong side of a stream gully. Looking both ways to make sure no one was watching, he pushed his bike between two houses and down into the trees of the undeveloped gully. A dog barked fiercely behind him and he heard a door slam as he tore his way through the brush. On the other side, he had to trespass again between two other houses before he was back on track.

Although the beacon's reception seemed to be holding steady, he didn't know its range, and he had no idea where the two men were taking Russ and the drone. As far as he knew they might be heading out of the state. He tried not to think of this, and concentrated instead on his navigation. All he could do was keep on course and see where it took him.

After a while he realized that the beacon was causing him to continuously veer to his left. This was good, for it meant that the drone was nearby. He cut hard to the left for a while. After a few streets he was satisfied to find that the visor now showed the drone's beacon off to his right. He was looking down a street that he knew emptied onto Little River Turnpike, a busy four-lane divided highway. He remembered that there was a Seven-Eleven near this intersection. Perhaps they were parked there. If so, he knew he'd better hurry, since they'd probably only be making a short pit stop.

In the near distance, the resonating peal of a bell rang out. It had a deep and mournful sound. The echoes faded away, and were replaced by the sound of rushing cars ahead.

CHAPTER EIGHTEEN

Tony drove Ahmed's car away from Jared's house, while Ahmed sat in the back seat gripping Russ's arm. He watched the rear-view mirror, waiting in a near-constant panic for a police car to appear. How could this have gone so wrong? All he'd wanted to do was get the drone from Jared. It should have been simple. His hysterical outburst had run its course, and Ahmed was now able to get a word in.

"The kid's father came home," he said calmly from the back seat. "What do you think I should have done, taken them both hostage? Perhaps I should have killed them both on the spot? Maybe just killed the father and politely ask this kid if he's Jared?"

"Nobody's getting killed!" Tony cried, feeling the hysteria rising again. "This is not some terrorist attack! We're just trying to get our hands on the TRAS."

"And we still can. Perhaps this kid knows where it is. Do you kid?" he asked Jared's friend, shaking his arm.

The kid looked scared, but his tone was defiant. "I don't know what you're talking about."

Ahmed sneered at him. "We have ways of confirming that."

"Look," Tony continued, tying to think, "we can't be driving around with this kid in your car. I'll take us to my car. I can hold him there while you go back to the house to look for the TRAS."

"And maybe we squeeze some information out of our little friend first."

Tony heard a squeak of pain from the kid. "Look!" he yelled. "No rough stuff! Nobody's getting hurt, I tell you. We're just going to grab the TRAS and get the hell out of here. We're the good guys here. Good guys don't hurt people."

Ahmed was watching the neighborhood houses glide by. "This is not an American western movie. There are no 'good guys.' There are only bad guys and worse guys. The American government is the worst guys. The American people elect their government, so you make the connection."

Tony looked over the kid's head at Ahmed. He realized that he had more on his hands than he'd bargained for when he solicited Ahmed's help. "See here, Ahmed, I don't know what organization you belong to, and I don't want to know. Right now we have a common goal to get our hands on this TRAS, but I'm calling the shots. You offered to help, and we do what I say, understand?"

Ahmed didn't answer.

"*Understand*?"

Ahmed looked at Tony before answering. "I understand you."

Tony drove on in silence for a while. When he finally spoke he felt much calmer. To Russ, he said, "I'm doomed now that you've seen me, kid. But that's okay, some things are just that important. What's your name?"

The kid looked at him, but didn't say anything.

"Oh come on, you're not a prisoner of war here."

"Russ," he finally replied. "Or, Russell if you're not my friend."

Tony smiled for the first time since leaving the house. "Well, I'll call you 'Russ' then if that's okay." He pulled Ahmed's car off the highway and into the driveway of a Lutheran Church, just past the Seven-Eleven. The parking lot was empty except for Tony's car. He parked next to it. Ahmed was lighting a cigarette. Tony opened his door. "I'm going to get my map," he said, climbing out.

He heard scrambling behind him, and Ahmed say, "Shit!" He turned to find that the kid had dived over the seat and rolled out onto the pavement. Before he could grab him, Russell tore off across the parking lot towards the church.

****

Russell ran up the front steps of the church, yanked open the door, and sped into the darkness within. He was in the vestibule. In front of him was the open hall of the main worship area, and in the dim light he could just make out doors to each side. Tony would be bursting through any second. Choosing randomly, Russell spun off to the right and was through that side door just as he heard Tony come through the main ones behind him. He prayed that Tony would be blinded by the sudden darkness and wouldn't see the side door close.

He was in what appeared to be a large coatroom, with storage boxes piled against the right wall. At the far end was a door with a window that led to the outside. He ran over and tried it, but it was locked. He could have unlocked it, but instead he instinctively slid in behind some black choir robes hanging next to him just as Ahmed's face appeared in the door's window. Russell heard Ahmed try the door, and then footsteps running away.

Crouching down in the corner, he pulled the dozen or so robes all to his end. The robes didn't reach to the ground, so he picked a small box off the piles and used it to cover the gap. He crouched down again and waited, heart pounding. He heard Ahmed come in the front doors and call softly to Tony, then enter the main hall. After a few minutes somebody opened the door to the coatroom, and Russell saw feet walk by. They tried the outside door, then walked back through the inner door again.

He knew he couldn't stay here for long. They'd eventually come back and make a more thorough search. After what seemed a significant amount of time and, not hearing anything, he eased himself from his hiding place. He crossed softly to the inner door. He still didn't hear anything. The door had an old-fashioned type lock with a large keyhole. He peered through and could see the form of Tony standing facing into the main room. Just then, he heard a sound behind him and, turning, saw to his horror the face of Ahmed in the window again, this time looking straight at him.

Ahmed called out, and when Russell looked through the keyhole again he saw Tony running out the front door. He opened the inner door and saw the back of Tony as he trotted down the front steps. He stepped out and dashed into the main church hall. Aisles immediately to his right and left led forward to the pulpit between rows of pews on each side. Aisles along the far walls also led forward. He ran to the left all the way to the wall where high stained-glass windows glowed with sunlight. When he got to the wall, he saw a door leading back into a small room that was opposite the one in which he'd hid. He tried the door and it opened. It was completely dark, and he entered, closing the door softly behind him.

He stood in the dark, trying to quiet his heavy breathing. He could hear Tony and Ahmed talking, but couldn't place their location. His eyes slowly adjusted, and he began to make out the room's interior from the cracks of light under the doors. Hanging in front of him was a large rope. That would be the bell rope, he guessed. Then he made out a ladder along one wall leading away up into the darkness. He started climbing. It was dark enough that he had to feel for each rung. He'd climbed about ten rungs when he heard the doorknob turn, and light flooded the room. He froze and looked down. He was about fifteen feet above the floor. Tony glanced quickly around and left, closing the door behind him. He rested a moment, then continued climbing in the dark.

Up, up, he climbed. The sounds of Ahmed and Tony talking to each other throughout the church faded away below him. He could see light above now. It was coming through a small hole and as he got closer, he could see that the rope passed through it. Directly above him it was still totally dark, though. From the hole he could tell that he was coming to a ceiling and, although he went slowly, he still banged his head, barely managing to hang on to the ladder. He reached above him and pushed, and a trap door opened easily. Light poured through and blinded him. He pushed the door higher and then it started to fall over the other way. He lunged to catch it, but missed. It banged loudly to the belfry floor.

He froze and Ahmed began yelling from below. They'd heard it.

He scrambled up through the trap door into the light of the belfry. Louvered blinds surrounded him on four sides so that he could only see directly down along the sides of the bell tower. He slammed the trap door shut and looked quickly around for something to put over it, but the belfry was bare. He went to the blinds and yelled out through the cracks. He couldn't tell if anybody was around outside to hear him. He stepped back and turned in a circle absorbing the four sides and the large bell in the middle. The rope was attached to a lever that tilted the bell when pulled. A bell striker hung inside the bell. Russell went to the rope and pulled. The bell tilted, but not far enough for the striker to hit the side of the bell. He pulled as hard as he could and the recoil lifted him right off the floor, but the bell barely tapped the striker. He abandoned the rope and went directly to the striker. Taking it in both his hands he could easily swing it against the bell. He got one good, satisfying ring out of the bell when the trap door flew open, and Ahmed emerged through the opening. He tried to keep away from the man, but there was nowhere to go and Ahmed quickly cornered him. Ahmed grabbed him by the arm and slapped him hard across the face. He cried aloud and fell back, but Ahmed pulled him up and slapped him again. It hurt, and he was terrified. He started crying. Ahmed raised his hand to slap him a third time, but held it. Instead, he dragged him to the trapdoor and ordered him to climb down. Russell sobbed as he climbed down the ladder. The room below was now lit, and Tony stood at the bottom waiting. About half way down Russell slipped and barely caught himself, wrenching his arm in the process. A few rungs from the bottom, Tony reached up and lifted him gently down.

"Take it easy, Russ. You're going to be okay."

He looked up at Ahmed climbing down then back to Tony. Tony put his arm around Russell's shoulder and sat him down in a chair. Although Tony's arm was resting lightly across his shoulders, he felt Tony's firm grip on his arm.

Ahmed reached the floor and turned to face them. "Enough of

these games! This kid is getting in the way. We have to take care of him now!"

"Forget it, Ahmed!" Tony said. "I told you, nobody's getting hurt!"

Russell sat listening to the two men arguing his fate. His life was a point of contention. Through the door he could see an ocean of pews and a lone alter on the far shore.

Chapter Nineteen

Jared pedaled like mad and could see the cars rushing by on the highway ahead. As he came to the thoroughfare, he could see the Seven-Eleven a short distance to his right on the other side. He placed the visor over his head to get a final bearing and suddenly was looking at ... Russ! The visor was now close enough so that it automatically connected with the drone, taking the tiny spy device out of its beacon-sending mode. The drone must still be clinging to the coat under the collar. He saw that Russ was sitting in a chair looking awfully forlorn. It appeared as though his friend had been crying. He saw that the walls were polished wood paneling—real wood, not the fake pressed-board kind. In the earphones he could hear an angry argument between the two men.

He took off the visor, letting the drone return to beacon mode. Where were they? Based on his experience with the drone's transmission range at the park, he guessed somewhere within a block or two ... but where? This section of the highway had not been developed for residential use. Behind him, and along his side of the highway, was undeveloped forest, part of Accotink Park. Directly across the highway was a commercial garage, and to the right, the Seven-Eleven. Farther to the right were more trees and brush. He didn't see anything that might have contained a wood-paneled room.

He slipped the visor back over his head. The man who unknowingly played host to the drone—the man who had held the knife to Russ's throat—had moved a bit. Through a door, Jared could now see rows of benches. He remembered the lone peal of the bell. These were pews! They were in a church! He yanked off the visor and looked around. There, beyond and behind the Seven-Eleven, he saw the stout steeple. He'd forgotten about that church that sat off the Turnpike. He could see the driveway was just beyond the Seven-Eleven. Barely missing the rushing cars, Jared sped across the highway, leaving the wailing horns to dissipate behind him.

Chapter Twenty

Riding in the back seat with his cardboard box, Ted looked up. He was perplexed. "Well, what the...?"

Stegorski glanced at him in the rear-view mirror. "What's up?"

"It seems we've lost the beacon signal—no, wait. Now it's back. Damn! Now it's gone again!"

"Should I turn around? Maybe we've moved outside its beam."

"The beacon's not directional; it transmits equally in all directions. No, I'm afraid that the signal has actually stopped."

"What does that mean?" Stegorski asked, sounding concerned. "It's been destroyed?"

"Well, that's one possibility, but not the only one."

"What other possibility is there? It can't be because the power's dead."

"My clumsy antenna might have a bad connection," Ted said, fiddling with the antenna. "Or, the drone may think that it has a control connection."

"How could that be?"

"Good question—wait, the signal's back! It must be a bad connection at my end here. Too many unsoldered wires."

They drove a couple of blocks before he lost the signal once more. This time, despite his fussing with the connections, he couldn't get it back. After another block of this, he suggested that Stegorski pull over before they got too far off the mark. The MI agent pulled over to the side of the road, and Sara and Jack pulled up behind them. They all got out and stood around arguing the situation. Ted stood off to the side pondering. He couldn't figure it out. Why would the drone stop sending its beacon signal? Was there a glitch in the drone's software? If that were the case, he'd expect the program to lock up, not keep coming back. Perhaps the drone was accidentally connecting to some other source, thinking that it had made contact with a controller. He knew that this was highly unlikely since the communication protocol was structured with safeguard mechanisms and encryption, specifically to avoid such a thing.

Sara pulled out her detailed Fairfax map and spread it on the hood of the car. Ted walked over, and Jack showed him where they'd started, and the streets they'd just been on.

Peering at the map, Ted said, "It appears that the beacon signal was coming from a southeast direction. However, I didn't get enough spread to guess a range." He scanned along the map in that direction from their present point. "We have a Community College," he said, tracing with his finger. "Going farther, we cross the Beltway. From there we have the Landmark Mall, the Pentagon, ... and, interestingly, National Airport."

"That's Reagan Airport," Jack corrected.

"Excuse me?"

"Sorry, I mean they renamed it Ronald Reagan Airport."

"You're right, I'd forgotten."

Ted looked around at the group. They had to do something. "How about we split up, maybe wind our way southeast looking for their car, and also for Jared, of course. I'll let you know if I get the signal back. Sara, could you alert security at the airport?"

"Already dialing," she said, putting the phone to her ear and stepping away to talk.

When she was done, Sara gave Stegorski and Ted the description of Ahmed's car, and they made sure they had correct cell phone numbers all around. Seconds later both cars pulled away and headed southwest.

CHAPTER TWENTY-ONE

When Jared arrived at the church parking lot, he found only two cars parked next to each other: one old, one new. He approached them cautiously and saw that they were empty. Checking the visor, he could see that Russ and the men were still in the side room of the church. Originally, he was intent only on getting the drone back to Tony Stone and Stelltech. Now, though, after hearing the ongoing arguments, both in the car and now in the church, he wasn't sure. There seemed to be more interests here than just Stelltech's.

He decided to check out the situation some more. He hid his bike in the weeds next to the parking lot and walked carefully up to one side of the church, avoiding the front door. He sat down in the warm sun where the ground was dry against the wall. He could faintly hear voices inside. In fact, he seemed to be just outside where they continued to argue. He put on the visor and saw that the man's coat must have shifted position, for his view was now mostly obscured by the fur of the collar. The fur itself was too close to be in focus; the view consisted of moving gray blobs with occasional glimpses of the room beyond.

The sound came through fine, though, and he heard the distinctive accent of the man who had grabbed Russ at his house, "... kid, you must know where it is. You can tell me, or I can hurt you. Your choice."

"Come on, Russ," Tony Stone's voice said, "we'll take the drone and leave, and this will be all over. Just tell us where it is."

"I don't know what you're talking about," Russ repeated. He sounded scared, which was not like him. In fact, it was obvious that his friend had indeed been crying. "And even if I did," Russ continued, "once you had it, you'd kill me."

"Don't take Ahmed's threats seriously. Nobody's going to get killed." Tony paused a moment. "But I don't know if I can continue keeping him from hurting you."

"*Keeping* him from hurting me? You haven't done a very good job of that yet."

"You tried to escape. What do you expect?"

"I expect that if I don't, I'm going to be killed."

Jared was clenching the grass as he sat listening. Hurt? Escape? Killed! The situation was clearly not what he had originally thought. There was no way that anybody representing Stelltech could be talking about hurting, let alone *killing*! So, what was going on here? He didn't know who this man with Tony was, but it didn't seem likely that he was an employee of Stelltech. Maybe he was a spy. But why was Tony involved? Had this other man—this "Ahmed"—taken both Russ *and* Tony hostage? This didn't seem to be the case either. Although it wasn't clear that Tony was in complete control, he certainly appeared to be a willing participant. Whatever the arrangement, the drone was obviously a lot more valuable than he'd realized.

He wondered whether he should call the police. On one hand he knew that this was probably appropriate. But he still felt deeply guilty about taking the drone from the lab, and just the thought of the police caused his stomach to clench. It would be better to call his father. Ahmed must have adjusted his coat, for the drone's view suddenly opened and Jared could see the room clearly again. Russ was sitting in a chair, and Tony was sitting next to him with his arm around his shoulder. He'd never seen his friend so scared and helpless. As far as Russ knew, nobody was even aware that he'd been kidnapped. He wished he could at least somehow let Russ know that help would soon be on the way. But how?

He saw that Russ was keeping a watchful eye on Ahmed, but

Tony gave most of his attention to Russ, trying to cajole him into telling where the drone was. He had an idea. He pulled the waldo gloves over his hands. Using the church wall for a surface he placed the drone into Walk mode. Then, ever so carefully he took a step forward. He couldn't tell how far he was under the collar. He took two more steps and remembered the Scan mode. He switched to this, and his view swung far to the right, and as it reached its extreme point, he saw that he was just at the edge of the collar. He changed back to Walk mode and took two more steps. Now when he switched to Scan mode, he saw that he was finally out from under the collar.

He felt frighteningly exposed. If Tony happened to take a look at Ahmed, or if Ahmed should brush his shoulder, it would be all over. He placed the drone in Articulate mode, locking the leg hooks into Ahmed's coat fabric. Then he began waving his arms at Russ. Sitting outside the church, Jared opened his arms out wide and then brought them together. The claws of the drone should be mimicking his movements.

He saw that Russ was looking at Tony who was talking. Ahmed added a point, and Russ glanced over at him. He looked back to Tony, but did a double take. Jared could see that Russ was staring right at him. Russ sat dumbly for a moment, and then his eyes went wide with surprise. Jared quickly put the drone back in Walk mode and scrambled backward for safety.

He'd taken only a couple of steps when Tony looked to see what had caught Russ's attention. To his horror, he saw Tony look right at him. He froze. Russ looked from Tony to Ahmed. In an instant he jumped out from under Tony's arm and dashed for the door of the room, obviously trying to create a distraction.

Jared's view swung bewilderingly as Ahmed reached out and grabbed Russ. He heard a sharp smack and then Russ cry out. His view steadied on Russ lying on the floor rubbing his cheek and glaring up at Ahmed.

"*I will kill you, brat!*" Ahmed screamed.

CHAPTER TWENTY-TWO

Sara divided her attention between driving and glancing periodically at the map as she listened to Jack call and leave another white lie-message for his wife. He said that there was a mix-up, and they were going to pick up Jared before coming to the airport. He shut off the cell phone, then said to her, "What do you know of all this?"

She glanced at him briefly. She could see that he cared about his stepson. "I knew nothing of this Tony Stone or the little robot an hour ago." She looked at him again. "You're not supposed to know what I'm about to tell you."

Jack nodded and she continued, "The bureau has been tracking suspicious foreign movements, mostly in the Newark area. These ... activities could include public disruption—"

"You mean terrorism."

Sara grinned. "We do like our euphemisms, don't we? We've been tracking a loosely coupled terrorist organization. To even call it an organization is probably an exaggeration. Ever since 9/11 the main focus has been on al-Qaeda. The general sentiment of most Americans has been a resurgence of patriotism, a rally around the flag, the good guys against the bad guys. And we like to have our good and bad guys neatly drawn and separated into distinct camps. Bad al-Qaeda, bad Saddam."

"You think they're *not* bad?" Jack said, looking at her in surprise.

"Oh, don't get me wrong. Osama Bin Laden and Saddam are

evil, no question. But, many of us—many Americans—aren't comfortable about issues that aren't black and white. We often don't know how to deal with shades of gray. Personally, I think it's the old argument about growing up with TV where, in order to keep the sponsors happy, all problems have to be resolved by the end of the show; all the gray tones divide nicely into either white or black by the end of the half-hour. What great literature ever got away with that? Was captain Ahab good or evil? Or, to put it in the political arena, are Palestinian suicide bombers good or evil? Most of us shove them solidly over to the evil camp. They're killing innocent people, after all, although it would be a lot easier to pigeonhole them if they didn't end up dead themselves. Few of us really try to understand what kind of commitment would drive young men to take their own lives."

Jack shrugged. "I'm not going to argue with all that. But I don't understand how it's connected to this Ahmed guy."

Sara smiled at him. She guessed that he wasn't comfortable with what she was getting at. "I know. It sounds philosophical, but that's exactly the point. I think there's a problem with our philosophy, our worldview. What do we make of the mothers and brothers of these suicide bombers who support them? What kind of family would act like that? We can't comprehend it, so we take the easy way out. We tell ourselves that they're crazy. We tell ourselves that they were driven mad, perhaps, by the stressful conditions under which they live. There are even some of us who believe that their real problem is that they're simply following the wrong religion. After all, we have our Christian fundamentalist groups, just like they have their Islamic fundamentalists. I imagine that it's easy for the small radical factions within their fundamentalist groups to focus on the small portion of American society that openly dismisses their religion, and even their whole culture."

Jack's brow wrinkled with skepticism. "I assume you're not throwing me into that pile, but, in any case, I still don't see where this is going."

"Right. I'm sorry. Here's my point: despite all our chest-pounding after 9/11, very few of us asked seriously why they hate us so much ... because they really do. I think the answer is simple, and it's not because they're jealous of us; you don't send your son off with a bomb strapped around his waist because you're envious. And it's not because they hate democracy; that's just plain silly. No, it's because they believe, first, that we—our government—are directly or indirectly responsible for their persecution, and second, that we—again, this is their perspective, focusing on the small proportion of fundamentalist Americans—dismiss their religion and their culture. You don't spend years planning and training to take an airliner hostage and fly it to your death into a building because you're jealous; but you might if you think that the people in the building and on the plane view you and your entire culture as primitive and immoral."

Sara glanced over at Jack. "Anyway, after 9/11 we had a middle-eastern community here that was horrified at what had happened, but were also hurt and nervous from our government's righteous proclamations and military strong-arming. Most carried on making the best of it and waiting out the storm, but a few got caught up in the emotions and began to take the verbal attacks from our politicians personally. They had no background of terrorism, they didn't come to America with links, and so they reached out to find an avenue to act."

Jack gave her a look of pained patience.

Sara laughed. "I promised to get to the point. So, this fellow we're trying to find; his name is Ahmed Mubara. He's a rough character—views himself as a Jihad warrior for his people. We think that the serious terrorist groups shy away from him because they think he's too much of a loose canon, so he's not all that useful in the big picture. But he's apparently managing to start his own personal terrorist war."

"Against a fourteen year-old boy?"

"I'm trying to understand this connection myself." She looked at Jack. "What can you tell *me*?"

Jack explained the family structure, that Ted and Alice had divorced six years ago, that she and he had married three years after. Jared idolized his father, Ted, but lately there'd been tension between them.

Sara decided to see if she could keep the ball rolling. "You seem to care a lot about the boy."

"Yes. Yes I do. He's a great kid, smart and gentle—like his father, I guess."

Sara glanced quickly at him. "Jared hasn't taken to you, though?"

Jack smiled wryly, watching the side streets for Ahmed's car. "It's a tough situation for him. Divorces, I guess, usually are."

"What about Dr. Martin—Ted—what's his company do?"

"Stelltech? I guess some people might call them Beltway Bandits, but they've been doing high-tech development for some years ... robot stuff. Only some of it's been for the military. I imagine it's hard to turn down money to do what you wanted to do anyway."

"What about this tiny spy robot that we're supposed to be chasing? I think Dr. Martin called it a drone."

"I didn't even know about it until an hour ago."

"And what about this Tony Stone?"

"Never heard of him before today."

"So, no idea how he'd be involved with Ahmed?"

"Not a clue."

Sara drove on. They both looked for Ahmed's car.

CHAPTER TWENTY-THREE

Tony came into Jared's view in the visor. He saw his father's colleague lift Russ roughly to his feet. Tony looked angry now as well. "You're just bringing this on yourself!" he said. Then to Ahmed, "Look, we've got to go back to Jared's house. The drone must be there."

"And him?" Ahmed asked. Jared could tell he meant Russ.

Tony looked at Jared's friend. He seemed to be weighing factors.

"I know where it is," Russ said calmly.

"What?" Tony asked in surprise.

"The drone. I know where it is."

"Where?"

"That would be pretty stupid—for me to tell you right away."

"Listen Russ," Tony said, "we're not playing games here. You *know* that Ahmed is serious. Now, where's the drone?"

Russ looked from one to the other. "Take me with you and I'll show you."

"Tell us now kid," Ahmed's said, "or you will truly be sorry."

"What, are you going to do? Torture me for the information here in the church? My screams won't attract attention?"

Tony held his hand out to halt the argument. "We'll take him along." Then to Russ, "This is going to be bad if you're lying, Russ."

Jared's view moved out of the room and into the main church hall. Tony was shepherding Russ with a tight grip on his arm. As they walked along the carpeted back aisle, Russ suddenly turned in Tony's grip and winked back at Ahmed. Jared saw Ahmed's hand reach out and cuff Russ on the head, "Keep moving, kid."

Jared smiled to himself.

The view moved out the main entrance, and Jared suddenly realized he was in full view lying there at the side of the church! The two cars were right there, just fifty feet in front of him. He was about to get up and run to the weeds at the edge of the woods, but the three of them were already outside. He could hear their steps directly now, mingling with those coming through the earphones. He lay down as flat as he could in the grass. He wiggled up tight against the cement foundation of the church where the lawn mower wasn't able to catch all the taller grass.

He hadn't even had time to remove the visor. From his virtual position on Ahmed's shoulder, he saw Tony and Russ walking ahead of him towards the two cars, and he heard Tony say that they'd take his car and leave Ahmed's. Tony shoved Russ in the back seat, and Jared's view swung around as Ahmed went around the car to get in the other side. His view from Ahmed's shoulder was now facing back towards the church. He could see himself clearly lying there against the wall. He felt panic grabbing at his chest. He was ready to take flight as soon as Ahmed cried out. His view swung into the car where Tony was climbing into the driver's seat. They hadn't seen him. Amazing! The scene through the car windows slid around and around as Tony backed out and headed out of the parking lot and onto the highway. A minute later it snowed away as the signal was lost.

Jared lay where he was, feeling too weak to move. Finally he sat up and took off the visor. The warm sun felt so fine there against the wall. He considered again for a moment calling the police, but shied away immediately. Instead he retrieved his bike from the weeds and pedaled over to the pay phone at the Seven-Eleven. He didn't remember his father's cell phone number, so he called again to his father's apartment as he'd done earlier.

"Dad!" he said when the voice-message announcement was done. "This is me again. Russ is still with Tony and another man named Ahmed. I don't think Tony is trying to get the drone back for Stelltech. I think they want it for ... I don't really know, but not for any good. They think the drone is back at our house—my house—but it's really in Ahmed's coat. I can watch what's going on. I'm going to follow them back to the house. Dad ... they sound like they might hurt Russ if they don't find it, and maybe even if they do. I don't think Jack's there. He had to go to pick up Mom at the airport. Anyway, I gotta go. Bye!"

The ride back to his house was much quicker this time; he knew where he was going.

CHAPTER TWENTY-FOUR

T
ed's jury-rigged direction receiver had been unresponsive for many minutes, and he'd stopped paying attention. Instead, he began scanning the cars as he and Stegorski wound their way southeast on Little River Turnpike. They'd already passed a Seven-Eleven store and the Community College and were almost to the Beltway where they'd have to decide on their next move, since it presented a solid barrier.

"Each passing minute puts them potentially farther from us," he said, studying the cars they passed. It seemed so hopeless now that the LEDs just flickered randomly. "And the area to be covered is growing at a squared rate."

Stegorski smiled slightly as he drove. "That would be true if the surveillance area were a circle. πr^2, right? But we have the advantage that we know the general direction they're traveling, so it's just a slice of the pie."

Ted smiled back despite his worry. "You've obviously had some training in the field."

He continued watching the cars as they passed and then added, almost as an afterthought, "But the area still grows at a squared rate, just not as fast—some constant fraction times πr^2."

Ted happened to glance at the circuit board. "What's this! We've got the signal back!"

He scrambled to get the wire loop into position and slowly turned it in arcs. "It's still off to the southeast, beyond the Beltway." He thought a moment. "But, we have to be careful here. We lost the signal for a good while. How do we know that we didn't overrun it? As far as I can tell with this antenna, it could actually be northwest of us now—behind us."

"Seems unlikely," Stegorski offered. "I say we continue southeast. We may lose it altogether if it gets too far away."

Ted pursed his lips in thought. "I don't like it, Bill. The drone should have been continuously transmitting. Why did the signal die, then come back strongly?"

"You said yourself that the connections were bad."

"I know, but I just don't buy it. Reception of the signal doesn't seem to be correlated to my fiddlings with the connections. I think that the drone is truly de-activating itself." Ted stared at the steady, hypnotic modulation of the LED. Almost to himself he added, "What's going on here?"

"Well I still say we continue in the direction we're on."

"Okay," Ted agreed with a sigh, "but, do me a favor, head off orthogonally so I can get a directional fix."

Stegorski gave him a quick glance. "That means 'at ninety-degrees', I presume?"

Ted nodded. "Sorry, yes."

At the next intersection Stegorski turned left and headed north on Lake Boulevard. After a half mile it dead-ended. A sign indicated that the trees in front of them were part of Accotink Park. They'd seen a similar sign some miles before. Ted remembered that Accotink was long and sinuous, following the stream by the same name.

"This is probably not enough distance to catch a deviation," Ted said, "but let me see what I have."

He rotated the loop until he found the peak spot. "I wish I had a compass. It sure seems to be indicating a direction more to the left of before, but I can't really tell for sure."

"Well, you gave it a try," Stegorski said as he turned the car around and headed back the way they'd come, "but we have to get back on track before they get too far away."

When he came to the highway, he turned left, back in the direction they were headed before Ted's diversion. Within a quarter mile they were on the Beltway overpass. The eight lanes below them were filled with streaming cars. Suddenly Ted told Stegorski to move right.

"That puts me in the Beltway entrance lane!" Stegorski protested.

"Bill, just do it, please."

Stegorski stayed in his lane, staring straight ahead, and only at the last minute whipped the car one lane over. Ted had to hang on to his armrest as they curved sharply onto the north-bound clover-leaf entrance to the Beltway.

"You know this will takes us away from the drone?" Stegorski said tersely.

"Maybe, but I have to be sure about this."

Stegorski accelerated and they hurtled northward. Ted concentrated on his loop antenna.

They were nearly to the next exit when Ted said, "Definitely! The signal is swinging to the left. Bill, the drone's behind us! It probably never got very far from Jack's house after all."

Stegorski took the exit, turned around, and put them on the Beltway back in the direction they'd come.

Ted called Sara. "We got the signal back. It's coming from somewhere between the Beltway and Jack's house. I'd guess that it's probably closer to the house than the Beltway. Where are you now?"

He heard her ask Jack. She then told him that they were just south of the Community College.

"Why don't you work your way back towards the house," he told her. "We'll do the same. Call if you find anything."

He closed the phone. Stegorski was just coming back to the exit where they'd gotten on the Beltway.

"You're quite certain about this?" Stegorski asked. "This seems like an awfully risky gamble. I don't like the idea that they could be getting away as we putz around here."

"You have to trust me on this one, Bill. You may be worried about the drone, but you have to remember my son's safety is at stake here. I'm not going to take any chances."

"We don't even know if he's with them."

"I hope he's not. But the drone is all I have to go on."

Ted's cell phone rang. It was Sara. She explained that they'd found Ahmed's car at a church just off the highway ahead. Ted felt a wash of relief that the drone, and possibly Jared, hadn't evaporated.

Jack and Sara where standing next to Ahmed's car when they arrived at the church.

"No sign of any of them?" Stegorski asked, getting out of his car.

"Not a clue," Sara replied. "The engine's warm. They obviously drove it here not too long ago. They must be nearby."

Ted was working the antenna. "The signal has died again. But I got a rough direction before it was gone." He pointed towards the church.

"Jack and I can check out the church," Sara offered. "Mr. Stegorski, Dr. Martin, why don't you stay here and watch their car." Then to Jack she said, "Be careful, no heroics. If you find anything come get me."

Jack nodded and they headed off towards the church.

While they were waiting, Ted used his cell phone to check for messages. He heard Jared relating what had happened. Ted jumped for the door of Stegorski's car and yelled, "Sara! Jack! They've gone back to the house!"

CHAPTER TWENTY-FIVE

A hmed held Russell tightly with both his hands, one on each of his shoulders. At every red light and stop sign, Ahmed's grip tightened, hurting him. They weren't going to let him get away a second time.

Tony parked his car in front of Jared's house and went to the front door. He rang the doorbell and waited. He rang it again. When no one came, he tried the door, and it opened. He turned and motioned to Ahmed. Russell winced in Ahmed's grip as he was hauled out and to the house.

Once they were inside, Ahmed gave him a quick shake and said, "Take us to the robot."

He tried to shrug off Ahmed's hand but the man gripped him even harder.

"Ow!" he cried, "Look, if you want me to show you, then you're going to have to stop hurting me. Now *let me go!*" With one good shake he was free of Ahmed.

Ahmed pulled out his knife and held it out for Russell to see. The blade was at least six inches long. "My friend here would love to kiss you. So I would be very careful if I were you, kid."

He looked at the shiny blade and then up at Ahmed. "Got it," he said.

He led them into Jared's room. Tony told Ahmed to watch him, and went off to make sure nobody else was in the house. When he came back, Tony nodded to him and said, "Okay, Russ, give us the drone."

He'd been pondering this moment of un-truth during the whole ride there. He had to stall until Jared could call for help. He assumed that this is what Jared would do, but there was a nagging, very distressing thought that Jared's falling out with both his father and stepfather would influence him. Maybe Jared would try something risky instead. He had to count on his friend's whimpy sense of adventure that he always teased him about. He pointed up at the vent, "It's in there."

Tony and Ahmed looked at the wall uncomprehending. "What do you mean; it's in the wall?" asked Tony.

"No, it's in the vent."

Ahmed looked like he was getting angry.

Tony looked concerned. "What are you trying to do here, Russ?"

"No, it is. We walked it back into the ventilation pipe for safekeeping. We didn't want Jared's mom to accidentally find it."

"What do you mean, you 'walked it'?"

"Using a waldo and a visor."

"What are you talking about?" Tony said. "What waldo? What visor?"

"Jared's."

Tony looked hard at him. "Russ, I know that the drone won't work with whatever controls Jared has. You can't afford to be playing games here. Ahmed is dead serious. I mean *dead* serious."

He looked at the blade in Ahmed's hand. "We configured them."

Tony looked skeptical.

"The visor was easy," Russell continued. "We only had to select the right frequency for that. We then programmed the visor to work as a relay for the waldo, since the visor could communicate with both the drone and the waldo."

Tony's skeptical look morphed into understanding. He looked impressed. He even smiled. "Kids are going to take over the world."

Ahmed was getting impatient. "So, how do we get it out?"

"We use the controls to walk it out, I guess," Tony replied. He looked to Russell.

"Jared probably put them in his closet," he said, walking over to it. He got down on his hands and knees inside and started tossing Jared's things around, pretending to be trying to find the controls.

"They're obviously not there," Tony eventually said, standing in the doorway.

He came out and shrugged his shoulders. "Let me try under the bed."

He got down on hands and knees and peered under the bed. He lay flat and looked in. Then he started crawling under. Somebody grabbed his ankle and pulled him back out.

It was Ahmed. He leaned down and looked for himself. "There's nothing under here," he said straightening back up and turning threateningly to him. "He's stalling!"

"Okay, Russell," Tony said, "We've about had it. Where else would Jared put them?"

"Hey," broke in Ahmed, "where *is* the other kid?"

"He probably went with his stepfather to pick up his mother at the airport," Russell offered.

"So ... why were you here alone?"

"I always come over and let myself in." He gave Ahmed his most sincere look. "This is my second home."

He led them to other places in the house to look for the controls. After peering under Jared's mother's bed Tony said, "Enough already! They're obviously not here."

"He must have taken them with him," Russell concluded.

"So what to do now?" Tony asked, almost to himself.

"We send the kid in," Ahmed said.

"Huh?"

"We put the kid in the vent to get the robot."

Tony nodded. "Okay."

They returned to Jared's room and looked up at the vent. It was very small even for a child.

"How far in is it?" asked Tony.

"I'd say about there," Russell replied, pointing to the wall about ten feet from the vent."

Tony went to the garage and returned with a toolbox. He pulled a chair under the vent and used a screwdriver to take off the grill cover. Then, standing on the chair, he hoisted Russell up. He managed to get one arm and his head in, but his other shoulder wouldn't fit. He pulled out and tried a different angle, but with no better result. Finally Tony lifted him down. He had scratches on his face and arms and could taste the dust in his mouth.

"What now?" Tony said.

"Through the wall," answered Ahmed.

Tony looked surprised.

"Through the wall," Ahmed repeated, picking up a hammer from the toolbox. He went to the spot that Russell had indicated and gave a swing. The hammer buried itself up to the handle in the dry wall. Tony shrugged and picked up a crowbar to join in.

CHAPTER TWENTY-SIX

J ared saw Tony's car parked in front of his house and swung his bike into the driveway. He'd pedaled as fast as he could the whole way, and was sweating despite the chill air. He suddenly realized that either Tony or Ahmed might be watching out the front window. If so, well, it was too late now.

As he was retrieving the visor and waldo controls from his bike, he heard dull thuds coming from the house. Wondering, he carried the equipment over to the far side of the garage. Sitting against the wall, he donned the waldo and then slipped on the visor. He was immediately greeted with a view of the wall of his bedroom ... with a large, gaping hole in it! Ahmed's arm was swinging a hammer and beating away at the edges of the hole. Wall studs ran vertically through the hole, and beyond the studs was a horizontal portion of the air vent.

"Okay, that's enough," he heard Tony say. "I'll see if there's any tin shears in the garage. "

He heard Ahmed say to Russ, "You're going to be real sorry if it's not there." At about the same time, he heard Tony rooting in the garage next to him.

He understood! Russ must have told them that the drone was in the air duct in order to stall for time.

He got up and bent over, doing the duck-walk as he passed his bedroom window. He then went around back and down into the basement. Using the phone there, he called his father and left another update.

115

What to do now? Within minutes they'd know that Russ had been lying. He decided he should probably leave a message for Jack as well, using the second line on the basement phone. Half way through dialing the home number, though, he quickly hung up the receiver. He remembered that the two men above would hear his message as the machine in the kitchen recorded it.

He donned the visor to check on Russ's situation. He saw that they'd cut away a large hole in the duct, and Tony was reaching in as far as he could. He pulled his arm out and turned to Russ. "It's not there." He sounded sad, resigned. "I think your time is up."

He had to think. He had to do something—stall for more time. His mind was blank. It was like he was pressing so hard against it that all the mental gears were jammed tight together, unable to move. His last image, that of the answering machine in the kitchen above, was stuck there, hovering in front of him.

And just like that, he had it. He dialed the number for the other line again and this time let it ring in the house above. He waited for Jack's announcement followed by the prompt-beep to finish, then said, in as calm a voice as he could muster, "Hey Mom, Jack, just wanted to let you know that I'm at the park—the barn. And, oh yeah, I have the drone with me. Tell Russ if you see him."

There was silence from the house above him. He slipped the visor on and saw that Ahmed was turning as Tony came through the bedroom door.

"Did you hear that!" Tony asked.

"Yes, was that the other kid, the one who took the drone?"

"That was Jared. He said he has it, that he's at the park." Then to Russ, "He said 'at the barn.' What did he mean by that?"

Russ looked at Tony with defiance. "Why would I give my friend away?"

For a moment Jared thought that Russ was confused, or didn't understand, and was thinking that he really *had* called from the park. He remembered what a ham his friend was, though, and decided that Russ was simply playing a convincing part.

Ahmed stepped forward towards Russ, "Because of this."

Jared saw the blade of a knife that Ahmed held in his hand.

Russ looked at the knife, then at Ahmed. "He means Accotink Park. The barn is an old building that they never tore down. They use it now as a storage shed."

"How far from here?" asked Tony.

"Five, maybe six blocks—north and east."

He saw Tony looking at Ahmed. Ahmed must have been gesturing in some way that Jared couldn't see in the visor's view. Tony nodded and left the bedroom with Ahmed following. Ahmed closed the bedroom door behind him. In a low voice he said to Tony, "We don't need this kid anymore. He's nothing but trouble."

The two men were standing close together in the hallway and he couldn't see Tony's face, but he heard him whisper, "What exactly are you suggesting?"

"Just what I said, we don't need him anymore."

"You're talking about *killing* him?"

"You just go to the car. I'll be out in a minute."

He saw Ahmed place his hand on the doorknob and heard Tony shout, "NO!" There was a blur as Tony shoved Ahmed aside and pushed into the bedroom first. Ahmed recovered and followed him into the bedroom to find Tony pulling Russ back through a window that his friend had opened and was halfway through.

"*See?*" Ahmed shouted, "Nothing but trouble!"

Tony turned to Ahmed, "He was just trying to save his own skin. You'd do the same in his position."

"I'm not *in* his position, but *you* will be soon!"

"Don't threaten me, Ahmed! This is my show. Hurting people is exactly the opposite of what I'm after."

"Your show? Your *show*? Yes, that's all it is to you—a show! You have some noble plan to help all of humanity: a goodie-goodie American going to make his God smile. And who will you help in the end? Why, other rich Americans so that they can drive maybe bigger cars and build bigger houses. In the meantime my people live like animals. They aren't even allowed to work to buy food for their children. No, my stupid American partner, this little toy will not be a part of your *show*. I know that this robot is very important to your military. They will give a lot to get it back. With this as trade, I can truly help my people."

"No way!" Tony yelled. "I should have known I couldn't trust you. I shouldn't have let the organization talk me into bringing you. I will not let this turn into some bloody terrorist horror."

Tony turned around to Russ, and Jared saw Ahmed raise his knife. "It already has!" said Ahmed as he drove the knife into Tony's back. Jared gave out an involuntary yell. Tony moaned as his shoulders came back and his hands spread wide in pain. Ahmed pulled the bloody knife from Tony's back. Tony fell forward onto Russ who cried out and scrambled to get out from under him. As Tony fell, he rolled onto his back, facing Ahmed. His eyes were wide with shock. He lay on the floor gasping for breath.

Russ was looking at Ahmed in absolute terror. "I'll show you the barn," he whispered, unable to talk. "I can help you get to Jared—he'll trust me."

Ahmed grabbed Russ by the shoulder of his shirt as Russ winced, waiting for the knife to fall a second time. Instead, Ahmed yanked Russ along. "If you make one bad move," Ahmed said, "I will kill you."

Jared sat frozen. His view showed him that Ahmed went back and pulled the car keys from Tony's pocket. Tony just watched him motionlessly. Ahmed then dragged Russ through the house and out to the car. They drove away and the view finally turned to snow, to be replaced by the blinking beacon indicator. Jared sat paralyzed. There was a man bleeding to death above him in his own bedroom. He couldn't really believe it. The horror was almost unbearable. He shook himself and shivered all over. He remembered the terror in Russ's eyes. Russ! He had to help Russ!

He yanked off the visor and ran out the basement door to his bike. He stashed the visor under the back rack clip, but didn't bother to take off the waldo controls. For the third time that day he pedaled away up the street, this time frantic with fear.

Chapter Twenty-seven

Sara had a lot to absorb. She and Jack had left the church in her car, and were on their way to meet Ted and Stegorski at Jack's house.

"Ahmed and this Tony are obviously after this spy robot," Sara said. "Dr. Martin said that it was attached to Ahmed's coat?"

"That's what I heard."

"How do you think it got there?"

Jack thought a moment. "I imagine that the boy's, either accidentally or intentionally, managed to get it there. I mean, if this Ahmed character knew it was there, he wouldn't be holding Russell hostage, would he?"

"Right. What can you tell me about the controls that Jared would be using?"

"I never paid much attention. It was a thing between him and his dad, really. I do know that he used this helmet—kind of like what I've seen used for virtual reality games, only this one was a lot more sophisticated. It was originally made for a remote-controlled robot that police apparently could use in dangerous places. With the helmet he could see and hear through the robot."

"How about controlling the robot?"

"That was actually pretty tricky. He has these sort of gloves that go all the way up past his elbow. By moving his arms and fingers he could control the movements of the robot."

"Dr. Martin said that Jared's controls wouldn't work with this tiny spy robot."

"Well, they must have figured it out somehow. I think that Ted maybe underestimates the ingenuity of these two kids."

They'd arrived at Jack's house. Ted was already parking his car on the street, and he and Stegorski got out and walked over to where Sara had pulled into the driveway. Jack got out as well, and she heard them talking quietly together. She reached over and took her gun from the glove compartment. She sat for a moment looking at it. She'd never fired it except at the practice range. The men, particularly Stegorski, didn't need to know that. She took a deep breath and got out.

"I'll go in first," she said to them. "Stay here until I come back."

She went to the door and quietly opened it. *Routine*, she thought, *just like training*. She stood back and pushed it slowly open. When nothing happened, she stepped quickly to the other side of the door-post and, holding her gun ready, she peeked in and pulled her head back immediately. She then took a longer, closer look and stepped inside, into the living room. There was only silence. She moved to the kitchen. Silence filled the house. Suddenly she heard a sound behind her and she swung around, gun pointed, index finger pressuring the trigger. It was Stegorski coming through the door.

"Damn you!" she said in a whisper. "I told you to stay outside."

He looked coolly at her. "Since when did I begin taking orders from you?"

Behind Stegorski she saw Jack stick his head in the doorway, followed by Ted. She rolled her eyes and motioned for them to come in. They went back to the kitchen.

"Look," Jack said.

Sara saw that he was pointing at the flashing light of the answering machine. He hit a button, and she heard a message left by Jared to Jack and Alice. It seemed very loud in the empty house as Jared explained that he had the drone at some park barn.

When it was done Jack said, "Let's go!" and headed for the front door.

Ted raised his hand, "Hold on. This doesn't quite make sense. In the last message to me, Jared was obviously in a state of ... distress, or maybe urgency. Here he seems to be calm, or maybe he's just trying to sound calm. Also, why would he tell you almost as an afterthought that he has the drone, Jack? I'm guessing that this message was actually meant for somebody else."

"Tony and Ahmed," Sara said.

Ted nodded.

"Well, in either case," Sara said, "we should head over to this barn since that's where they would've gone. They're apparently not here."

Ted called out to the house, "JARED, RUSSELL! ARE YOU HERE?"

Stegorski came out the hallway from the first floor bedrooms. Sara hadn't even seen him leave. "I think you'd better indeed head over to the barn," he said grimly. "My guess is that the boys are there and probably in trouble. Tony's in Jared's bedroom."

Sara started in that direction, but Stegorski held up his hand to stop her. "He's been stabbed. It doesn't look like he's going to make it."

"What!" they all said at once.

Sara pushed past Stegorski and looked into Jared's bedroom. Tony was lying on the floor looking at her with glazed eyes. She could see blood beneath him. Stegorski put his hand on her shoulder. "You go find the boys. I'll call for help and stay with Tony."

She nodded dumbly and headed for the front door. Jack and Ted followed. The front door slammed behind them, leaving Stegorski alone with Tony.

CHAPTER TWENTY-EIGHT

J ared pedaled frantically. He pedaled to help his friend, but, more urgently, he was pedaling away from the bleeding man in his bedroom. Some small part of him—abstract, disassociated from the raging storm that filled his head— whispered that he should get help for Tony. It nagged at him, but onward he pedaled, his legs pumping rhythmically, carrying him away while his mind was paralyzed.

He came to a stop sign and didn't even slow down. He didn't see that there was a car on his left about to make a left turn. The car started into the intersection just as he came flying through. Caught by surprise, he swerved to the right and off the road. The front wheel of his bike hit the curb at an angle and he flew headlong onto the sidewalk. He felt the scalding burn of scraped shoulder skin. The waldo controls had protected his elbows. He looked to his left and saw the car passing him by. It wasn't even slowing to see if he was okay. To his astonishment, there was Russ looking at him in the passenger seat. Russ gave him a secretive wave with his fingers, hiding the action from the driver with his body. The driver was Ahmed, looking straight ahead, intently focused.

He struggled to sort this out. He decided that Ahmed must have made a wrong turn, and he'd managed to overtake the car on his bike.

He heard a voice behind him. "Are you all right, son?"

He rolled over painfully and saw an elderly lady working in her yard. She must have seen him fall.

"Son, are you okay?" she repeated.

"Uh, I think so," he finally replied. He got up slowly. He felt dazed.

The woman came over and put her arm around his shoulder—to hold him up in case he fainted, he guessed.

"Come inside and let's get you cleaned up," she said.

He let himself be led away. It was good to have an adult in control. She sat him at her kitchen table and went away to get her first-aid box. As he sat there, the pain of his throbbing shoulder was overwhelming. Both the pain and the image of Russ trapped in the passing car put some distance between him and the vivid image of Tony stabbed and lying helpless. The woman returned with the iodine bottle and bandaide box and he asked, "Could I use your phone?"

"Well, of course! It's right there behind you, on the wall."

He turned, lifted the receiver, and punched three buttons. He heard two rings then, *"Emergency. Your name and location, please."*

"My name is Jared Martin. I'm at some lady's house now, but there's a man, Tony Stone, who's been stabbed at my house. The address there is 2951 Southwick Street."

There was the slightest pause before the woman at the other end said, *"Is there an adult there I can talk to, boy?"*

"There's the lady here where I'm calling from, but she doesn't know me ... look, I have another emergency I have to take care of. Just send an ambulance to that address, okay?"

"Hold on, *don't* hang up the phone!"

"Sorry," Jared said, "I have to go."

As he hung up the phone he said to the elderly woman, "Thank you ma'am for the help, but I have to go. My friend's in trouble."

He dashed out the door, leaving her standing wide-eyed, holding the bottle and box.

He jumped on his bike and took off. The street he was on ended at another one that ran parallel to the park: a large, open grass area—the same place that Jack often took Birgy, and where they'd earlier rescued the drone. The barn was to the right, set back in among bushes and small trees. As he pedaled towards the barn, he saw Tony's car parked in the dirt driveway.

He dropped the bike along the sidewalk and approached cautiously until he could see that the car was empty. He went back to the bike and got the visor. He walked to the car again and, squatting down behind it, slipped on the helmet. The view was mostly dark. He could see the bright vertical cracks of sunlight shining between the planks of the barn walls. He could vaguely make out the shape of Russ in front of him. He heard Ahmed say quietly, "Call for him again."

"Jared!" Russ called, but not very loud.

After a moment Ahmed asked, "Where would he hide in here?"

"I don't know."

He saw a vague blur as Ahmed's hand jabbed out towards Russ.

"Ow!" Russ exclaimed.

He pulled off the visor. He hadn't really thought past buying more time and getting Russ away where he might have a chance to escape. What to do now? From inside the barn, he heard Russ call his name again, louder than before. He had to keep Ahmed on the hook here. Judging from his memory of the barn's layout, he guessed that Ahmed and Russ were in the large, open area in the middle. Taking the visor with him, he took off into the thicket along the left side of the barn. The deciduous bushes were bare, and it was fairly easy for him to find a path through them. He made his way around to the middle of the left wall. He put on the visor and cupped his hands against the outside wall so that he'd be calling through one of the larger cracks. He yelled out, "Russ!"

Through the visor he heard Ahmed say, "Shhh." After a few moments he heard Ahmed whisper, "Tell him to come out."

It worked! Ahmed thought he was inside the barn.

"Jared!" Russ called, "Come on out."

Jared cupped his hands against the wall and yelled, "No!"

He then whipped off the visor and, as quickly and quietly as he could, he made his way through the bushes back to the front door.

He checked the visor again and heard Ahmed instructing Russ what to say next. When he took off the visor he heard Russ from inside call out, "He's not going to hurt us, Russ! Cross my heart!"

Jared smiled to himself. *Cross my heart* was a phrase they used when messaging. They abbreviated it as CMH. Like some other messaging phrases, they used it as the opposite of its original meaning. He knew what Russ was telling him: Ahmed *would* hurt them.

The large double doors at the front of the barn were open a crack, but he moved on to a side door on the right instead. Although this door was supposed to be padlocked, the boys routinely entered through here. The wood around the padlock clasp ring was dry-rotted, and they simply pulled it, with the clasp and padlock still attached, from the rotted screw holes. When they left, they placed it all back in place. The park maintenance workers never used this door, otherwise they'd have found the flaw and fixed it.

Walking on tiptoes, he quietly entered the deep darkness within. He was familiar with the layout. The door through which he'd just entered led into what was originally a grain storage room. The room was now cluttered with bags of fertilizer and lime for the open grass areas. Their forms began to take shape around him as his eyes adjusted to the darkness. To his left was a door that let into the large, main open area of the barn where the tractors and lawn-mowers were stored in summer, but which was mostly empty now. It was here where Ahmed and Russ stood, facing the far left wall where they thought he was.

Ahead of him was another door that led into another small storage room, similar to the one in which he now stood. This room, though, was filled with a jumble of unused and broken maintenance equipment. It had a door into the main barn area on the left, but it also had another door that led to the outside on the right. That outside door was two-piece, split horizontally along the middle so that the top part could be opened with the bottom remaining closed, keeping some long-ago animal inside. That door was not used anymore, and, in fact, bushes covered it on the outside. He was sure that there was no padlock on the outside, so whatever kept it closed had to be on the inside. He decided on a tentative plan of action. Its success depended on how that outside door was locked.

Carefully, ever so carefully, he made his way among the fertilizer bags to the door ahead of him. He heard Russ call out to him again. He got to the door and saw that it was open about three inches. He slowly swung it out enough to let him slide through. His heart was pounding as he waited for the inevitable hinge squeak. Instead, the door brushed across a piece of paper bag lying on the floor, rattling it slightly. He froze, and he sensed that Ahmed and Russ did the same. He heard Ahmed whisper something, then he heard Russ reply, "Rats."

"Rats?" he heard Ahmed say louder.

"Rats," Russ responded, "the place is full of them."

Ahmed whispered something urgently, and Russ said "Ow!" again.

There was just enough room now for Jared to slip through the inner door. He had to be careful when he pulled the visor through behind him. He wasn't sure he could make it through the tangle of unidentifiable machinery.

Russ called out again, "Jared! Ahmed says that he's going to hurt me if you don't come out!"

There was a pause as Ahmed whispered something else. Then Russ added, "... but he won't hurt you."

Jared shook his head. Did Ahmed think he was a total idiot? He slowly made his way through the metal jungle. Twice he accidentally made scuffling sounds that caused Ahmed to pause, and Russ to reaffirm the rat theory. By the time he made it through the maze of crammed machinery to the outer door, he suspected that Ahmed must be doubting that he was a rat. This was confirmed when he heard them walking across the main barn floor. He slipped on the visor and dimly saw that Ahmed was indeed slowly walking towards him, presumably with Russ in tow.

He felt panic beginning to rise when he realized that he was totally trapped if he couldn't get the outer door open. He pulled off the visor and studied the door. This wasn't easy since there was equipment pushed right up against it. With his hand, though, he could feel that, just about at the height of his head, there was a clasp. If a padlock hung on it he was cooked. He felt around. There was only a turn-latch! He'd be able to open it.

"Hello in there!" Ahmed called.

Ahmed was right outside the door to the main area. This was it. He had no choice, really. Taking a deep breath, Jared said, "What do you want?"

He heard Ahmed's sharp gasp. "Jared?"

"Yes, what do you want?"

"Jared, come here."

"Why?"

"I want to talk to you."

"I can hear you from here."

"I want to see you."

"Then come here."

He heard Ahmed jiggling with the door latch. He heard him try to open it, but it was stuck. The terrorist tugged on it a few times, then with a bang it swung open. He could now see Ahmed's head silhouetted against the cracks of the far wall. He had to fight back an overwhelming panic of being trapped.

"Come on out, Jared. I won't hurt you," Ahmed said.

"I don't think so," Jared replied, "I think I'll stay right here."

Ahmed tried to take a step into the room, but it was obviously difficult with one hand holding on to Russ. But he persevered. He slowly worked his way into the tangle of metal. With much scuffling and cursing, he made it halfway through. Russ was now being pulled into the clutter with howls of "Ouch" as he was dragged across the metal pieces.

Jared hadn't anticipated this. Soon Ahmed would have them both. He lunged for the outer door clasp. Behind him he heard Ahmed make an all-out effort to get him.

"*Run, Russ, Run!*" Jared yelled as he fumbled with the latch. The clatter of Ahmed's struggle seemed right on top of him. He got the latch open. He pushed against the door, simultaneously realizing with terror that it might only swing inward. But it gave way, and daylight streamed in. He saw that only the top half had opened. He slammed his shoulder against the bottom, but it must have been jammed with dirt deposited against the outside over the decades. Ahmed was almost on top of him. He wriggled his way up and over the bottom half. He had his hands over the door and was beginning to pull himself up and out when the strong hands of Ahmed closed on his shoulders and pulled him sharply back. Jared lost his hold on the visor and it fell to the ground outside.

Chapter Twenty-nine

I should have called the office, Sara thought as she drove her car towards the barn. Jack was in the front seat, and Ted in the back. First things first. She placed a call with the Fairfax police, giving them her destination with Jack's help.

She looked in the rear-view mirror. "I'm sorry, Dr. Martin, did you ... er, do you know Tony Stone well?"

"Yes," he replied "I've worked with Tony for over ten years: six years at Stelltech, and four years before that at a previous start-up. It's really impossible for me to believe that Tony is mixed up in this kind of thing. He's the opposite of what you'd expect from the situation: conscientious, honest, honorable—just a good Joe."

Sara looked at him again in the mirror. "It's my experience that there's almost always more to situations like this than meets the eye. I've read that people fall into four broad categories of trouble: greed, passion, error, and crusade. Greed draws people into banks with hold-up notes, passion to shoot their spouse for infidelity, error to leave the rat poison where their neighbor's kids can get it, and crusade, ... well this can be toughest to deal with. This can tap the most capable of people who are willing to work for months or years to achieve their goal. And, as Jack and I were talking about this earlier, we Americans like to separate issues into distinct good and bad camps, black and white, us and them. When we do this, we miss the fact that these crusaders truly believe that they *are* doing the right thing. They believe that they hold the moral high ground. We shouldn't forget that history sometimes favors their view. We don't like to recognize that if England didn't also have to deal with the French during the Revolutionary War, George Washington might be remembered today as a dirty traitor who was hanged in the square."

She glanced in the mirror again. She realized she was going off on a soapbox speech again. But Dr. Martin was staring out the car window, as though he was wasn't even listening.

"So, how did Tony end up lying on the floor back there?" she continued. "Error, greed, crusade? Whichever one, I doubt there's some secret side to him that he kept hidden from you. I expect that when—if—we understand, we'll see that it was just a combination of decisions which happened, by bad luck, to be categorized as 'wrong' ... at least by our society at this point in time. A criminal-Tony today might be a hero-Tony a century from now."

Ted looked up, and his smile was pained. "He's paying a terrible price for his decisions."

Sara nodded. "The world really can be a dangerous place, especially when you step outside society's defined paths."

"You're quite the philosopher for a cop," Jack observed.

Sara said nothing for a moment. "I started college with a philosophy major. I switched to law enforcement when my six-year-old niece was raped and murdered. They never caught the guy." She smiled. "So you see, even in the most abstract philosophical sense there are some actions that I believe are truly evil. There are things a person can do for which he should not then be allowed to live."

She laughed. "And you see how I automatically assume that my niece's murderer was a man."

"A fair assumption, I'd say," agreed Jack. He then pointed down the street to their right as they came to a stop sign. "That's the barn down there."

Sara gave Ted and Jack instructions. They were simple. They were to stay in the car and wait for her and the police. If anybody came out of the barn they were to only watch to see where they went. She pulled up along the street near the dirt driveway.

Taking her gun, she told them that she was going to go around to see if there was a back entrance.

As she got out of the car, she thought, *I seem to be getting a lot of field experience today.*

****

Once Sara disappeared around the corner of the barn, Jack rolled down his window and stuck out his head. He listened. He opened the door, got out, and slunk up to the bushes along the sidewalk to better hear. After a moment he came back to the car.

From the back seat of the car Ted said, "You never intended on following Sara's direction to stay here, did you?"

Jack shrugged quickly. "I can hear voices from inside. I'm going to go over near the front entrance. I won't go in, I just want to make sure that Jared's okay."

"I'll go," Ted said, "you stay here."

"You have a cell phone. Maybe you should call the police and tell them that—"

Just then Russell came running out of the barn at full speed. When he got to the sidewalk he stopped and turned around to look back at the barn. Jack called softly to him. Russell jumped, startled, then ran over.

"Oh man, Mr. Brassard, am I glad to see you!"

"Where's Jared?" Jack asked.

"He's still in the barn. There's this man—he stabbed this other guy. I think he got Jared. Jared tried to trick him into letting me go, but I think he—"

Without saying a word, Jack sprinted off for the barn.

****

When she rounded the corner of the barn, Sara found thick brush. Squatting down, she saw a narrow path that led through the thicket. It appeared to be a trail used by some animal, or maybe kids. She could hear voices from within the barn. One, presumably Ahmed's, sounded angry, while the other, obviously one of the boys, was scared. Placing her gun in her holster she made her way on her hands and knees. The trail angled left towards the back corner of the barn. The sun was now low on the horizon directly ahead of her, and it flashed and winked as she passed through the complex pattern of the bushes.

She was about to round the back corner of the barn when she saw that the top half of a door was open. She could hear the voices more clearly through it. Ahmed was clearly threatening Jared. She could see that she wouldn't be able to open the bottom half of the door, as it was bound by the deposits of erosion and vegetation. Then she saw some kind of high-tech helmet lying on the ground. She grabbed it and continued around to the back of the barn looking for an entrance, and hoping the police would soon arrive.

CHAPTER THIRTY

Ahmed pulled Jared back through the stored machinery of the small room. Metal edges scraped and bruised him, and tore his clothes. Ahmed dragged him into the large central area and pulled out his knife, holding it out threateningly. "You will now give me the robot," he said.

Jared looked at the knife in front of him. It seemed a whole lot bigger than through the eyes of the drone. "I don't have it," he replied.

Ahmed shook him. "Tell me where it is."

"I don't know!"

Ahmed twisted the shoulder of Jared's jacket in his hand to get a tighter grip and held the glinting blade to Jared's throat. "*Tell me!*"

Russ was gone. Why not? "My friend, Russ—he has it!"

Ahmed paused a moment absorbing this. "You lie! I've had enough of this bullshit." Ahmed pressed the flat of the blade against Jared's throat for emphasis.

He was terrified. He knew that Ahmed might really do this. He reached up with his right hand to feel under Ahmed's coat collar.

"Watch it!" Ahmed said. He pressed the knife harder.

Just then he felt the small, hard body of the drone. With his thumb and finger he plucked it from its safe home and held it up for Ahmed to see. "Here! Here it is!"

Ahmed removed the knife from Jared's neck and held him away to better see what was in his hand. "Bah! You won't fool with Ahmed!"

Jared realized that Ahmed had never seen the drone. He only knew that it was a small robot. He was probably expecting a toy-like man with arms and legs.

"HOLD IT!"

It was Jack's voice coming from near the entrance! Ahmed backed away, pulling Jared with him. After only a few steps he came up against the back wall. He stood waiting, holding Jared hostage. "Who are you?" Ahmed asked. "Stay back or I will kill the boy."

The low sun shining through the cracks of the barn wall behind them threw bright, vertical stripes across the figure of his stepfather as he came cautiously forward. He was holding a pipe like a bat. Jared heard somebody say something indistinct behind them, just outside the barn. It sounded like, "Sit!" Ahmed turned in surprise at the voice, and Jared tore himself from Ahmed's grip and stepped away. Jack advanced with his pipe. Jared looked and saw through a knothole in the barn wall that a woman was outside the back of the barn holding a gun ... and she was wearing his visor!

Jack raised his pipe, and just as be started to swing, a shaft of sunlight caught him in the eye. He swung blindly, but missed Ahmed as the terrorist leapt forward, planting the knife into Jack. With a cry Jack fell backwards. Ahmed stood wild-eyed grasping his twice-bloodied knife.

Jared's heart was in his throat. The terror of Jack being stabbed was devastating and he nearly fainted. But through the knothole he saw, again, the woman with the gun wearing his visor. She was holding the gun towards the wall, as though she was going to try to shoot Ahmed. Then Jared understood that his woman was seeing through the drone he held in his hand, and was trying to gauge Ahmed's position. Jared held the drone out at arm's length towards Ahmed.

CHAPTER THIRTY-ONE

When Sara rounded the back corner of the barn, she saw that the brush here gave way to open grass, and she was able to step out to the middle of the barn's back wall. She looked at the visor in her hand that she'd picked up. What the hell? Why not? She put it on. At first she only saw darkness and was about to take it back off when she began to discern shapes. Yes, she could make out the interior of the barn and there was Ahmed's face. The view was rather hard to follow as it kept swinging around. Through the earphones she heard someone say "HOLD IT!" in a weird, synthesized voice, and then Ahmed's response. Then, as the view swung to the left, she saw Jack advancing with a pipe.

"Shit!" she exclaimed involuntarily. Inside, they must have heard her, for the view then shook so violently that she could hardly make anything out. She heard Jack's cry of pain, and at one point she saw Ahmed holding the bloody knife. She then caught a glimpse of Jack lying on the ground.

She had to do something. The only thing she could think of was to try to shoot Ahmed through the wall. But the sun was at her back and she wouldn't be able to see through the cracks into the dark interior. Her only hope was the visor. Just then her view became stable and centered directly on Ahmed. It was as though the drone somehow knew what she needed. She could see Ahmed silhouetted against the bright vertical stripes of sunlight shining through the cracks. And she knew what to do.

****

Jared stood holding the drone out, and Ahmed took a cautious step forward to finish Jack off. His instincts screamed to pick something up and hit Ahmed, but he held his position with the drone. Then, outlined by the bright cracks, Jared saw the figure of the woman outside the wall. She was holding one arm up and running it along the wall just behind Ahmed. Through the visor she would, of course, be seeing the same image. Through the drone, she would see Ahmed and herself, and know where to aim the gun. Ahmed took another step forward and a thunderous shot rang out. In the distance Jared heard the wail of a police car, and the next instant his father was there, gathering him into his arms.

CHAPTER THIRTY-TWO

J ared sat in Sara's car and listened to the comforting murmur of his father and Sara outside talking to the police in the soft light of the evening dusk. The ambulances had already left with Jack on route to the hospital, and Ahmed to the county morgue. His father had turned the engine on and had cranked up the heat, but Jared couldn't stop shivering.

He had tried to wipe Ahmed's blood off of his jacket, but he'd only managed to smear it in deeper. He couldn't get rid of the image of Ahmed's chest exploding outwards. He'd seen this kind of thing a hundred times in movies, but to have it happen in reality, ten feet in front of him, was like nothing he'd experienced, ever. His father had told him that they'd get him a new jacket on the weekend. He liked the thought of that. In fact, he clung desperately to the thought of him and his father shopping together in a mall for the jacket: normal, safe.

Russ sat in the back seat. He seemed in much better shape. He'd been a prisoner for the last three hours, and although he'd seen Tony stabbed, he hadn't had a knife pressed against his throat, nor had he witnessed Jack getting stabbed and Ahmed being shot to death less than a half hour before. And, well, Russ was just like that: nonplussed by life in general.

"Man, that was some stunt you pulled in there," Russ said. "Stupid, but brave. And I'll tell 'ya, Martin, I'm glad you were both."

Jared smiled a shivering grin. He welcomed his friend's banter: normal, safe.

"What did you think you were doing?" Russ asked.

His answer came through chattering teeth. "I knew that Ahmed would have a hard time getting through all that junk, so I was going to wait until he let go of you, and then I'd open the door and escape before he could even get near to me. I was supposed to jump up and surprise him and get him all excited so that he'd rush in. But instead, he just sort of found me there and didn't let go of you right away. Then the stupid door wouldn't open all the way."

"Well, you couldn't have known that."

Jared was mildly surprised at Russ's response. Encouragement and support were not normally his strong points. Maybe he was shook up more than he let on. "It *was* pretty risky," Jared said, "but I didn't know what else to do."

"You know what they say, 'All's well that ends with us alive and Ahmed dead.'"

Jared shivered again at the thought of Ahmed's fate. "I don't know, Russ. I know that he was a real bastard, but I don't think that I'm ever going to get that image out of my head."

"You're still young, my boy." Russ was back to his psychologist routine. "Why, you haven't even started dating yet."

He thought of something. "What about Tony Stone? Is he okay?"

"I'm not sure, but I heard the police telling Sara about somebody being dead. I imagine it must be him."

His sadness deepened. He'd always liked Tony. It was hard to believe he was gone. Actually, the remembrance of seeing Tony stabbed helped ease the horror of witnessing his murderer's death. In a way, justice was done. That was probably a morbid connection, but he decided it had the ring of truth.

Russ broke his musings. "When the heck did you get the drone on Ahmed's shoulder? Now *that* was a stroke of genius."

"I wish it was. What really happened was that I let it slip off the doorframe and it just accidentally fell on him. I had to scramble to get under his collar. But I sure took you by surprise in the church eh?"

Russ laughed. "That was great, seeing the drone there waving at me. Up until then I didn't think anybody knew where I was. Hey! Wait a second ... why didn't you call the police?"

He had to think about that himself. "Now I wish I had right away. At first I thought we were just in trouble with Stelltech, and the last thing I wanted was the police. Then, at the church when I realized that we were in a whole lot more trouble than that ... I don't know. I guess I still had the idea that I was in deep doo-doo over stealing the drone and ... actually, I had the idea that my dad could take care of everything if I could just get to him. I left a couple of messages."

He remembered his last bike ride. "I *did* call on the way to the barn, although that was just for Tony. God, Russ, I guess I could've gotten you killed!"

His friend scoffed. "Ah, Ahmed probably would've killed me anyway if the police had shown up earlier."

He decided that Russ was definitely suffering from mild shock.

"By the way," Russ asked, "what ever happened to the drone?"

Jared didn't have a chance to answer as the door opened and Sara got in the car. She told them she was going to take them to the hospital to have them checked out. It didn't look like they had any real injuries, she said, but they could have their cuts and scratches cleaned and maybe get tetanus shots.

"Can I see Jack?" Jared asked.

"We'll see. The police are taking your father to pick up Jack's car. He's going to meet us there. You can talk to him."

They drove in silence for a while until Russ asked Sara how she'd gotten involved. She explained how her department had been tracking Ahmed's activities and how she'd connected with the others by accident.

"I didn't know the FBI allowed women to be agents," Russ said, then added, "that didn't come out right."

"That's all right," Sara replied. "That's most people's reaction. Actually, women are usually more surprised than men. Shame on us, eh?"

Jared felt a lot calmer, but still hugged his arms to his sides. He saw Sara look over at him. "Ahmed was a very bad man," she said. "You know, he killed Tony Stone. He would've hurt either or both of you in the end."

"You mean," Russ said from the back seat, "that we shouldn't feel bad that you killed him. It was either him or us."

Sara laughed. "You don't mince words, Russ. Yes, I guess that's what I was trying to say."

****

When they arrived at the emergency room, Russ's parents were waiting for them and there was a gush of tears and hugging before they spirited him away. Russ managed a wave to Jared from under his mother's smothering arms as they walked off. Sara stayed with Jared until Ted arrived, then excused herself, telling them she'd be seeing them later.

Jared was beginning to feel better. Distance from the barn helped, and sitting in the busy emergency room, even though the activities surrounding him were, by definition, emergencies, was somehow comforting. He took comfort in the general air of competence and control, and that none of the emergencies he saw were very serious. When a nurse took him to a small room and cleaned his scratches, the sting of disinfectant actually felt good. The sting was "germs dying," as his mom used to tell him.

Back again in the waiting area, he began to think about Jack. He prayed that he'd be okay. The staff hadn't told them anything, so he had no idea if he was even alive. He remembered how good it had been to hear his voice in the barn and how he'd rushed in, without pausing. It suddenly struck him that Jack had done that solely for *him*. Jack wasn't a policeman or an FBI agent. Under any other circumstances he would have stayed well back where it was safe. His throat felt tight. He blinked back tears.

A nurse's aid came up to them and asked if Jared's dad was Dr. Martin. She then took them to an elevator, up three floors to intensive care, down a hall, left, down another hall, and pointed into a room. He walked in after his dad, and there was Jack, lying in bed with tubes sticking out of one arm and his left shoulder all bandaged up. His mom sat in a chair next to him. Somehow she had gotten here from the airport. Jack looked awful. He was pale and seemed like an old man lying there. Although he was awake, he didn't seem to be really there. Jared understood that this was the effects of the heavy-duty drugs they'd have given him, but the appearance was still one of somebody more than half-dead. His mom was holding his stepfather's free hand and his father walked over and placed his hand on her shoulder.

"The doctor told me that he's going to be okay," his father said.

His mom glanced up at his father briefly, "He lost a lot of blood. Another five minutes and he wouldn't have made it."

She stifled a sob. She seemed to see for the first time that he was there. "Jared, honey!"

He fell into her open arm as his father stepped back. She started sobbing uncontrollably. It took a moment for him to understand that she was overwhelmed with gratitude that both he and Jack were okay. At first he'd thought she was crying because he was in so much trouble over the problems he'd caused.

After a few minutes she recovered and wiped her eyes and blew her nose. She looked up at his father and said, "They got mixed up in your spy business, didn't they?" Her stuffed nose muffled her words, but the anger behind them was obvious.

His father looked straight at her and nodded slowly. "Yes, they did."

His mom made a disapproving sound and, shaking her head, turned her attention back to Jack.

This was unexpected. Jared had stolen the drone, but it was his father who was apparently in trouble. Although it was certainly a relief to be avoiding the hot seat for a while, he vaguely resented the idea that he couldn't be considered responsible for his actions, like an infant who shouldn't be left alone by his father where he might pick up something dangerous. Almost worse than being punished was the realization that, unlike his mom, his father was treating him more like an adult ... and he'd betrayed his father's trust. Worse still, his father wasn't holding it against him! It was almost too much to bear.

Finally, there was Jack. He lay there, his life seemingly hanging by a thread because he had, without hesitation, stormed in to save him from Ahmed. This man, this intruder in their lives, was his mom's new husband. He had always resented the fact that the word "father" was even part of his stepfather's title. He'd never tried, not in the least, to hide his disdain for this man. He had, in fact, gone out of his way to show his dislike. And now here he lay, terribly wounded as a result of his unselfish concern for him. The kettle boiled over in a rush, and suddenly Jared was sobbing with his mom. She hugged him, and his father put his hand on his shoulder. After a few moments his mom suggested that he stay with his father that night. His father responded, "Of course," and the two of them left the room.

When they arrived back at the waiting room, Sara was there with a policeman. She explained that they'd all have to go to the Fairfax police station to give formal statements.

"Couldn't this wait until tomorrow?" his father asked. "We've already given our accounts at the park."

"No sir," replied the young officer, "I'm sorry. There have been two deaths and we're going to have to follow the rules to the letter on this one. The accounts at the scene were just preliminary statements."

Two deaths, Jared thought, so Tony Stone definitely hadn't made it. He felt as though a huge rock were crushing down on him. He was too numb to even respond.

CHAPTER THIRTY-THREE

J ared rode with his father as they followed the policeman to the station where they met Sara. Russ had already been there and gone, having finished relating his account. Jared waited while his father gave his version in a separate room. It took a long time.

After about twenty minutes Stegorski walked in and stopped short when he saw Jared. Stegorski studied him closely and looked as though he was going to ask him something, but then he glanced around at the people present and approached the night duty officer instead. Jared heard him ask the officer if he could question him now. The policeman told him that he'd have to wait until Jared gave his report to the detective. Stegorski tried to argue with the officer who simply pointed him to a seat, and with a scowl Stegorski complied. Stegorski flipped through a magazine, but Jared caught the MI agent eyeing him.

After what seemed like hours, his father walked out, followed by the detective who called Jared. As he got up to follow, his father asked him if he wanted him to be there. Jared shook his head and followed the detective into the small room. As he was about to enter he glanced over and saw Stegorski glaring at him. Jared was glad to see that Sara was waiting in the room and apparently would be participating in the interview.

Jared thought he'd see the sun come up before it was done. They began with his visit with his father at Stelltech. They already knew about the drone, probably from his father's interview, and simply let him tell the story, pausing now and then to ask for more details. They seemed to get lost when he explained how Russ and he had configured the visor and waldo controls to work with the drone, but the detective patiently waded through it all. Understanding lit up Sara's face when he explained that the visor automatically turned itself on when placed on the user's head. "That's why Dr. Martin kept losing the drone's beacon signal," she said to the detective. "Every time Jared put on the visor, the drone connected with it and stopped sending the beacon."

Sara seemed most interested in what Ahmed had said, and also Jared's brief encounter with Stegorski at Stelltech. At one point the detective made a call and a few minutes later an officer brought in the visor and waldo controls, which Jared had taken off at the barn. Jared showed the detective how he used them, although there was no drone to provide a signal. He was relieved to see that, although scratched from all the abuse, the waldo controls seemed in good shape.

His story flowed along fairly smoothly until they got to the point when he was hiding in the basement while Ahmed and Tony argued in his bedroom with Russ held hostage. Jared described how Ahmed had ruthlessly stabbed Tony in the back and then taken Russ to the car. The detective asked to go over that again. After he'd gone through it a second time, filling in as many details as he could recall, the detective looked at Sara without saying anything. He then went through a third time, only now they asked him to just relate the few minutes before and after the stabbing.

The detective pulled Sara aside and spoke to her in a low voice. Jared pretended to be absorbed in the grain pattern on the table, but he could hear what they were saying.

"What's the possibility that he couldn't see it all through this robot?" the detective asked Sara.

"It's possible of course," she replied, "but from what I saw, the view in the visor is wide and clear. Then again, there's always the trauma factor."

The detective came back and nodded, and Jared continued his tale uninterrupted until the final scene in the barn when Jack was stabbed. With a quick nod from the detective, Sara left the room. Jared then had to go through this part multiple times as well. The detective seemed particularly interested in establishing that Ahmed was clearly about to stab Jack again when Sara shot him. When they were through and Jared got up to leave, the detective opened the door, shook his hand, and said, "You did fine, Jared."

As he walked out of the room, he heard Sara say to the detective behind him, "What happened to a detective's objectivity?"

The detective laughed. "Hey, what can I say? I'm a fan. The kid's a hero."

He felt his spirits lift for the first time since leaving the barn. But then he saw Stegorski's eyes stalking him. Jared felt uneasy about this and his heart sank again as Stegorski motioned him into another room. He sat in a chair and Stegorski closed the door behind them.

"Hello, Jared." Stegorski was smiling now. "You remember me? We met last Saturday at your dad's company."

Jared knew a sincere smile, and this was not one. "I do."

"Do you know who I am—I mean my position?"

Stegorski stood waiting for a response. Jared gathered that this was not a rhetorical question. "I think you're with the military ... intelligence, I guess."

"Intelligence, yes. But there are various levels of military intelligence. You should understand, Jared, that I work with a very powerful group. We talk regularly with the President."

Jared nodded, his eyes following Stegorski as he paced the room. He could guess what was coming; he wished that Stegorski would get on with it.

"You stole the drone from the lab Saturday, didn't you?"

Jared looked straight at him. "Yes."

"And you threw the display material into the trash can."

He hesitated, confused. "No, I just took the drone away in my pocket."

Stegorski's eyes flashed but his cold smile quickly returned. "You know that I *will* get the drone back?"

He nodded.

Stegorski paused in his pacing. He leaned on the table so that his face was a foot away and asked, "Where's the drone, Jared?"

"I must have dropped it in the barn. I guess it's still there."

"You dropped it? Why would you drop it?"

"I dunno. I was scared when Ahmed was shot, I guess."

Stegorski's eyes were piercing. He was so close to Jared that his face completely filled his view. "I've searched the barn. The robot's not there."

Jared shrugged.

"Do you think somebody else picked it up?"

He shrugged again.

"What do you think? Do you think it's possible that somebody else picked it up? Maybe one of the police? Maybe one of the rescue squad?"

He shook his head. "I don't know. It's pretty small, maybe it got crushed, or maybe it fell into a crack—"

"Or maybe you never dropped it?"

He returned Stegorski's stare. "I dropped it."

Stegorski stood up. "Then you wouldn't mind emptying your pockets for me?"

He continued to return Stegorski's stare. After a few tense seconds he stood up and began placing the contents of his pockets on the table. They consisted of a quarter, a house key, and a small, beat-up pocketknife. When he was done, he sat back down.

Stegorski nodded. "And would you please turn your pockets inside-out for me?"

He stood up and did so, holding his hands out as well so that Stegorski could see that he was not holding anything.

"Okay," Stegorski said, making as though the interview was now over. "Anything else you'd like to tell me before I find out for myself?"

He ignored the last part of Stegorski's question. "Tony Stone never wanted to hurt us. In fact, he died trying to protect Russ."

Stegorski waved it off. "That's all very nice. Maybe his family will like to hear about that, but as far as I'm concerned he was a terrorist. This country maintains zero tolerance for security threats." Stegorski gave him a knowing look.

As he put his things back in his pocket, he concluded that he did not like Stegorski at all.

Almost as though Stegorski could read his mind, the MI agent called to him as he was walking out the door. He turned and Stegorski was holding a new, brown pocket knife. It appeared to be of fine quality, one that might be used by Special Forces.

"A gift from the military for your help," Stegorski said, handing it to Jared. Jared took it and put it in his pocket with his old beat-up one. He still didn't like Stegorski.

****

In the waiting area, the clock on the wall showed that it was 9:30. This had been the longest day of Jared's life. It was hard to believe that it was just this morning that they'd managed to configure the waldo controls and played with the drone in his bedroom. Within minutes after his father drove away from the station, he was sound asleep. Sometime later he vaguely remembered being carried to his bed at his father's Baltimore apartment. His father hadn't done that in years. It felt good.

CHAPTER THIRTY-FOUR

The next morning, Jared's father woke him very early. It would be a long drive to Virginia, and he'd told Jared that he had to get back for meetings at Stelltech. The visor and waldo controls were sitting on the chair next to his bed. His father must have brought them along.

Clouds had sneaked in overnight, and the dreary side of winter in the Mid-Atlantic States returned. Even though he and his dad left before dawn, they were still caught in the rush hour Beltway jam that was a fixture around Washington DC. When they finally arrived at the house, the police were already there, continuing their investigation. His father gave him a hug and left for his long, slow drive back to Baltimore. Jared couldn't even go into his bedroom. Police tape was strung across his door, and men in street clothes were constantly coming and going. There hadn't been this many people since the housewarming two years ago.

Russ walked in through the open front door. "I hope they haven't found your stash of pot," he said loudly.

One of the men walking past shook his head and gave him a sorry look out of the corner of his eye.

"Listen, Martin," Russ said, "if my mom calls, tell her I'm not here."

"Why not?"

"I'm not supposed to come here."

He wrinkled his brow. "Just today, or, like, forever?"

"My mom didn't say exactly. If I'd asked I'm sure she

would've said forever, but she'll soften in a few days."

This gave him pause. He'd never thought of himself as the kind of kid other parents would want their kids to avoid. This wasn't all *his* fault! He had an image of his conscience wagging its finger at him. In fact, he had indeed stolen the drone, which in turn had set off the whole chain of events. Maybe he *was* one of "those" kids.

He and Russ watched TV in the living room and talked about the events of the previous day. "That was a good one about the rats in the barn," Jared said at one point. "Did you know it was me then?"

"No, but I had a pretty good idea. After all, why else would you have left that message on the machine? I figured you must have had some plan at the barn."

He felt sheepish. "Actually, I had no idea what I was going to do. I just knew that I had to buy some more time. I didn't come up with any plan until I got to the barn ... and even then it was pretty lame."

"Oh, I don't know. I'd say it worked beautifully. I'm still here."

He wasn't sure if his friend was kidding. His mom came in and told them that they could use his bedroom again. When they walked in, they found that she'd cleaned up the general mess and laid a carpet on the floor where Tony had died. This was obviously to cover the bloodstain. The large, ragged hole in the wall still gaped at them. These were the realities of yesterday's horrors and he found that they prevented the events from fading away safely into memories.

Russ whistled. "Man, your room looks like a bomb hit it."

He nodded, then turned slowly to look at his friend. "Wait a second. It was you who made up the story about the drone being in the duct. It's your fault that my wall's torn apart."

"Because you didn't call the police."

Russ had him there. Time to change subjects. "Hey, did you get the third-degree last night?"

"You mean the police?"

"Yeah, first the detective, and then that Stegorski guy."

"Oh yeah. The detective wanted every detail. It took forever."

"Was Sara—the FBI agent—there?"

"Yeah, she asked some questions—mostly about Ahmed."

"Did they ask a lot of questions about Tony being stabbed?"

Russ thought a moment. "Not that many, really. We went over it a couple of times."

"What did you tell them?"

"It was all kind of a blur, but I guess that Ahmed stabbed Tony twice."

"Twice, huh?"

"Yeah, why?"

"Nothing. So, how about Stegorski?"

"He was the MI guy, right?"

"Military, yes. Intelligence, I'm not so sure."

"Geez, Martin, that joke's as old as the hills. But, in this case you're right. What a bone-head he was. He was determined to get me to admit that we still had the drone. He wouldn't let up. He even made me empty my pockets."

"Me too. So, how'd you leave it then?"

"He accepted the fact that you had the drone last. He knew that was how the FBI agent was able to shoot Ahmed."

"Right, so now he's turning the spotlight on me."

Russ picked up the visor. "Man, I'm sure gonna miss that little guy. I wonder what *did* happen to him? He must be back there in the barn somewhere—probably squashed into little pieces from all the feet tramping around."

Jared smirked. "You know, the MI goon really thought that kids carry everything in their pockets."

Russ eyed him quizzically.

Jared reached down, pulled up his pant leg, and rolled down his sock. The drone tumbled onto the floor where he picked it up. It was curled into the auto-fall position.

"Martin!" Russ cried, "You sly son-of-a-bastard, I could kiss you!"

"Shhh, my mom'll hear you. I haven't tried it since the barn.

Its batteries *have* to be dead by now."

Russ grabbed the visor and slipped it on. "Oh man! Martin you're as ugly as ever," Russ said from inside the visor, "but a *most* beautiful sight! This thing has the most amazing batteries on earth. The video's fine, and I can hear myself talking in that weird, wonderful voice."

Russ took off the visor and pulled on the waldo controls, then donned the visor again. He worked the legs out from their curled position as Jared held it in his opened hand.

From under the visor Russ asked, "You didn't even tell your dad that you have it?"

He didn't answer at first.

"Maaartiiin?" Russ finally repeated in a singsong voice.

"No," was his simple answer.

"Why not?"

He'd asked himself this during the ride from Baltimore. "I'm not really sure. At first everything was chaos at the barn. I hardly even *remember* putting it in my sock. It was in my hand when my dad and Sara sat me down near the entrance, and I had to put it someplace. I was hugging my knees, and so my hand was there right next to my sock. I wasn't trying to hide it, I just needed someplace to put it."

He prodded the little bug with his finger. "And then I actually forgot about it until we were at the station and they started to ask all those questions. Mr. Stegorski gave me a creepy feeling, and I didn't want him to know I had it. I wanted to get it to my dad. He built it anyway; it's really his. Then when Stegorski was hammering me for it, I *knew* I wasn't going to give it to him. Man, I wouldn't want to be caught alone with him. I don't trust that guy."

He shuddered, suddenly remembering that Tony had died the day before in his room. Why had he thought of that now? "After that," he concluded, "I was so tired I was only half awake."

Russ had walked the drone up Jared's arm and onto his shoulder. His friend waved at himself. "So, what about this morning? Why didn't you tell your dad then?"

Again he was silent.

"Deniiiaaal," Russ sang in the same irritating voice.

"I don't know," he finally replied. "There just didn't seem to be any rush. I was so used to protecting it, and he didn't ask about it at all—"

"Frodo and the ring," Russ said.

"What do you mean?" he asked, even though he knew what his friend was implying by his comparison to the *Lord of the Rings* story.

"Frodo couldn't bear to give up the ring. In fact, when he finally stood, holding it over the lava inside Mount Doom—"

Just then they heard the doorbell ring. He stuck his head out into the hall to hear better. When he leaned back he said, "It's Sara, the FBI agent."

"I wonder what she wants?" Russ said. "I'll bet that she's come to arrest you for taking the drone. It's good you kept it. Maybe you can use it now to negotiate a lighter sentence—maybe only five years."

He shook his head in mock sadness at the joke. "She stopped to drop off my jacket that I left at the police station last night. Come on, you'd better take off the visor and controls. She'll be suspicious if she sees them."

"So, you don't intend on telling her you have it?"

After a moment's pause he said, "No."

"Good, I would've talked you out of it anyway. Hey, let's listen to what they're saying."

"I don't think so. We've had enough adventures for one month."

"Come on, Martin. What good is it if we don't use it? We'll have to give it back soon anyway. We might as well have one last trek."

He was actually curious about what was being said between Sara and his mom. "Okay, I'll take it out and get it as close to them as I can."

He picked it off his shoulder and quietly left the bedroom. He crept down the hall and heard his mom and Sara talking about the events of the day before. He placed the drone on the floor up against the wall. It looked like a dead fly that had fallen there. When he returned to the bedroom, Russ was listening intently. Jared dug out his portable MPEG player from his desk and took off the earphones. There was a jack on the side of the visor labeled, *aux. audio*, and he sat down next to Russ and inserted the earphone plug. *Voila!* Jared heard Sara talking to his mom.

"—all we knew when we left your house for the second time was that Jared had left a message on your machine explaining that he was at the barn at the park. We didn't know then that, along with us, he'd been tracking them, although much more effectively. We also didn't know that he'd left the message to bait Ahmed and Tony, but that didn't matter since it got us to where we needed to be."

"I didn't quite understand that part," Jared heard his mom say. "So, you say that Jared left the message on the machine specifically to fool these two men into thinking that he was at the barn?"

"Yes, he wanted to get them out of the house. He was stalling for time."

"Why, it sounds like something from a movie. On the other hand, he's probably spent half his life in front of the TV."

Jared heard the musical tones of a cell phone ringing. "Hello," he heard Sara say. "Hi, Bill."

"... I'm at the Brassard residence."

"... okay, sure."

He heard the click of the cell phone being closed. "Alice, could I use a phone?" Sara asked. His mom must have given her a questioning look since she'd just hung up a phone, for Sara continued, "I'm sorry for the inconvenience, but we avoid using cell phones for agency business when we can. They're not very secure."

"Of course." his mom said. "In fact, use the phone there in Jack's den. I'll close the door so you can have some privacy."

Jack's den was a small, windowless room—more a large closet, really—right off the living room. The doorway was only a few feet from the drone.

Jared heard the muffled sound of Sara's voice mingled with the clattering sounds of his mom in the kitchen. Then Sara's voice slowly became louder while his mom's activity faded. He guessed that Russ was walking the drone closer. Sara's voice suddenly became clear, as Russ must have maneuvered the drone under the den's door.

"—of course, Bob. But the Fairfax police seem to be handling the evidence okay. This is no Mayberry force here."

"... I'm okay. I don't think there's any question that Jack's life was in eminent danger. I agree that it could be tricky defending the fact that a view through some Sci-Fi miniature spy robot constituted unquestionable evidence that a citizen's life was in immediate danger, but Jared has given clear testimony, and, besides, I don't think the DA here has any interest in pursuing it. Everybody knows Ahmed for what he was."

"... yeah, well, there's some discrepancy there. Jared's testimony has Ahmed stabbing Tony only once, in the back. He misses the frontal attack. But the other boy, Russell, confirms Ahmed stabbing Tony twice."

"... of course. Russell was in the same room. But, I have to say, the view is surprisingly clear through the drone. Jared was under a lot of stress, and the later trauma in the barn could have dented his memory even more."

"... that's right. We've been trying to figure out ourselves how the robot's display ended up in the trash. Our best guess is that Tony must have seen Jared take the drone. Tony then put the display in the trash can himself to support the ruse that the whole thing had gone out with the trash. Dr. Martin and Mr. Stegorski say that Tony himself later advanced this theory."

"... not sure on that one, chief. We haven't found any mutual connections between Ahmed and Tony. Somehow they were already hooked up, though, because as soon as Tony managed to get the address of Jared's house from Dr. Martin, he met Ahmed at a local church, and they got to the house before Dr. Martin. Ahmed must have obviously been ready to go. They both had to come from the Baltimore area as did Dr. Martin."

There was silence for a while as Sara listened to her boss.

"... Stegorski? Nah. He seems like the admin type, the kind who worked his way up through the military ranks by politicking. I don't think he really understands how the technology works. Pretty tough cookie, though."

"... he was a commando? You're kidding!"

"... okay, I guess they don't call them that anymore—'Special Forces,' right?"

"... his tenacity does seem a bit odd. He's just determined to get the drone back. He acts like it's the Holy Grail. Dr. Martin tells me that they have other prototypes almost ready, there's nothing particularly unique about this one, other than the power source. He wouldn't tell me any details. I didn't expect him to. We'd have to go through channels to get that."

"... right. I'll check in again later. So long Bob."

He heard Sara hang up the phone, then the loud rustle of her feet walking inches away from the drone.

"Alice," he heard Sara call to his mom, "is Jared here?"

From the kitchen, but getting louder as she talked, came his mom's reply, "He was here with Russell last time I checked." She called to him, "JARED! YOU HERE?"

Shit! He ripped off the headphones and ran to the bedroom door just as his mom was coming down the hall. It wouldn't do to see Russ all geared up.

"Hey mom. What's up?" he said, trying to be casual.

"Sara, the FBI agent, is here. She'd like to talk to you."

"Sure."

He walked out to the living room.

Sara gave him a big smile. "Hi, there, Jared. How are you today? A lot better than last night, I hope."

He waved. "I'm fine."

"I didn't get a chance to talk to you after your interview with Mr. Stegorski. How did that go?"

He shrugged and looked down at the floor. "Okay, I guess."

"Did he ... scare you at all?"

He shrugged again. "Nah. He just wanted to know if I had the drone ... the spy robot."

Sara studied him. "Well if you think of anything that you didn't tell us, have your mom give us a call," she said, handing his mom her card.

"And, Jared," she said as he started to walk away, "let me know if Mr. Stegorski gets ... pushy, okay?"

He nodded and walked back to the bedroom. He immediately put on the earphones.

"—I wouldn't worry about it," he heard Sara saying to his mom. "Mr. Stegorski is probably harmless. You know these military types, though; they can get a little enthusiastic, and he probably doesn't know how to deal with kids very well."

He heard Sara make her farewells and leave. He then heard his mom return to the kitchen. He took off the earphones and Russ took off the visor.

"I didn't like this Stegorski guy the first time I saw him," Russ said.

"Yeah, he really gives me the creeps."

"Did you hear what Sara said? He's Special Forces. This is his mission. They sent him to get it back ..." Russ peered at Jared conspiratorially, "... at all costs."

He looked at his friend, realized he was teasing him, and gave him a shove. "Get outta-here! He's not part of Special Forces *now*, her boss told her that he was *before*."

"We'll see. You'd better go get the drone back, though. It's still in the doorway of Jack's den."

Jared hesitated. "Just a minute, Russ. What do you remember about Tony being stabbed?"

Russ thought a moment. "Gosh, it all happened so quick. I was trying to crawl out the window, then Tony pulled me back. Then they argued. It was like a power struggle. Then ... then Ahmed stabbed Tony."

"Okay, where?"

"Right there," Russ said, indicating the carpet his mom had put down.

"No, I mean where on Tony's body did Ahmed stab him?"

"Heck, I don't really remember. In his chest, I guess. I do remember Tony lying on the floor looking up at us."

"How many times did Ahmed stab him?"

"I don't really know ... wait! Tony was facing me when Ahmed stabbed him. He almost fell on me. I had to move real quick to get out of the way. I couldn't see Ahmed actually stab him, ... but ... that would mean he would've stabbed him in the back, not the front! I'm pretty sure that Ahmed didn't stab him any more after he fell. Why did I tell the detective that he stabbed him twice?"

"Maybe the detective wanted to hear that?"

"Yeah, maybe."

They heard the doorbell again. Thinking that it must be Sara returning after having forgotten something, Jared was surprised to hear a man's voice in the living room. It was a gruff voice. He and Russ looked at each other. It was Stegorski.

CHAPTER THIRTY-FIVE

Before either of them had a chance to react, he heard his mom call again for him, and again he hurried out to the hall to meet her.

"Honey," she said, "Mr. Stegorski would like to talk to you." She seemed a little concerned. "It's a regular parade through here today."

He walked out to find Stegorski smiling knowingly. A leather briefcase stood on the floor next to him, the kind that stands upright and opens from the top. "Hello, Jared," he said. "How are you today?"

Stegorski was a lot more polite now than the previous night at the police station. Jared guessed it was due to his mom's presence. "Okay," he replied.

Stegorski turned to his mom. "Mrs. Brassard—"

"Alice," she offered.

"Alice," he started again, "I'm sure that you know that your son ... took a very important piece of government property—"

"Stelltech," Jared interrupted.

"Excuse me?" Stegorski asked, surprised.

"The drone belongs to my dad—to Stelltech."

"Jared!" his mom admonished. "Don't be rude."

"That's okay," Stegorski said, "we won't quibble over these details, even though the device *was* developed with government funds." He turned back to him. He could see, though, that the agent was irritated. "Jared, you claim that you lost the device in the barn yesterday."

He nodded.

"You're sure you didn't keep it?"

He nodded again.

Stegorski paused as though relishing a triumphant moment. He reached down and pulled a metal box from his briefcase. It was obviously something electronic, but it didn't appear to be mass-produced. Rather, it appeared to have been built in a lab. It was thin and rectangular, about the size of an envelope. "Do you know what this is?"

He shrugged.

"This," Stegorski said, holding up the metal box so that they could all see it, "is a directional finder that I borrowed from your dad." He paused, waiting for them to absorb this information. "It's tuned to the frequency of the drone's finder-beacon and it's able to decode the beacon's transmission."

He shrugged again questioningly. He was trying to look calm, but he could feel his palms sweating.

"I've been using this the last hour or so. Once I hit the south side of the Beltway I began to pick up a very distinct signal." He looked to make sure his mom was catching this. "You realize, Jared, that this device's beacon transmission is very specialized. It encodes a type of ... signature that is unique to it alone. The chance that something else would transmit a similar signal is about zilch."

Stegorski waited for a response from him. He resented that Stegorski was being so dramatic and trying to force him to play a submissive role. He pushed back. "So?" he finally said, as though he was waiting for Stegorski to make a point.

"*So,*" Stegorski continued a little sarcastically, "the beacon led me here!"

He stared at him expressionlessly.

"Mr. Stegorski." His mom's stern tone surprised Jared. "If you're trying to accuse my son of something, then I think you'd better be plain about it. Don't play games with us."

He could have kissed his mom. He could see that Stegorski was barely containing his anger now.

Tight lipped, Stegorski fumbled with the box. "Why don't we

just let the direction finder make the accusations?" He held a button down and turned the box to the left and then to the right. Muttering, he flipped a switch and repeated this. They could see that a yellow LED glowed continuously on the box. A green LED next to it remained dark. Stegorski moved to a different spot in the room and tried again.

"Okay," he said, struggling to stay calm. "He's de-activated it somehow, ... or maybe it doesn't work this close."

"Mr. Stegorski," his mom said beginning to lose her patience. "Please make your point, or leave."

Stegorski's anger boiled over. "Mrs. Brassard, your son stole government property!" he yelled. "And I'm convinced that he still has it and refuses to give it up. He's in serious trouble, and it's getting more serious by the minute!"

"Mr. Stegorski," his mom said, containing her reaction to his anger. "I perceive a threat in your words. I will not allow that in my house. If you have a serious accusation to make, I suggest you return with the police—and a search warrant."

Stegorski closed his eyes and took a deep breath. "Mrs. Brassard—Alice—I'm sorry. I didn't mean to yell. I'm simply trying to recover some very valuable property. Nobody will be in trouble if I can just get it back."

His mom stared at Stegorski for a few seconds. "So," she said more calmly, "what exactly do you want from Jared. He's already told you that he doesn't have it."

Stegorski seemed at a loss. He clearly didn't expect the direction finder to fail at the last minute. "Can we take a look at Jared's bedroom? I haven't seen it since ... since Tony was killed."

His mother turned and looked at him for approval. He felt panicky. Russ was obviously in there fully geared up; otherwise the green LED would be lit on Stegorski's box. But, how could he refuse? What pretext could he give? His mom was able to push back against Stegorski's bullying, but he was just a kid. He nodded dumbly.

He led the way. Stegorski followed, holding the button of the direction finder while the yellow LED glowed serenely and the green remained dark. His mind raced, trying unsuccessfully to prepare an excuse for what they were about to see. He paused a moment with his hand on the doorknob, then pushed the door open. Stegorski pushed past him into the bedroom, still holding down the button on the box.

There was Russ sitting at the desk, facing the wall next to the computer. He was wearing the visor, but he'd put one of Jared's jackets to cover his arms. His hands were underneath the desk. They couldn't see that he was wearing the waldo controls. Jared also saw that Russ had left the auxiliary earphones plugged into the visor, but had put the earphones themselves underneath the desk, out of sight. This gave the appearance that the visor was wired into the computer. Russ gave no notice of them, as though he was intent on something going on inside the visor. Stegorski didn't notice Russ at first either, watching instead the box in his hands. Jared was catching on to what Russ was up to.

Stegorski finally noticed the visor that Russ was wearing. "Hey, isn't that the drone's remote viewer?"

He shrugged. "Yeah," he said, as if people wore these things around all day.

Stegorski looked from him to his mom. He was a lion, seconds away from sinking his claws. "What's he doing?" he said, indicating towards Russ.

He shrugged again. "Watching a DVD movie." He stepped to the middle of the room where the computer screen was more visible and pointed. Stegorski stepped over next to him and looked. Sure enough, there was an actor performing amazingly coordinated feats of marshal arts against a whole host of attackers.

Stegorski looked from the wired helmet to the screen. He looked questioningly at Jared.

"It looks better in the visor," Jared said simply.

Stegorski was at a loss. He stepped over to where Russ was sitting. "Son," he said. "Russell!" he said more loudly.

Russ didn't move.

Stegorski tapped him on the shoulder.

Russ moved his head to the side, but kept his hands under the desk.

Uh, oh! Jared stepped up and, taking the visor in his hands, lifted it off of Russ's head just enough so that Russ could see.

Russ looked at Stegorski and said, "Oh, hi!"

Once the helmet was removed, of course, the drone would begin sending the beacon signal. As Jared stood holding the visor over Russ's head, he glanced down and saw that the green LED on the box in Stegorski's hand was now glowing brightly. Stegorski hadn't noticed it. Russ had to keep the visor on—to keep that green LED off.

He jammed the visor back onto Russ's head. Stegorski stepped back, a bit surprised at his sudden action, but didn't say anything. Jared saw that the green LED had been replaced again with the yellow one.

Stegorski looked at the box in his hands, saw only the yellow LED, and let go of the button. He then returned his attention back to the hole in the wall, as though it was a work of abstract art to be appreciated. Stegorski crouched down at the carpet his mom had laid down. The agent looked up at his mom as he reached for the edge of the carpet.

She cut him off with a shake of her head. "Not while the boys are here," she said.

He waved it off, standing back up. He seemed finally to have had enough. Stegorski left the room, followed by his mom and then Jared.

Just before he stepped out of his bedroom he glanced back at the unmoving figure of Russ and shook his head wonderingly at his friend's resourcefulness.

Back in the living room, Stegorski didn't seem very sure about what to do next. Jared guessed that things hadn't gone at all the way the MI agent had expected. Stegorski dropped the direction finder box into his briefcase and picked the bag up, holding it in front of him with both hands. He just stood there watching his mom, as though he was hoping she'd say, "All right, Jared, go get the damn drone for Mr. Stegorski already."

Instead, she said, "Well, Mr. Stegorski, unless you have anything else, I guess that will be good day?"

He nodded curtly at her and just threw a look at Jared. As he was walking out the door, Jared's mom called to him, "And, Mr. Stegorski, I don't want you talking to my son when I'm not around. Do you understand?"

Stegorski paused and turned around. "I understand, Mrs. Brassard." Then he added, "I just hope *you* understand the seriousness of this."

And with that he closed the door behind him. They heard his footsteps fade away.

His mom said, "Honey, I want you to stay away from that man."

She headed back to the kitchen. He didn't need his mom to tell him that.

He went to his bedroom and opened the door with a sigh of relief. Russ was in the same position as before, except that he now had his hands on the desktop. He was working his fingers continuously, sometimes pausing to make pinching motions with his thumb and forefinger. Jared figured that he was moving the drone to a more secure place in Jack's den.

"Hey, Russ!" Jared said, knowing that his friend could hear him through the visor. "That was mighty cool thinking about that movie gimmick. What a pickle! When I lifted the visor off your head..."

He realized that Russ wasn't listening to him at all. Surely he could hear him talking. He walked over and nudged Russ's shoulder, but his friend just shrugged him off without lifting his hands from the desktop. He sensed not to push it.

Finally he said, "Look, Russ, why don't I just go out and pick up the drone, my mom won't see me, she's in the kitchen."

Russ shook his head sharply. Jared was perplexed; what was Russ up to? Why didn't he just let him go out and pick it up?

Suddenly Russ yanked off the visor and jumped up from the desk. "Come on, we gotta' go!"

"Where?"

Russ was already at the bedroom door. "We have to follow Stegorski!"

Jared was still standing in the middle of the room. "Why? *How*?"

"He has the drone." And Russ was gone, away down the hall.

Chapter Thirty-six

They pedaled their bikes as fast as they could. Every so often Russ stopped and checked the direction with the visor, just as Jared had done yesterday, so long, long ago.

"It's in his *briefcase?*" Jared exclaimed. "How the hell did it get in his briefcase?"

"I moved it there," Russ replied.

"You *moved* it there? Are you *crazy?*"

"Look, Martin, layoff. I thought it was Jack's briefcase sitting there. Stegorski put it right against the wall."

"So why would you put it in *Jack's* briefcase?"

"I thought it'd be safer there than in the open." He continued pedaling a moment, then added, "And I wanted a better view."

"Great! A better view?"

Russ didn't answer. His friend checked the visor again. "Good. It looks like he went to the barn. That makes sense."

Russ took off pedaling again with Jared in close pursuit. "I was perched nicely on top," Russ went on, "and when Stegorski reached in to get the direction finder I fell inside. I spent the rest of the time trying to get out. I couldn't climb the leather sides."

Jared sighed. His thoughts were starting to catch up with the situation. "Wait! Now that we're out of connection range the drone will be transmitting the beacon. Stegorski will see it!"

"Duh! That's why we have to get there before he has a chance to check it. He probably won't try while he's driving."

"Yeah, he didn't seem to understand that the finder can be set to continuous scan."

Russ looked over at him. "What are you talking about?"

"I know that box. I've messed with it at my dad's lab. There's a switch you can set to make it continuously active. The push-button was added in case you want to save battery power, but nobody uses it ... except mister genius MI super-agent. What a dork-head!"

Russ finally smiled. "You don't like him, an' he don't like you."

"You can say that again. I don't think he even understands that the beacon only comes on when there's no control connection with the visor."

"Lucky for us."

They pedaled on in silence for a while before Russ said, "You were starting to make a point back there about Tony getting stabbed. I thought Ahmed stabbed him twice, but it might have been only once. But on the phone, Sara was saying that he *was* stabbed twice. You told them he was stabbed only once, didn't you?"

"Yeah."

"They think you were confused," Russ said.

"Yeah."

"*Were* you?"

He furrowed his brow. "Last night I was sure that Ahmed stabbed him only once ... I just don't know now."

Russ stopped more often now as they got closer to the barn.

"It's pretty obvious that he went to the barn." Jared said after one stop, "why are you stopping so much? It's just slowing us down."

"Think about it, Martin. You just said that the drone transmits its beacon only when there's no connection."

"Right ... oh, I get it. We want to make connection as soon as we're in range to stop the beacon."

"Good morning, Martin. Hope you had a pleasant sleep."

The next time they stopped, Russ didn't take the visor back off right away. "We're right on the edge," he said from under the visor. "It's coming in and out." He lifted the visor so that he could see, but didn't take it all the way off. He pedaled madly to the end of that block and slipped it back down. "That's better, now it's stable ... blackness."

"Huh?" Jared said, then, "Oh yeah—it's at the bottom of the briefcase. I guess that's good news. If he found it, you'd see him holding it in his hand."

"Brilliant," Russ said from under the visor. "A veritable modern-day Sherlock Holmes."

He ignored the jab. "So, what do we do now?"

"You walk me to the barn. I'm stuck with the visor over my head now."

"Right, I guess we don't have any other choice."

"The blind leading the blind, I'd say."

"You should remember, Russ, you're pretty vulnerable right now. I could punch you and you couldn't do anything about it."

"Contain your sadistic fantasies and lead on, Martin."

It was another block and a half to the street that ran along the park, then another block or so down to the barn. He thought a moment. How was he going to lead Russ when they both had to walk their bikes? He told Russ to hold his bike with his right hand, right at the middle of the handle-bars, then Jared did the same with his own bike, only he used his left hand. Then he hooked his free right arm with Russ's left, like they were father and bride walking down the aisle. He'd led his blind cousin to the bathroom that way. This didn't work so well here, though, because inevitably one bike or the other would veer slightly inward and they'd get tangled. He abandoned that idea and opted to just walk behind Russ, giving him "left/right" instructions to stay on the sidewalk. This worked somewhat better, but was still slow going. Russ finally got frustrated and suggested that they just hide the bikes in the weeds.

He took the bikes one at a time and lay them in the longest weeds, twenty feet back from the street.

"I see some light," Russ said.

When Jared came back from hiding the second bike, Russ was squatting on the sidewalk, walking his waldo fingers on the cement.

"Going someplace?" Jared asked.

"Back at the house I tried to get the drone out of the way and into a fold at one corner of the briefcase. I'm worried that it may have fallen out of the fold. I don't want that box to crush me. I'm trying to make sure I'm still out of the way."

"I thought you couldn't see?"

Russ worked at it a moment before replying. "I can lift the front of me up along the briefcase wall and see the opening far, far above, so I can sort of tell if I'm in one of the folds at the end."

He made a last pincer grab with his thumb and forefinger and locked it down. He then stood up and groped around for Jared.

"Come on, blind boy, let's go," Jared said, taking Russ's shoulder in his hand.

After a while they found that it worked better if Jared just walked ahead and Russ hung on to the sleeve of his jacket. He'd seen his cousin do that as well.

"Hey, Russ," Jared said as they were walking along, "how do you think the visor knows that it's on someone's head?"

"You mean, how does it know to activate itself. I was thinking the same thing as we were riding back there. If we could fake it into thinking it was on a head I wouldn't have to walk around like one of the Three Stooges with a bucket on his head."

"Any ideas?"

"I was curious about this last Saturday when we were first playing with it. I couldn't see any switch or sensor. Of course, that was just idle curiosity. I didn't do a real close search. Who'd have known then that I'd be walking along now trapped under it?"

"You know, though," continued Jared after some thought, "even if we had an idea how it worked, it wouldn't really do us any good now."

"Why not ... oh, I see. How would we know if it was actually de-activated or not? We couldn't take any chances."

"So I guess we won't be stuffing any volleyballs inside as a dummy head."

"With coconut husk for hair?"

"Precisely."

They'd come to the corner. The park was in front of them, and the barn was down to the right. "I don't think we should walk down along the sidewalk," Jared said. "We don't know where Stegorski is, and we're not exactly invisible walking along like a lost Martian with his human guide."

"Through the park?"

"Yeah, I guess so. We'll take the bike path."

The bike path was paved and about five feet wide. It ran along the middle of the park which itself followed the windings of Accotink Creek. They followed a feeder path from the sidewalk down to the main path. On weekends it was a bicycle rush-hour, and even now at lunchtime on a Tuesday in January, a bike whizzed by every minute or so. The bicyclists looked at them oddly as they flew by, but, being kids, the pair could do almost anything and not be questioned as long as they weren't causing damage.

They came to a point on the path where Jared could see the roof of the barn between the trees. Now he had to find a way back up to the barn. They came to a dirt path heading in that general direction. Poor Russ. The path wasn't wide enough to keep the branches of the bushes from their faces. The helmet protected his head, but every now and then he'd let out with an "*Ouch!*" as a bare twig caught him on his throat.

As they struggled on, the bushes became thicker and higher, and soon he could no longer even see the barn. He wasn't sure if the path was going to take them there at all. Then, suddenly, they were at the edge of the open, grassy field behind the barn. This was where Sara had stood yesterday afternoon trying to understand what she was seeing under the visor.

What now? He wanted to avoid crossing the open area. He couldn't tell who, if anybody, was in the barn to see them. There was no choice, really; they'd have to go around the open clearing, keeping just inside the bushes. The day continued to be overcast, and Jared felt chilled each time they stopped. The cold made each scratching, slapping branch sting even harder. It was worse for Russ who couldn't see them coming.

They plunged into the thicket of the surrounding bushes. It was impossible. He couldn't fight through the bushes and hang on to Russ at the same time.

"You just go ahead. I'll follow the sound of your thrashing," suggested Russ. "Just don't go too fast and leave me behind."

This worked a whole lot better for Jared, but helped hardly at all for Russ. Blind under the visor, Russ parted the branches ahead of him and stepped forward as best he could. Often he heard his friend fall and groan behind him as he was scratched mercilessly. They seemed to be in the middle of an endless sea of gray branches with a gray sky above. If Jared were claustrophobic he could imagine a major panic right now. If he were in Russ's position he thought he'd be panicking in any case.

Finally, after what seemed like hours, they could see, through the branches, the movement of cars passing ahead of them on the street. They went more slowly and tried to make less sound since they were getting close to the front of the barn. Luckily, high weeds now replaced the brush.

Jared whispered for Russ to lay quiet and he continued on his hands and knees. About twenty feet farther, he found himself at the edge of the mowed area in front of the barn. He saw that the entrance was covered over with police tape. There were three cars in the dirt parking area, one of which was a police patrol car. He guessed one of the other two would be Stegorski's; he hadn't gotten a look at it when the agent came to the house. No one was around. They must all be in the barn. He wriggled his way, infantry style, back to Russ and brought them both up to within a few feet of the clearing's edge. He could now peer through to the barn and still talk to Russ.

"I can hear voices," Russ said.

"Can you make out what they're saying?"

"Some. It sounds like maybe there's a forensic guy ... he's getting annoyed at Stegorski. Stegorski keeps trying to go where he's not supposed to."

Russ listened a moment longer. He chuckled. "Stegorski's

being pushy. He reminded this guy that he's 'with the government,' but this guy told Stegorski 'yeah, so's the toll-booth collector.'"

Russ listened some more. "Stegorski got mad and told this guy that he'd have his job, and the guy replied, 'good, I always wanted to be a musician anyway.'"

He could now hear raised voices himself coming from inside the barn. Russ continued his commentary. "Now the forensic guy is calling over another guy that must be a patrolman and telling him to restrain Stegorski—by force, if necessary."

"And, here comes Stegorski out of the barn," Jared said. "And he does look mad. He's carrying the direction finder, but not the briefcase. It must still be in the barn."

Russ laughed. "I can hear the two guys talking about what an asshole he is."

"Stegorski's probably ready to give up on the direction finder," Jared said. "He hasn't had a signal in some time. You know, we have to think what we're gonna' do. He may give up here soon and take off for who-knows-where. Then we'll really be sunk since once he drives away from us he'll see the signal next time he looks. It won't take even his pea-brain very long to figure out that he's had the drone all along."

"So, what do we do?"

He didn't answer right away. What *do* they do? "We have to keep Stegorski here until we think of something." He was more thinking out loud than offering anything.

"Okay, you run out and tackle him, and I'll jam the visor on his head so he can't see anything. Then you run into the barn and yank out the drone and hold it up to your face. The shock of that sight should then immobilize him until we can explain things to the cop there."

"That's very helpful, Russ. Any other actually useful ideas?"

They were both silent, mulling it over. "We have to convince him that the drone is actually here," Jared said finally.

"Okay, so I just take off the helmet and we can go home for lunch?"

"No. I'm serious, Russ. I think that we can make him think that it's here without giving it away."

"Pray tell."

He explained his plan to Russ who grudgingly agreed that it seemed like their best shot. Jared crawled along the edge of the parking area towards the road. Stegorski was putzing around near the barn entrance. He waited until Stegorski had his back to the road, then stood up and walked into the dirt parking lot as though he'd just come from the road.

"Mr. Stegorski!" Jared called.

Stegorski looked up and just stood staring at him. This wouldn't do. He waved. Finally Stegorski headed over his way. He noticed that from where he stood, he could see some of the visor on Russ's head. He took a few steps towards Stegorski and when he glanced over, Russ was now hidden, so he stopped there and waited for Stegorski to come to him.

"Jared!" Stegorski said, surprised. "What are you doing here?"

"Just wanted to get out. Russ is watching that movie so I thought I'd come see what's up here."

Stegorski stood looking at him. He figured the agent was suspicious. He was probably born suspicious.

"Well, you can't go in," Stegorski finally said. "You can see the police are doing their investigations."

Stegorski looked like he was beginning to adjust to the situation. He gave Jared a cold look. "Your mother forbade me to talk to you. Maybe you shouldn't be here, ... or are you just trying to make trouble for me?"

Russ should have acted by now. "Nah, Mr. Stegorski, Mom over-reacts sometimes, that's all. Hey! How does that box work?" he asked, pointing to the direction finder Stegorski was holding in his hand.

Stegorski looked at him. He was obviously trying to decide whether Jared was trying to pull something on him. He finally held the box up without looking at it. "I push a button and it tells me if the robot is sending a finder signal." As he spoke, he absently pushed the button.

"And that green LED goes on?" Jared asked.

"*What!*" Stegorski said, looking at the box. Sure enough, the green LED was glowing. He quickly turned towards the barn and the LED brightened. He swung it back and forth and the LED was clearly the brightest when the box was facing the barn entrance. "Well, I'll be damned!" he said as he headed at a trot towards the barn entrance.

"Geronimo!" Jared yelled. He hoped that Stegorski would think that he was calling encouragement to him, but it was actually Russ's cue to put the visor back on.

CHAPTER THIRTY-SEVEN

Jared watched Stegorski pause on his way to the barn. The agent jiggled the box and pushed the button repeatedly. "Damn-it-anyway!" the man said.

He ran along to catch up. He reached Stegorski just as he arrived at the barn's entrance, still shaking and cursing the box. "Millions! Millions we give them!" he was muttering to himself. "And all they build is crap that doesn't work."

Stegorski noticed Jared next to him. "You can't come in here. Can't you see the tape?" Stegorski seemed really pissed. Scowling, he ducked under the tape and was lost in the darkness.

Jared glanced quickly back at the weeds, but was relieved to see that Russ was still hidden from the entrance. He turned back and peered into the darkness. The overcast sky helped, blocking the sun's blinding light. There it was! Stegorski's briefcase sat off to the right side, not too far from the entrance—too far, though, for Jared to reach in and grab. He contemplated making a sneaky dash for it, but decided that it wasn't worth the risk.

Out of the gloom within appeared the uniform of the patrol policeman. Jared's defenses were up at full shield power and he automatically assumed that the police were suspicious of him and ready to grab him at the slightest provocation. His heart skipped a beat as the officer came to the entrance.

"Hi kid," he said in a kindly tone. "Now don't go in there, we're conducting an investigation."

"Really?" Jared said, pretending ignorance. "What happened?"

The policeman knelt down to Jared's level. He could always tell when adult men didn't have children of their own; they invariably spoke to him as though he was in first grade. The policeman pointed his thumb inside. "We had a lot of excitement in here last night. A man was killed attempting to murder somebody."

He continued to play dumb. He shrugged his shoulders. "Really? I think I did hear something about it. Was it in here that it happened?" He peered into the darkness and could make out the form of Stegorski bent over in the middle of the large open area, searching the floor.

The cop smiled at him. "You bet, son. Now run along."

He took one last look at the location of the briefcase and slowly strolled back towards the road and his hidden friend. He kicked stones along the way, thinking about what to do next. He noticed that the policeman was walking to his patrol car. The man opened the door, sat down in the front seat and picked up the radio hand unit to make a call.

Jared glanced over at the weeds. The visor was clearly visible! Yikes! With the visor on, Russ, of course, had no way of knowing what was visible, or even who was around at any moment. Jared was pretty much in line between Russ and the police car. If the policeman happened to look over that way, he'd see Russ for sure. How would they explain *that* to Stegorski who'd certainly find out what was happening? He thought about distracting the cop by going back and making like he was actually going to enter the barn, but even though the cop had been kindly, Jared was still wary.

He did the only thing he could think of. He played a reprise of the dumb, innocent kid. He strolled over towards the police car, trying to keep himself in front of Russ. He was betting that the policeman wouldn't notice something in the background weeds if he was in his view. He stopped about ten feet from the open car door and just stood staring at the cop. The officer was telling the dispatcher to relay a message to his buddy about meeting for lunch. The cop glanced up at him and looked at him questioningly. He just stood there. The cop finished his call and said, "What's up kid?"

Well, he'd have to say *something*. "That's a two-way radio, huh?"

How stupid! Couldn't I think of something a little more intelligent?, he thought.

"Uh, yeah...." The cop looked like he wasn't sure he should be patronizing with this kid now.

"My dad makes things like that." *God! Not any better.*

"That's nice. Now why don't you go along and play with your friends, eh?"

He toed some pebbles around, but didn't move away. The cop finally got out of the car and closed the door. He waved at Jared like he was shooing away a bothersome cat and walked back to the barn.

Well, at least it had worked.

He strolled to the sidewalk and, glancing around to confirm that the cop went back into the barn, headed down the street. When he was out of view of the barn entrance, he cut into the weeds and made his way back to where Russ was lying. "It worked," he whispered.

"I know."

"How?"

"I could hear Stegorski come into the barn cursing the box. He's going to, quote, 'jam it up Dr. Martin's ass.' So, what do we do now? This is like sensory deprivation torture inside this dark briefcase."

"I'm going to grab the drone from the briefcase."

"Huh?"

"I think I can sneak in the side door and get to the briefcase."

Russ sat silent, obviously thinking this over. "I guess we don't have any other choice. I can't just stay here forever, and Stegorski will leave eventually. I don't think that there's anything else in this briefcase, at least not that I've run into. I'll move an inch or two away from the end so I'll be easier to grab. It's risky, since I could get crunched if he throws the tracking box in. I'll also curl up my legs so you won't damage them when you grab me."

"Okay, good. It's going to take me a few minutes to get around to the other side of the barn and get inside. I'll have to wait 'till nobody's looking. So, it may be a while. You'll have to be patient."

"Maybe I'll take a nap."

As he was leaving, Russ added, "By the way, I think I'm at the end nearest the entrance. The light above me seems to be a little brighter at my end."

Jared retraced his path back to the sidewalk and shuffled past the barn, hands in his pockets. When he was out of sight in that direction he ducked into the weeds and brush. He had an uneasy feeling when he realized he was following the same steps as the evening before. Maybe they should just hang a sign with his name on it above this side door: Jared's own reserved entrance.

The brush was thicker on this side of the barn, and he gathered a few more scratches before he arrived at the door. Luckily, it was still open from the previous night. It was virtually inaccessible from the parking area, and they hadn't bothered to lock it or put police-tape across it. The door was open a couple of inches. He slowly eased it open some more. One of the rusty hinges gave a single small squeak. He froze, but heard no reaction from inside. With three of them in there working, he realized, they would each assume that random small sounds were made by one of the others.

He stepped into the gloomy room full of agriculture bags. It smelled of fertilizer, wood preservative, and rat droppings. Straight ahead was the door to the next room full of abandoned machinery, but on his left was the door to the main area. Through this door it was only a few steps to Stegorski's briefcase, and then a few more to the main entrance. Jared made his way quietly to that door. It was closed. He pushed against it lightly, then more strongly. The bottom of the door gave slightly, but it was firmly attached at about the height of his head. It was obvious that it was latched from the other side, most likely padlocked to keep kids like him from getting at the bags of chemicals.

He considered going around through the room full of junk, but abandoned that immediately since he could never get through without creating a storm of ruckus. Besides, that would put him near where the forensic guy was working.

He looked up. Like other barns he'd seen, storage lofts above created ceilings for the rooms below. He'd often climbed around through them with his friends; this was one of the main draws of the forbidden structure. The lofts consisted of loose planks laid across small cross-beams, themselves attached between the barn's main structural beams. Built-in ladders located here and there in the barn led up to the lofts. One such ladder was built into the wall separating this room and the next one full of junk, and provided access to the loft area just above him. The larger loft above the main area was about four feet higher still and could be reached by another short ladder from the loft above him.

He tiptoed over to the ladder and climbed the hewn wood step-rails worn smooth by a century of use. As his head rose above the walls of the side rooms he could see into the main area. The forensic man was kneeling in the middle. Between him and the entrance lay the various boxes of his trade, arranged in a neat line. The policeman sat on a crate just below Jared, facing away from him. Stegorski was poking and probing the floor around the far wall. Every minute or so, the forensic guy glanced over to check on the unwelcome agent.

Cautiously now, Jared climbed farther until he could step onto the planks of the first loft. They were bare except for a loose covering of rat and squirrel droppings. He made his way one careful step at a time to the corner near the main entrance. Each step lightly crunched some droppings, but the men below took no notice. He climbed the next ladder to the loft above the main area. The briefcase was below him now. He could see it through the wide cracks between the planks below his feet.

He knew from past excursions that this loft was littered with old ropes attached to pulleys and hooks. These were presumably once used to lift things, like maybe bales of hay, up to the loft. He was going to go fishing. He remembered when he was younger and his grandfather had given him a fishing pole. That pole was made for little kids and, instead of an actual fishhook, it had a large plastic hook, which the angler tot used to snag toy fish off the floor via rings stuck in their mouths. He'd played with it about three minutes before realizing how stupid it was. He was back at it now, but this fish was made of leather.

Searching among the ropes, he found one that had a large, rusty hook attached. The rope led off into the tangle of others lying around the floor, but he was able to quietly gather the eight or ten feet he needed to reach the leather bag below. He carefully lifted one end of the plank that was immediately above the briefcase. A cloud of dust drifted down. He froze. The forensic investigator paused and looked over, but after a moment, went back to his work. Jared began breathing again and placed a thick rope beneath the raised end of the plank, then lifted the other end and lay it to the side. He was then able to go back and move the first end aside as well, leaving a gap in the loft floor where the plank had been. He started to lower the hook, but decided that a briefcase rising towards the loft would be way too obvious. He'd have to wait for a better opportunity.

He left the hook dangling a few feet from the loft and sat back. He wondered if Russ could see him, as he was now right above the drone. He waved down at the briefcase, then sat back again to wait. Seconds dragged into minutes. He got tired of sitting and lay back. He knew that he was lying in rat dung, but he didn't really care. His life seemed to consist now of one uninvited adventure after another. No, he knew this wasn't the truth; he *had* invited it the moment he stole the drone. He and his friends used to play out imagined adventures right here in this barn. In these very lofts he'd fought off pirates with wooden stick swords. He wished that this were a play adventure where he could call time-outs at will.

He heard the sound of a car in the parking lot. He eased himself to the front wall and saw, through the cracks, that a van with *Stelltech* written on the side had pulled in. Jared recognized the two men that got out. They were some sort of managers. He saw the policeman come over and talk to them. The cop was shaking his head and waving towards the barn. Pretty soon their voices raised in volume as they argued, and he could make out that the Stelltech men wanted to search for the drone, but the policeman insisted they had to wait until the police investigation was done. The police officer finally returned to his car. The two men stood talking together for another couple of minutes, then got into the van and drove away.

Jared carefully worked his way back to his opening in the floor and hugged his knees to his chest. The seriousness of his theft weighed heavy on him. He could have given the drone to his dad the night before. He could have yelled through the cracks to the Stelltech men just now and told them it was in Stegorski's briefcase. Was Russ right? Was he indeed like Frodo and Gollum: unable to give up the *precious* treasure? He knew there was some truth to it, but there was more. Something about Stegorski smelled bad to him. He couldn't say just what, nor did he quite know what he was after by refusing to give up the drone. He felt certain, though, that the answer lay in the little robot marvel below him.

It was chilly and his hands were getting cold. He put them in his jacket pockets and lay back down on the dirty floorboards. He could hear the whoosh of cars passing by outside. Lying there, he saw that there were small holes in the tin roof above him. In the darkness they looked like a handful of tiny, lonely stars in the night. He could feel that the excitement and adrenaline were beginning to catch up with him. He suddenly felt tired, bone weary. He pressed his arms against his sides in an attempt to hoard his body's warmth. He felt like this little ball of warmth floating in a cavern of cold winter air.

He awoke with a start. After a half-second of confusion he remembered where he was. He lay completely still, worried that he'd made some noise when he'd jerked awake. After a few seconds he heard the soft shuffle of the forensic man below— apparently not. How long had he been asleep? It might have been a couple of minutes, or it might have been an hour. He sat up stiffly. The briefcase was still below him. Out in the weeds, Russ was lying, probably hugging himself trying to keep warm and wondering what was taking so long. He felt bad about falling asleep. There was just enough room for him to lower his head slowly through the gap. He could see the forensic man packing up his gear. The cop and Stegorski were gone. He pulled his head back and looked out through the cracks in the outer wall. The patrol car had left and Stegorski was sitting in his car. It looked like he was eating something.

This was it! He started lowering the rope, but just then the forensic guy picked up some gear and headed for the door. The hook was dangling half way to the floor but he took no notice; the barn was full of ropes and hooks. He guessed that the man would make multiple trips to gather his equipment so he waited. Two more trips back and forth, and there was just one box remaining. The forensic guy picked it up and paused at the entrance. He looked over at the briefcase. Then, shifting the box to one arm, he stepped over and picked up the case. As he stepped through the barn entrance he yelled to Stegorski, "Hey! Don't forget your bag!"

Jared was stunned. This couldn't have happened! It wasn't fair. He was there, in position, *ready*. He felt tears welling in his eyes.

Well, the bag wasn't going to come back. There was no reason to stay here. He retreated, following the same path back, only this time, he didn't have to be careful at all since he was the only one left in the barn.

When he was outside, he was unsure how to get back to Russ on the other side of the lot. Both the policeman and the forensic man were now gone, but Stegorski remained. It would be far too obvious if he were to just happen to come strolling past on the sidewalk yet again.

His problem was solved for him as Stegorski started his car and pulled out of the lot, spitting pebbles in his wake.

He ran to where he'd left Russ. He found him lying on the ground with his arms wrapped around him. He shook his friend's shoulder. "Russ, it's me."

The visor-clad body stirred and sat up slowly.

"They're all gone," Jared said.

He wasn't sure Russ had heard him. After another moment Russ took off the visor and said, "The picture just snowed out."

Russ blinked at the daylight. "Martin, I'm frozen solid. Where have you been? I guess you didn't get it." He was shivering now. "I need some hot soup."

"Later, Russ. We have to follow Stegorski."

His friend looked at him wearily. "The game's up. Who knows where he's going in his car? We can't follow him around on our bikes."

"We have to try."

"No we don't. Look, so he finds the drone in his case? He won't have any proof or even any idea how it got there. It'll be back where it probably belongs anyway. All's well that ends well. Let's go get some hot chocolate."

What Russ was saying made sense. But he knew he couldn't give in yet.

"No," Jared said. "You can go home if you want, but I'm going to try to follow him. Russ, I have a feeling about Stegorski. I don't know what it is, but I don't trust him. There's something ... bad. I don't know, there's just something bothering me."

"Yeah, probably hypothermia."

He ignored the comment. "Besides, there's too much invested now."

"What investment? We've given up half a day of holiday vacation. Big deal."

"No, Russ. Tony gave his life."

Russ looked at him as though he'd just pinched him. "Tony lost his life trying to steal the drone ... like you're trying to do now."

"Exactly."

"Martin, you've lost it. This is crazy!"

"Whatever. Give me the visor so I can track him. You go on home."

Russ stood up stiffly shaking his head. "As they always say in the movies, 'I know I'm going to regret this....' "

Chapter Thirty-eight

R uss walked stiffly as they left to retrieve their bikes. Jared imagined Stegorski getting farther and farther away every minute, and he had to restrain himself from dragging Russ by the arm. By the time they got to the corner, though, Russ was coming back to life, and they sprinted to their bikes.

Checking the direction indicator of the visor, they saw that the drone was somewhere to the southwest of them. That was the direction back to his house. They guessed that the agent had gone back intending to grill him some more.

"At least our trick to make him think the drone was still lying around somewhere in the barn worked," Jared said as they pedaled along.

"Oh yeah? What makes you think so?"

"After we let him see the drone's beacon he completely ignored me. He didn't think he needed me anymore."

Russ absorbed this for a minute. "So now he believes you really did drop it, but he just couldn't find it. So he's going back to your house maybe to try to see if you can remember exactly *where* you dropped it."

"That's my guess."

But when they got closer to the house they could see from the visor that the drone was not there; it was farther away, still off in the southwest direction. They dropped their bikes in the driveway and Jared ran inside, calling for his mom.

"Was Mr. Stegorski here?" he asked breathlessly when she came up from the basement.

"No!" she replied, looking him up and down. "Has he been bothering you? Jared! You're a mess! Go change, and I'll make some lunch for you and Russell. You must be starved—it's after two."

He rolled his eyes. "No he hasn't been bothering me." *Just the opposite*, he thought. "No time, Mom. We gotta go."

"Well at least take a sandwich with you!" his mom yelled, but he was already out the door.

As they headed down the street, Russ said, "Man, that sandwich sounded mighty good."

"Yeah," agreed Jared, "but we can't let him get too far away. We'll eat later."

"He could be in Maryland by now."

He shook his head. "The drone's beacon only has so much range. I think my dad said about five miles."

As they got closer to Little River Turnpike, they saw that the drone's position was now off to the west more.

"Maybe he's at the Fair City Mall," Russ offered.

"We'll head west on Little River. He probably took that route, wherever he's going."

A quarter mile along the highway they could see that the drone was even farther west than the mall. They stopped every so often to check the position. After about a half-mile they stopped, and Russ just sat silent under the visor.

"Well? Where is it?" Jared asked.

"Darkness," was Russ's reply.

"Darkness? That means you've got contact!"

"Yep," replied Russ, taking off the visor. "Let's hope he hasn't used the direction box and found it. If we're lucky, the darkness means that it's still in the briefcase."

He looked around them. Now that they were back in contact range, he was feeling anxious about being discovered by Stegorski. He feared what would happen if Stegorski found them spying on him. "Come on, let's keep going," Jared said, already pedaling ahead.

After another hundred yards, they stopped and checked again.

They were now out of range to connect to the drone, but its beacon told them that it was now behind them. They'd passed it.

"This is a bit of a pickle," said Russ. "We can only get a direction from a distance. We could take four careful readings from different corners and plot the intersecting lines on a large-scale map."

He was looking at his friend levelly.

"Martin," Russ continued, "I was only kidding."

He looked around and pointed to a street heading off perpendicular to the left of the highway. "Let's take this one and see if we can come in behind him."

This street went a good distance before ending at another street parallel to the highway. They checked the visor but it still showed darkness; they were still close enough to be connected. They went left again and checked at the next corner—still darkness. At the corner after that they regained the beacon and, as expected, it pointed back towards the highway behind them.

"We can't take the time to continue this direction stuff," Jared declared. "He might have only stopped for a while and could be leaving at any moment. We'll just have to go back and look for his car along the highway."

They went back the way they'd come, and at the next corner, the one they'd just passed, turned right, back towards the highway. This should put them in the general area of the drone. When they were about a hundred feet from the cars zipping by on the highway Jared paused. "We have to be careful. He could be anywhere. Let's leave our bikes here somewhere."

There were no convenient weeds this close to Fairfax City, so they set them against the wall in a small, private parking lot and chained them together with Jared's bike-cable. They walked out to the highway and looked cautiously up and down. Here, garages, real-estate offices, pool and spa stores, and fast-food restaurants elbowed each other trying to grab the attention of passing motorists.

"Maybe we should check the Burger King and KFC," suggested Russ, indicating towards the restaurants up the street.

"No," Jared replied. "Stegorski was eating a sandwich in his car."

Russ looked longingly at them. "You never know ... as long as we're there we could grab something."

"Russ! He could be leaving any second! We have to find him."

Russ pouted. "Besides, I have to go to the bathroom."

"Oh cripes! Look, go ahead. I'll walk along the other way and we'll meet back here. But don't take long! Remember, we're looking for a big green Taurus."

He headed east along the highway while Russ sprinted off to the west. He walked along, poking into the small parking lots, and peering across the highway at the lots on the other side. It seemed to be getting colder and the overcast heavier. He wondered if it was going to rain or even snow. He heard the pounding of footsteps behind him. Realizing that Stegorski must have seen him pass by and was about to pounce on him, he spun around, and there was Russ running after him as fast as he could.

"I've found him!" Russ gasped. "I saw his car!"

He followed as Russ ran back. Between the street they'd come in on and the cluster of fast food restaurants, there was a small, dumpy, two-story motel set back a ways from the highway. Out near the sidewalk was a large, beat-up sign sporting a neon arrow and the words, *Little River Motel*, then in smaller letters below it, *TV, phones*. Russ pointed, and there, in one of the faded parking spaces, was the green Taurus.

"I'll be damned," Jared said. "We have him."

"We need to get out of sight," Russ said, looking around for somewhere to hide. "He could be looking at us out of his window right now."

This thought gave Jared goose bumps.

"Come on." He grabbed Russ's sleeve and pulled him back along the sidewalk. He went into a small, empty parking lot next door. The faded sign on the front of the old wooden building read, *Palm Reader*, and had a picture of an open hand with a lone eye floating in the middle. From there, they were able to make their way through a pushed-out section of a chain-link fence to the back of the motel.

Rows of barely discernable parking spaces bordered the building and the back of the pot-holed lot, optimistically ready to accommodate any overflow from the front. The spaces were all empty. The motel sat on slightly sloping ground so that the first floor rooms were about four feet above the back lot atop a cinder-block foundation. Back entrances led in from each end, and next to the entrance on their side was a small, open alcove set in to the foundation. Here, there were boxes of motel supplies and bags of trash that somebody had been too lazy to carry across to the far corner of the lot where the large trash bin sat. A small puddle of water sat in one back corner of this recess, but otherwise it was covered and dry, albeit dirty. They ran down the bank below the fence, and over to the alcove. Pushing aside a large box of toilet paper, they squatted down between it and a box of paper toilet-seat bands: the ones the maids attach to prove that the bathroom had been cleaned.

Russ held the visor in his hands. "We need to keep this on continuously again," he said. "Stegorski could check his direction box at any time." He looked morosely at Jared. "You know, I don't think I could bear another minute under there. It's really torture to be trapped in the darkness."

Jared nodded and took the visor from his friend. "Don't worry, it's my turn." Placing it over his head he said, "So long, world."

Chapter Thirty-nine

Jared heard nothing through the earphones, but he could hear Russ scraping and scuffling around beside him. Eventually his friend told him to lift up a second. When he sat back down he was now on something smooth and clean.

"I tore off a box flap for you to sit on," Russ told him.

He felt Russ placing the waldo controls on his arms and hands. "I bequeath my kingdom to you, my good knight."

He grinned. "And a land of perpetual darkness it is, my Lord."

"Yes, fraught with danger, but ripe with possibilities. Listen, Martin, I'm ready to pass out. I'm going down the street to the Burger King and grab a sandwich. What do you want?"

"I'm broke."

"Don't worry about it, we'll call it even for saving my life yesterday."

"In that case, it'll cost you fries as well."

He heard Russ's footsteps fade away, then the rattle of the chain fence, then silence. He sat in the cold, surrounded by darkness. With his friend gone, his imagination insisted on exploring the possibilities of his surroundings: drug addicts sneaking around back for a fix and finding him, rabid dogs, serial killers overjoyed with an easy victim. The slightest sound caused him to jump. After a few minutes he heard a strange dragging sound. It came from off at the other end of the parking lot, near the garbage bin. It was faint at first and seemed to start and stop, then start again. He could hear it coming closer. It scraped, then paused and clicked, then scraped some more. This repeated over and over. It was dragging itself across the parking lot towards him. The scraping sound was ... maybe a cripple pulling along a limp foot behind him. No, it sounded more like somebody dragging something behind them. Yes, something heavy—a dead body. The clicking sound ... this was clearly a butcher knife the murderer was tapping—against his teeth.

In a panic, he reached in his pocket and found the pocketknife that Stegorski had given him. He pulled it out and unfolded the largest blade. This took some time since he had to do it by feel, and he thought he'd have to scream before he finally got it opened, as the dead body was dragged closer and closer, and the butcher knife tap-tapped against the yellow teeth. Immersed in darkness he held up the knife defensively in front of him. The deranged murderer was not intimidated in the least by his fancy little pocketknife, for the scraping came closer and closer. One quick swipe of the huge butcher blade and his puny knife would go flying, fingers and all.

With an involuntary squeak, he yanked up the visor. There was no ragged murderer dragging a dead body. Slowly sliding across the parking lot, was a scrap of cardboard. One flap was folded back, and it caught the slight breeze and propelled the scrap along the parking lot. Then when the gust ended, the flap would fall back with a click and the progress would stop until the next puff of wind.

He hastily pulled the visor back down. He felt simultaneously relieved and embarrassed. Mostly relieved. Although extremely unlikely that Stegorski would be pushing down the direction box's button at just the few seconds that he'd lifted the visor, he nevertheless listened carefully for signs that they'd been found out. Still, all was silence.

He sat feeling nothing but the cold seeping into him. Finally, he heard the rattle of the chain fence and knew that Russ was back. Footsteps came close, and then rustling as Russ pushed boxes aside to make more room. Then came the most heavenly of all heavenly smells: hot fries!

"How you doing?" Russ asked in a low voice.

"Cold, hungry, and miserable, but otherwise, great. What took you so long? Did you decide to eat in the warmth of the Burger King?"

"I was tempted, for sure. No, I've got mine here with me. The motel manager—I assume it was him—was standing outside smoking. I didn't want him to see me so I kept walking. He must have smoked a whole pack out there."

He sensed that his friend had something else to say. Finally Russ continued, "Martin, I have to tell you; I couldn't stop myself. I ... I ate my fries, then half of yours while walking around waiting for that guy. I couldn't help myself!"

"You paid for them, you dope."

"Uh, yeah. Right. Here's your Whopper."

He unfolded the wrapper and could feel the juices dripping as he ate. It was absolutely the most delicious meal he'd ever eaten.

They finished their sandwiches, and he was feeling around for the last couple of stub fries when Russ asked, "What motel would advertise that it has TVs?"

He smiled. "I guess a motel that was built when TV was a luxury," he replied.

"I guess so," Russ said. "So, what now? It must be about three. It's going to be dark in a couple of hours."

He took a deep breath, but didn't reply. He'd been thinking about this. He had dragged them over here on a hunch. Back at the barn it had seemed certain that following Stegorski was the right thing to do. He still felt there was something about the guy he didn't trust, but now he was questioning his own motives for the chase. Was it just to get the drone back? He knew that he was totally infatuated with it. The fact that he'd actually had possession of it for only a short time in the last two days made it all the more intriguing. Like a girl playing hard to get at school, something about possessing this toy was seductive.

A ringing phone interrupted his ruminations. He was hearing a call coming in to Stegorski's room. "Here we go," Jared said. Bed springs squeaked, and he heard the receiver picked up.

From inside the leather briefcase the sound was muffled, and he had to concentrate to hear what was said.

"Dr. Martin," Stegorski's voice said. "Thank you for calling back.

"... I'm having trouble with the tracking box.

"... no, it seems to operate intermittently. The signal comes and goes.

"... no, I'm just holding it when it happens.

"... but sometimes I also get a signal that doesn't seem to have any direction. It's the same response in *all* directions.

"... batteries? How do I tell?

"... hang on, let me check.

He heard movements.

"... when I push down the activate button I see a yellow LED through a hole. It's set into the box.

"... no. No red LED.

"... so, even when that red LED inside the hole comes on, I still have an hour or more of use, and that's an hour of time only when the button is pushed, right?

"... so the batteries are fine.

"... right, I didn't think about that. I was assuming that the problem was the tracking box. But, you're right, of course; the drone itself could be sending an intermittent signal. Would that mean that it's broken somehow?

"... no, no—the power pack is good for ... well, there's certainly zero chance that it's depleted yet.

"... right. The whole point of this was to prove out a virtual unlimited life usage. But we shouldn't be talking about that on the phone. What about this non-directional signal? If the drone is having problems, could that just be a symptom?

"... I see. How close would the box have to be to the robot to lose directionality?

"... did you say ten *feet*? That's awfully close.

"... that's okay. I don't really care about the details. I believe you.

"... yes, I got a strong, highly directional pick-up at the barn. That's my current assumption. I searched, though, and couldn't find it, nor did I get the signal back again ... except when I got back to the motel. That's when I got the non-directional signal. How's things at Stelltech?

"... I see. I'm sure Tony was respected and liked there. He chose his own path, though.

"... yes, it is a real tragedy." Stegorski's voice was acquiring an edge of impatience. "But destroying the drone wouldn't have been an answer. He would've just found some other way to get himself into trouble. Like I said, he made the decision himself to get involved.

"... yes, I know you were just making a point, but understand that people have lost their lives in the protection of security matters of lesser importance than this.

"... what's the cost of a life you ask? I can tell you: when my boss declares information to be highest security, *that's* worth losing a life to protect.

"... I understand. But you don't need to concern yourself. Your only responsibility is to follow the documented security procedures. You'll never be asked to decide on a life.

"... well, this is just an academic exercise in philosophy since neither of us is going to convince the other, and it's not necessary anyway.

"... yes, I understand that your son was in harm's way, but that was not my department's doing. You know yourself that the danger that he was in came about because both he and Tony—completely on their own—managed to get themselves tangled in terrorist activities. I did absolutely nothing to add to that danger.

"... of *course*, the terrorists would have no leverage if the drone wasn't important, but blaming us for that is like blaming the government for building roads when motorists have accidents.

"... like I said, Dr. Martin, I don't think this is going anywhere."

"... okay, thanks for calling back."

He heard Stegorski hang up the phone and mutter to himself, "Ten feet, huh?". He then heard water running in the bathroom.

He took off the visor. Russ was looking at him questioningly. "He's in the bathroom," Jared explained. "I have a couple of minutes before he'd try the box again. That was a call from my dad. Stegorski thinks that either the box or the drone is broke. We've got him confused. He still thinks that the drone's in the barn, though.

"But, get this," he continued, "Stegorski now knows that when he gets a non-directional signal it might mean that the drone is within ten feet. It's more important than ever that we keep the visor connected at all times. One more non-directional pickup and he might start looking in the room for the drone."

"We can't stay here forever," Russ said, wrapping his arms around him. "I vote we just give up and go home. Let them have the stupid thing."

"I don't know, Russ," Jared replied, musing. "Stegorski and my dad argued about Tony's death. My dad seemed to be saying that maybe it would've been better if the drone had never been made, but Stegorski was all hot about how important it was to security—even if lives had to be lost protecting it. Stuff like that."

"Shit, Martin! Even *more* reason to give the drone up."

"I don't know," Jared said, shaking his head. "I just don't know."

"Well, you'd better get the visor back on. In the meantime, I have to go and call my mom. I told her I'd call before noon. I'm gonna be in hot water."

He placed the visor back over his head, submerging into the featureless darkness, and heard the familiar sound of the chain fence rattling. When Russ was here with him, it seemed worth trying to stay on top of this. He just couldn't shake this dire feeling about Stegorski, particularly after that conversation with his dad. But when Russ was gone, like now, he felt lonely, and the danger seemed to loom much larger.

The sound of Stegorski rattling keys brought his attention back to the motel room. He heard the motel door slam, then silence. Stegorski had left? He listened ... only silence. He wished he could get out of the briefcase somehow while Stegorski was gone. He'd then have a lot more freedom with the visor. If, for example, he saw Stegorski lay down and take a nap, then he wouldn't have to keep the visor on continuously. He could just take a peek now and then to check on him. As it was, he never knew what Stegorski was up to unless he did something obvious, like leave. And even then, if he missed the keys jingling and the door closing he wouldn't know if he was there or not.

But how could he get out? Russ had said that he'd tried unsuccessfully to climb the bag's sides. Maybe, he thought, he could get a hold on some stitching at a seam ... if he could just *find* a seam. He worked the waldo controls against the cardboard he was sitting on, but he immediately realized that with just a sense of sight and sound he couldn't tell if he was stuck pushing up against a wall, or making his way across to the other side. It sure would be nice to have a tactile sense, a sense of feel. Maybe he'd suggest this to his dad ... if he ever had a chance to tell his dad about this.

He wondered how he could tell his position at the bottom of the bag. Maybe the light from the opening at the top? This had made him dizzy before, but he activated the Scan mode to get a wider view. As the view swung from side to side, Jared saw a strange thing: whereas he was expecting to see some rectangle of light above him, instead he saw what appeared to be the two ends of a lit rectangle on each side *behind* him. He didn't understand this. Had the direction box crushed him and he was lying head-down? A sense of kinesis—the sense of position—would be nice along with the tactile. Then it hit him. The bag was on its side!

CHAPTER FORTY

Once he got the drone turned around so that he was facing the bag's opening, Jared simply walked himself right out along the side of the briefcase, now his floor. As he approached the opening, the light resolved into definition, and he saw that a zipper flap presented a wall ahead of him. The flap was higher than he was long, and, rather than trying to crawl over this picket fence, he walked his way to one corner where he could easily climb the folds and stitching. Up and over he went.

He paused, relishing the moment. Freedom! It was like a release from days of solitary confinement. He was facing a wall of the motel room. To his right, he could see a lamp and clock radio. They were obviously sitting on a nightstand. To his left was a doorway leading, apparently, to the bathroom. He must be facing the wall opposite the window. Stegorski had presumably walked in, taken out the direction box, and plopped the bag on the bed where it fell over on its side.

He crawled out onto the bed. There was another couple of inches to the edge—a dozen yards in his miniature view. He turned around, but the briefcase was like a four-story building hiding his view of the rest of the room. He walked along the bed's edge toward the nightstand. He came to a pillow mountain. The maid had tucked a fold of the bedspread under the pillow so that a glacier-sized overhang loomed above him. He walked along it until a wrinkle brought the bedspread up to touch the overhang.

Here he could reach up, get a grip in the threading with his leg hooks, and pull himself up onto the pillow. He climbed, one leg after another, up and over the feather-filled berg until he was again horizontal. He turned himself around to see the rest of the room, and there, standing next to the door, was Stegorski!

Stegorski hadn't left after all! He was standing there looking right at him. No, he was holding the phone handset to his ear and staring off into space. He must have decided to check messages before walking out. Just a slight glance downward a few degrees and Stegorski would be looking right at him.

He felt on the verge of panic. A merest flick of Stegorski's eyes and he'd be doomed. Should he scurry for cover, or stay frozen to avoid movement? Too late, Stegorski was suddenly looking right at him! With a curious expression, he looked Jared right in the eye. He took a step in the drone's direction, then apparently heard something in the message that caught his attention, for he grabbed a pencil and began writing on a pad.

Jared crawled as fast as he could towards the back of the pillow. This put his back to Stegorski and he gasped with the anticipation of a hand smashing down at any moment. Over the back slope of the pillow he went. When he was starting to tilt dangerously downward he turned to the right and made his way to the edge where his pillow met a second one on the far side of the bed. He dove into the crack between the pillows and lost his grip, tumbling into the darkness.

He lay motionless, listening. He heard Stegorski hang up the phone, and then he heard the door open and again slam closed. He'd apparently forgotten about the curious black dot that he'd seen on the pillow. Stegorski must have simply thought that he was a fly, which, in itself, was unusual in January.

He wondered whether he could get out of this blanket crevice, though. He seemed to have jammed himself headfirst into the tapering crack between the two pillows. He tried to pull himself backwards out of the chasm, but his leg hooks were designed to catch only when walking in a forward direction; now they just slipped along the pillow cover without grabbing. He pedaled his legs faster, but he only managed to tilt the drone to one side a little. He could feel his brow sweating inside the visor. He felt the panic of claustrophobia. He worked his legs as fast as his waldo fingers could manage, but the only result was to tilt himself a bit more to the side.

He stopped completely and closed his eyes. He took a deep breath. He reminded himself that it wasn't really him stuck in the pillow crack. He could breathe fine, and if he wanted to, he could just whip off the visor and run home.

This helped considerably. As he calmed down, the solution was obvious. He had already started to tilt to one side. By pushing slowly with the downside front leg, and simultaneously pulling up with the upper leg, he easily turned himself completely sideways and was able to crawl out of the crack.

He emerged in the middle of the bed. Where now? Someplace safe, yet where he'd have a good view of the room. He decided on the curtains. Here, he could keep a fly's-eye view of the room, and maybe look outside as well. Plus, what would be more natural than an old, dead fly still hanging onto a curtain? The motel was dingy enough that dead flies would come as no surprise.

He made his way to the edge of the bed opposite the briefcase. The old bedspread rolled away before him down into the canyon depths of the open area between the bed and the window. He edged his way over. He started to tilt down towards the floor. He remembered that the leg hooks caught backwards, appropriate for climbing in a forward direction. He realized that he'd have to back down the blanket canyon wall for the hooks to take hold. Maybe he should move back up to a more flat area to execute his turn. Not knowing why Stegorski had left, though, he was afraid that the agent could be back at any moment. He began his turn where he was. Suddenly his view spun as he fell, tumbling to the carpet far below.

The view settled, and he could see that he'd rolled under the bed. Maybe it was okay not to have those tactile and kenesis senses after all, as these falls might then be far too real. As he expected, the drone had automatically folded in its legs, and he had to work them back out before proceeding across the seemingly huge expanse of floor carpet to the drapes. Luckily, the carpet was the cheap, short-fiber indoor/outdoor type that his tiny legs could easily navigate.

He was nervous crossing the open carpet, but he made it to the safety of the curtains without Stegorski walking in to find him. Reaching the drapes, he found the next problem: they didn't extend all the way to the floor. They were only about an inch or so above him, but that was as high as a second-story window to him, and well out of reach of his claws. In the worst case, if Stegorski came back now, he could hide up against the wall, but he really wanted to get a good view of the room. That would provide the precious release from the purgatory of continual visor duty. He walked to the near end of the drapes without finding any way up. He walked the length to the other end, right next to the door, but still it was too high.

He noticed, though, that there was a thread hanging down from the sheer inner curtain—more like a remnant end of stitching that hadn't been cut off properly. Jared switched to Articulate mode, and was able to grab the hanging twists of thread with his claws and pull himself vertical. He found, though, that his view didn't allow him to see where his legs were, and he couldn't tell if they were hooked into a twist of thread-braid, or just dangling in space. He tried the Scan mode. He was able to see his feet at the far excursions of the scans, but he quickly exited the mode, as he found himself becoming rapidly nauseous like the previous times he'd used it. Finally, while making a blind grab, he missed and tumbled back to the carpet. He decided that this was a waste of time. Fortunately, the fall was not far enough to activate the auto-fold of his legs, and he was immediately back on his feet.

It looked like he wouldn't make it up the drapes after all. He reverted to plan B and moved himself to the wall underneath the curtains. As he waited for Stegorski to return, he noticed that the surface was not painted. Rather, it was wallpapered with fabric-type material that had been popular back in the seventies and eighties. Over the decades, the wallpaper had become dirty and dinged, but the fabric-like material might still provide a grip for his leg hooks.

He turned himself around so that he was facing the wall. He wasn't able to get a grip with his claws to pull himself up, but he found that the hooks worked perfectly in the fiber texture, and all he had to do was reach out his front legs and walk right up. It was as though this was exactly what the drone was built for. He climbed the wall like he was walking across a flat surface. Up, up he went. Ahead, he saw a dark line that grew into a wall before him as he got closer. This must be the sill of the window above, extending out from the wall. It presented an impassable barrier. It was aluminum and there was no way for him to get a grip. Stegorski had never opened the drapes, so Jared was now safely hidden inside the gloom, but he still had no view of the room.

He turned away from the door and made his way along the bottom of the sill. When he got to the end, he was still behind the drape, which extended beyond the side of the window. He continued up along the edge of the window towards the ceiling. He guessed he was about halfway up when he heard the door open and close. He paused a moment but saw no reason to take caution. Thinking he'd try to get a view outside, he moved over to the window's edge. It was set into the wall, with drywall casings around the inner sides. The wallpaper covered this area so that he had continuous footing around the corner ... if he could just *get* around the corner. This was a problem he kept running into: he had difficulty reaching around corners with his legs. He turned himself so that he was facing upwards, then found that he could ease himself around the corner and grab the wallpaper on the inner surface with his right two legs. He was now on the window's casing facing the top of the window. He could see the flat white light of the overcast day off to his right. He turned himself so that he was facing the window, and as he did so the images of cars and bare trees swung towards him. He could finally see outside!

The problem with the view was that it was sideways. This was disconcerting. He had the urge to twist his head to try to right it. He studied the skewed image and saw that Stegorski's room was on the second floor. He couldn't tell which room, but it seemed as though they were at the left side of the building, the opposite end from where his own flesh-and-blood body sat right now on a piece of cardboard among the trash.

There, out on the sidewalk he could see somebody walking along. It looked like a boy about his own age. In fact, it looked a lot like Russ ... oops; it *was* Russ coming back. Jared realized how dangerous it actually was for them to walk around out there in front of the motel.

He heard the room door slam, then Stegorski dialing the phone. He then heard him talking, but the drapes absorbed enough sound to make the words almost impossible to make out. He eased himself back around the window casing's edge and crawled horizontally to the edge of the drapes. As he was crawling his way there, he heard Russ arriving. Russ must have seen him absorbed in walking the waldoes on the cardboard because, except for a quick, "I'm back," he remained silent, waiting. The drone reached the edge of the drape and he could now clearly hear Stegorski's say, "... it's okay, I'm on a land line at my room."

"... the unit hasn't been located. That's negative. I have evidence that it's at a barn in a park here. That's where the FBI agent shot Ahmed.

"... shit! really? How far up in the FBI are the questions coming?

"... but, we can bring the lid down there—hell, we could get the President to intercede if it comes to that.

"... yeah, I expected that we might have problems with this FBI gal. She's young. She still sees her role in life as a noble agent of good, protecting American citizens from harm.

"... his name was Tony Stone. Yes, he was the blind agent.

"... no, they still think Ahmed killed him.

"... I couldn't take that chance. It wasn't clear that Ahmed's wound would be fatal. I couldn't wait very much longer to call in rescue. In fact, it turns out that the kid actually placed his call before I did.

"... a kitchen knife—about the same size blade as Ahmed's. They're not even suspicious. They won't bother to do a forensic match of the two stab wounds.

"... the kid apparently gave testimony that he saw Ahmed only stab once, but from what I gather, they're discounting this as unreliable—a traumatized kid viewing through some miniature camera. In any case, his friend claims he saw Ahmed stab twice, and he was in the same room.

"... well, here's a status assessment: Tony Stone was the prime risk, obviously. Dr. Martin and the FBI agent will both probably honor their security restrictions. We'd have to keep an eye on Jack Brassard, the kid's stepfather. He heard enough to be dangerous. He's a teacher—could be viewed as credible. There's the kid, of course, and his friend. I gather that they're tech-geeks—probably surround themselves with science fiction. Maybe they'll be seen as suffering from active imaginations. In any case, they're too young to be credible.

"... right, the whole bunch will require some monitoring for a while. You're still sending backup, right?

"... two staff, tomorrow morning around 10:00 AM—got it.

"... right, you too. So long."

He heard the sound of the phone being hung up. He slowly took off the visor and returned to the cardboard boxes and trash bags of the alcove. Russ was kneeling in front of him watching him. Jared looked at him, stunned. "Stegorski murdered Tony."

CHAPTER FORTY-ONE

"Stegorski," Jared repeated, still dazed. "He murdered Tony."

Russ held out a piece of apple pie in a cardboard container to him. "What are you talking about?"

"I just heard him talking to ... I guess his boss, or maybe a co-worker on the phone. He stabbed Tony after Ahmed stabbed him. I guess he did it after everybody left to find us. He used one of our kitchen knives!" Jared said this as though he'd never before realized that a kitchen knife, or at least one in his house, could be used to kill somebody.

"What!"

He shook his head quickly and looked at his friend. He felt like he was waking up from a bad nightmare, except that the nightmare was still in the motel room above them. He took the offered apple pie without comment.

"Russ," he continued, "they've assessed the risk of the rest of us, like we're pieces on a chess board."

"Are you sure you heard right? What exactly did he say?"

"I don't remember the exact words, but I'm telling you, Russ, he killed him. I think they were afraid that he'd talk."

"About what?"

He shrugged his shoulders. "The drone, I guess."

"But that doesn't make sense. There must be at least twenty people at your dad's company that know about it."

"He called him a 'blind agent.' "

"Huh?"

"I just remembered that Stegorski called Tony a blind agent."

"What's that?"

"I dunno ... maybe that he used to be part of MI?"

"Maybe he was acting as their agent, but he didn't even *know* that he was; you know, he was blind to the fact."

"Yeah, that could be." He tried to remember more. "Sara's reports must be causing some ripples up the ranks in the FBI. Stegorski said that—get this, Russ—they might have to get the President to step in to keep the FBI off their backs."

Russ looked at him skeptically. "Come on, the *President*?"

"That's what he said."

"Maybe it's the president of their country club."

"It sure sounded like *the* President. Russ, we gotta *do* something."

"We have to tell the police. How about Sara?"

"No, they won't believe us. Like Stegorski said on the phone, we're 'too young to be credible.' "

"We could try. They might."

"No. We'd just be wasting time, and Stegorski might find out that we're on to him. He talks to the police, you know."

"Well, what then?"

He stared at the visor. "We have to get evidence."

"You already heard him talk about it."

"They won't *believe* me. We need hard evidence."

"Okay, we'll confront Stegorski and demand a written confession. If he refuses we'll threaten to put the drone down his shirt and tickle him to death."

He rolled his eyes. "Big help, Russ. Thanks."

"Well, then how about this: I'll go get my tape recorder and we'll catch his next conversation."

Jared smiled. "We'll tap into the aux audio jack of the visor! Russ, you're a genius."

"If only the world would accept it gracefully."

He looked to Russ in surprise. "I just remembered! Stegorski said that two more men are going to come to help him. They're supposed to be here tomorrow morning. Once they get here, they'll be looking for us. We won't be able to hide here much longer after that."

Russ looked at him. "One of us will have to stay here listening."

"I'm staying, Russ. You go get the tape recorder."

"Martin, I mean one of us will have to stay all night."

He nodded. "I know. You'll need to bring blankets for me ... and some food."

"What will you tell your mom?"

He thought a moment. "I'll tell her that I'll be at your house."

"And if your mom calls our house tonight?"

He lifted his palms. "Then I'm busted."

"Okay, then," Russ said, getting up, "I'd better get going if I'm going to come back and still get home before dark."

As Russ was leaving, he said, "Stegorski thinks we're tech-geeks."

His friend shrugged. "We are."

CHAPTER FORTY-TWO

Jared put the visor back on and heard the sound of the TV in Stegorski's room. This surprised him. Even though Stegorski was not sitting at a desk, he still had a job, and here he was relaxing in front of the tube. It seemed like cheating.

He crawled the drone farther out from behind the drapes. Perched on the wall, though, he could only orient himself in one plane: towards the back wall, the ceiling, the drapes. He could, however, hear the TV clearly. Stegorski was watching Oprah. He found this even more surprising than the fact that he was watching television at all. Stegorski was a soulless, calculating murderer, but still interested in exploring the everyday human condition, however sensationally presented.

He had to find a better place to hide, someplace where he could hear *and* see what was going on in the room. Had the drapes been open, the windowsill would have been ideal. Go for the high ground. Up, and up to the top of the drapes he crawled, trying to find a flat surface to position himself for a view. The drapes never touched the wall and remained always tantalizingly just out of reach. He worked his way over to the drapes and curtain brackets. He might be able to crawl out along one of these, but as he positioned himself at one of their bases, he reminded himself that the drone didn't do well on smooth surfaces. He'd likely fall, and, although he'd survived a few tumbles already, they'd all been onto soft carpets. He didn't think he'd survive a fall onto the windowsill, so far below. No, it wasn't worth the risk.

Instead, he made his way back down to the floor between the window and the edge of the drape where he could remain hidden from Stegorski. This was a very slow process since he had to back down, step by step, so that his leg-hooks could get a grip. By the time he was below the sill and about two feet from the floor, he was so tired of the process that he turned around and, sure enough, as soon as he took his first step the view spun away in the now-familiar tumbling free-fall. It sure would be nice, he decided, to have hooks facing both ways.

The image settled, and he quickly worked his folded legs out. He stood up and was startled to see that his fall had rolled him out onto the carpet. He was half way to the bed. Oh well, there was nothing for him back at the wall; he scurried under the bed.

From there he angled across to the opposite head corner. He crossed in front of the small bed-stand dresser and found a one-inch crack between the bed-stand and the wall. He backed himself into here with just his head sticking out. From this position, he could hear fine, and he could at least see Stegorski walking around.

He hadn't seen Stegorksi since he'd returned to his room, but he could tell by the occasional squeaking bed-springs that he must be lying on the bed watching the TV. From his new spot, he could see just the top third of the TV screen. His mom occasionally watched Oprah's show and he had always thought it was dumb. It had seemed to him to be just a bunch of adults whining about problems brought upon themselves through their unwillingness to control themselves. Now, however, trapped in a tiny drone, but simultaneously feeling the winter cold numbing his corporal flesh and blood, he found it fascinating. Despite her guest's somewhat bizarre circumstances, he found the easy banter of Oprah comforting. These people and their unusual problems seemed very normal, part of the everyday world he'd stepped out of. Oprah made everything hopeful. Her optimistic chatter gave him solace and he was sad when the show finally ended.

As far as Jared knew, Stegorski might also be after some comfort. In any case, the agent must have specifically tuned in, for as soon as the credits rolled, he clicked off the TV, rolled off the bed, and put on his coat. His feet were right there in front of him. Stegorski wore comfortable shoes with soft rubber soles, a bit out of place with his characteristic gray suit and tie. He heard the jingle of car keys, and then the slam of the room door. He had seen Stegorski's head as he walked out and, unless he'd stooped and jumped back inside just as the door swung closed, he was definitely gone this time. Still, he waited a few minutes, listening, before sliding the visor off his head. The TV, carpet, and dirty walls of the room glided away and he was back outside, huddled in the trash alcove. The cold, diffused light of the winter day was starting to weaken as the afternoon eased to its end.

The sight of cold surroundings brought home the actual cold he was feeling. He wasn't exactly sure what hypothermia was like, but Russ had talked about how Shackleton's men were always fighting it as they battled for their lives while drifting among the Antarctic ice floes. As he sat shivering, he wondered what it must have been like to be one of those men. He knew that if he really wanted to, he could get on his bike and be at a warm, safe home in twenty minutes. He closed his eyes. What if he was floating on an ice floe now? He imagined what it must be like: it's been continuously dark here below the Antarctic circle for over a month. I've been eating nothing but raw seal meat and a mixed, reconstituted slop called "goosh" that was prepared and dried in England over a year ago. I'm not sure when, or if, I'll ever get off this floating slab of ice, but it certainly isn't going to happen tonight, or this week, or probably even this month.

His eyes snapped open. This wasn't the kind of thing to think about in these circumstances. He wished Stegorski had left the TV on. He ate the apple pie Russ had left him. It was cold. He was licking the sugar off the box when he heard the fence rattle, and there was Russ ducking under—finally. His friend was dragging rolled-up sleeping bags and a green plastic garbage bag behind him. He got up stiffly to go help him. Together, they carried the goods and dumped them in their cave.

"Man," Russ said, out of breath, "what a job that was

carrying all that on my bike. I must have dropped stuff five times along the way. The garbage bag got a hole one time, and I had to tie it shut."

He looked over the pile. Inside the green bag was snack food, sandwiches, cookies, and a thermos. "Wow! What a haul! Shackleton's men would've been dancing with joy."

He looked closer at the rolled-up sleeping bags. "Hey, one of these is mine. How'd you get that?"

"It was quite a show, let me tell you. My mom caught me leaving with the food and my sleeping bag and wanted to know what was up. I had to think quick. I told her that we were going to have a camp-out in your bedroom. She started to get mad until I told her that you were scared to be alone. She fell hard for that one, boy." He continued, imitating his mother, " 'Oh that poor, poor boy! You tell his mom that if there's *anything* I can do just let me know.' "

He smiled. "But, how did you get *mine*?"

"That charade worked so well I figured I'd stop by your place and give a reprise performance. I told your mom that you were engrossed in a game and had sent me to pick up your bag so you could stay with me tonight."

"*My* place! Are you nuts? My mom's going to figure out what's up!"

"Think about it, Martin," Russ said as he started to untie the sleeping bags. "You've got to have some story to tell your mom about why you'll be over my place tonight, and I figured that you were definitely going to need another bag. There's a chance of snow flurries tonight."

He helped him unroll the bags. "I guess you're right."

"Just let Uncle Russ take care of things ... oh, I almost forgot: your mom wanted you to call right away. You'd better hurry. She'll be expecting that I would've been back at my house ten minutes ago."

He sighed. He dreaded talking to his mom. He was going to have to lie, and he hated that. He checked his pockets. "Russ, have you got a quarter for the call?"

Russ reached into his own pocket and handed over a quarter. "Your tab is growing young man. By the way, I brought new batteries for the visor. I'll change them while you're gone."

He crawled out through the fence and walked to the sidewalk. It felt good to be moving. Watching for Stegorski's car, he walked to the McDonald's. He had to wait for an older kid to get done talking to his girlfriend. He shuffled back and forth while the kid gave him dirty looks. The light was beginning to fade. Russ still had to ride his bicycle twenty minutes home.

He finally tapped the kid on the shoulder. "I'm sorry, but I really have to make a call," he said.

The kid turned his back to him, but he heard him tell his girlfriend that some little jerk wanted to use the phone, so he was going to go. He hung up and walked away with a menacing glance. Sometimes the world seemed like a hard place.

He dialed his house and his mom picked up. *"Hello."*

"Mom, it's me."

"Jared! Why did you wait so long to call? We're supposed to leave for the hospital in five minutes!"

Yipes! He'd forgotten! They were supposed to visit Jack. "I can't go, mom."

"Jared! Why not? I know that he's only your stepfather, but you could at least show some *concern."*

His heart sank to his toes. What could he say to make this better? Nothing. "I ... I just don't want to go, mom."

"Jared! I can't believe this. This man is in the hospital because he was trying to save your life. *He almost died!"*

"I know. I just don't want to go. Hospitals make me nauseous." He actually did feel nauseous right now.

"I'm not going to argue with you now. You have your fun with Russell and we'll talk about it tomorrow. But, I want you to think about Jack lying there in the hospital, and I want you to think about why he's there in the first place."

"Yes, mom. Bye."

He wanted to tell her to say "Hi" to Jack for him, but he sensed this would not be good. It would only make her more angry.

He started back to the cold cave, hands in his pants pockets. He couldn't remember when he'd felt so shamed.

Darkness was settling fast. He sprinted back to the motel. Russ was on his bike, ready to leave.

"Where will you go now?" Jared asked.

"I'm going to go and hang out with Sam for a while. Later, I'll head home and tell my mom that we had a fight or something. I'll be back first thing in the morning."

"Okay," Jared said.

They stood looking at each other. Russ seemed about to say something, but he just stood there, straddling his bike. On impulse Jared reached out his hand. His friend looked at it, smiled and took it in a firm handshake. They'd never shaken hands before.

"Chin up, old boy," Russ said, imitating the English accent of Sir Shackleton. "I'll return for you, don't you fear. The Admiralty will be proud of you."

"Very good, sir," Jared returned, saluting and smiling.

Russ jumped on the pedals and sped away. His salute dropped slowly as Russ rounded the corner and disappeared into the gathering darkness.

CHAPTER FORTY-THREE

The cold pressed in again as Jared made his way through the fence and back to the cement cave. Feeling bold, he emptied the remaining few toilet-paper rolls from one large box and tore open its glued panels so that he could lay it flat on the cement floor. On this, he put the sleeping bags, one inside the other. A paper towel roll from another box made a pillow. As a final touch, he imitated homeless people he'd seen in the city; he lay scrap pieces of cardboard box across the sleeping bag to break the wind.

One last preparation: he crawled under the fence and walked back to the McDonald's. He toyed a moment with the idea of doing his toilet business there in the back motel parking lot, maybe behind the trash dumpster, but decided to maintain a minimum level of decency. The inside of the fast-food restaurant was brightly lit and noisy, full of parents trying to control their kids who were boisterously dancing their way through their evening meal. He felt like a ghost among them. He'd once lived in this world. He used the bathroom, which had a sign on the door: *For Customer Use Only*. He didn't have a penny on him. Oh well, Russ had bought the apple pies here. He still had some of the sugar around his mouth for proof. On the way out, he lingered a moment, reveling in the wonderful chaos of squealing kids and scattered sandwich wrappers, before plunging through the doors and into the night.

Outside, in the cold winter air, he felt like he was awakening from sleep. The world separated into the part that was him, and all the rest that was coldness. There was no deep violet sky that he loved so much at this time of evening. The overcast clouds threw back the electric lights of suburban DC with a slightly ominous radioactive glow.

He found his way under the chain fence by feel and hurried across the empty parking lot to the pitch black hole in the motel wall that would be his home for the night. Only one window in the rooms above showed light behind closed drapes. He felt around and found the flashlight that Russ had remembered to bring. When he flipped the switch, its beam seemed starkly alarming, like a warning beacon to the world that something irregular was going on here. He arranged his possessions as quickly as possible, then flicked it back off. He took off his shoes and lay them next to his head where he could find them, then slid into the freezing cold interior of the sleeping bag. For a while he shivered, but the warmth of his body gradually won the day, and before long he was actually cozy. In the darkness, he dug out Russ's cassette recorder and connected it to the visor. He was familiar with the controls since it was the same model as his own, a hand-held unit the same size as the early Sony Walkman. With a last look around at the platoon of shadows surrounding him in the parking lot, he slipped on the visor.

Complete darkness met him. He told himself he should be glad that Stegorski hadn't returned, yet he would have welcomed a lit room even if he could only see and hear it. Not for the first time, he contemplated walking the drone to the door to see if he could fit under the crack at the bottom. He could then retrieve it and go home. He could sleep in his own bed, and in the morning call his dad and confess. It would be over. So, why didn't he? Because, he decided, it felt like surrendering. He was sure they wouldn't believe him about Stegorski. The murderer would get away clean.

He lay in the darkness, his body warming up in the layers of cloth and cardboard, his head disconnected and tucked in virtually between a dingy motel dresser and a dirty motel wall. He realized that he'd dozed off only when the sound of the door opening and the glare of returning light woke him. While he struggled through the confusion of becoming fully awake, Stegorski tossed his coat on the bed and headed for the bathroom. He heard the toilet flush, and the agent came back out zipping up his pants. He flopped down on the bed and the TV came to life. Stegorski flipped through several channels and finally settled on a sitcom. Jared thought that watching TV would be the best thing he could imagine right now. The top third of the screen, though, was just a tease. He decided to try to find a better angle. He told himself that, in any case, he should be keeping a better eye on Stegorski.

He pulled himself out from his crack, and crawled along the front edge of the dresser and back under the bed, keeping a wary eye on the top of the bed cliff above him in case Stegorski's enormous head should appear. He then followed the edge of the dresser to the back wall.

Here he paused, reconnoitering. The bedspread never touched the floor, so, like the drapes, that avenue was denied him. The smooth polished legs of the bed would not, he knew, provide him any grip. He continued around to the backside of the dresser. He found that, as with almost all furniture manufactured in the last fifty years, the backside consisted of thin pressed fiberboard. He tested it and found that if he was careful, he could grip it with his leg hooks.

Up he went. He followed one of the columns in the grid pattern of indentations made when the fiber material was pressed together to form a flat board. He found that he could use the indentations like steps, and his progress was swift. When he reached the top, however, he encountered a familiar problem: how to get around corners. His legs just weren't long and agile enough to easily reach around and get a hold. He turned sideways and eased up as far as he could manage, pushing with his downward-facing legs. He groped around along the top surface of the dresser, and although he couldn't see his upper legs nor feel what they were grasping (that lack of tactile sense again), he could tell that he wasn't getting any purchase. No surprise, since the top of the dresser would be some polished veneer.

He eased back down so that all four legs were again gripping the fiberboard. What to do? He felt a little foolish, taking all these risks just to watch some TV. No sense turning back now, though. He carefully turned his butt down and rotated himself over so that he was facing the other way, towards the wall. Ahead of him, the cord for the dresser lamp spilled over the edge and fell away far below. Perhaps this could serve as his ladder over the edge. He crawled over to the plastic cord. It looked like an extended version of some dinosaur's tail hanging over the edge. He reached up and tried grabbing it with his front leg hook. It caught tentatively in the plastic material. He pulled back very slightly. It held. But when he then pulled back firmly on it, his hook lost its grip. He wasn't sure whether this was going to work. He edged over as far as he could, lifting his right two legs so that they were above the cord. He brought them down and pulled them towards him. He could sense that they'd gotten some kind of hold, since he saw his view shake slightly as the drone's body was pulled over the cord. But he couldn't tell whether the hooks were still holding, or whether they'd already drug across the cord's surface and were now up against the drone's body. Yet again, he was hampered by the lack of tactile and kinesis senses.

He took a deep breath and simultaneously pushed with his left two legs while pulling gently with his right. He slid satisfyingly up and onto the cord. He paused, but whatever was gripping held and he didn't fall. He slowly lifted his left legs and brought them down onto the cord next to him. He could see the very end of his front leg, but not his back. He reached them forward and gripped the plastic. He pulled with his left legs and started to move, but then fell back with a jerk as the legs hooks gave way. He froze, but his right hooks held.

There was nothing to do but try again. This time he slapped his legs down onto the plastic in an attempt to dig in the hooks. This apparently worked, because he was now able to pull himself forward a bit. He proceeded with the slapping and pulling until he followed the cord up and over the edge of the dresser. As he hauled himself over the dresser's edge, the flashing color-bursts of the TV climbed into view and then, off to his left, he saw Stegorski's head. He almost lost his grip, but he saw that Stegorski was lying on the other side of the bed and his attention was totally on the TV.

He had a great view of the TV now, but he was too exposed. He'd be obvious, perched on the lamp cord with nothing but a plain wall behind. Other than the base of the lamp, the only other object on top of this bedside dresser was a towel that Stegorski had tossed down on the other side of the lamp. He considered hiding under a fold of the towel, but he feared that Stegorski might pick it up again. He looked off to the left and saw, beyond Stegorski's head, the lamp on the other dresser. In a feeble attempt to introduce some class to the room, the management had replaced the typical nondescript lampshade with an exotic version. Besides an oriental type pattern on the shade itself, there was a fringe of little balls hanging from threads all around the bottom edge. He looked at those balls hanging down. When he tilted himself up by pushing up on his front legs he could just see the balls hanging down from his own lamp. He had an idea.

He crawled down from the lamp cord and nearly slid right off the dresser. The polished surface was like ice. He'd read that flies have sticky pads on their feet—this is how they can "stand" upside-down on a ceiling. He wished he were more like the insect he so resembled. Feeling like a clumsy first-time skater, he paddled and slid his way around the base of the lamp to the towel. Reaching it was like making the edge of a frozen lake. His leg hooks dug satisfyingly in the towel fabric and he scampered up.

The towel was a mountain rising above him. One portion brushed the lampshade near the peak. As he began to navigate the myriad folds and crevices, he couldn't tell which ones were taking him in the direction he wanted to go. Now and then he had to pause and look around to gauge his progress. Finally he was looking up at the fold which would take him to the shade. He pulled himself up this last slope, and reached the pinnacle of his climb. From here he could survey the entire room. There, off to the left on the other side of the bed was Stegorski engrossed in the TV, lying with one leg crossed over the other. On the near side of the bed were various possessions dropped casually: the briefcase, his coat, a pad of paper. On the long dresser next to the TV was the direction-tracking box.

He turned from the room's vista to the lampshade at his back. The cloth material was ideal for the drone's leg-hooks, and he climbed easily on. He immediately turned right and made his way a few inches along the bottom edge, towards the bed. He picked a thread below him and, hooking his left back leg into the edge of the shade he switched to Articulate mode and reached down with his right claw and grabbed the thread firmly. He then switched back to Walk mode and let go of his leg. His body swung down; he was swinging from the thread, the ball just below him. He mentally crossed his fingers that Stegorski wouldn't look over, for he could tell by the swaying view that he had set the ball swinging. Back to Articulate mode, he let himself down, claw over claw, until he could tell that he'd come to the ball below by the fact that he was starting to tilt forward.

He paused. He was apparently grasping the ball now. He couldn't see it, as his vision didn't extend beneath him, and he was facing the thread, the TV behind him. It took a long time to work his way around to the back of the ball since the drone was not very much smaller than it was, and he didn't have much working room. When he did finally make it to the back of the ball, he found that he was still tilted up towards the ceiling. He could see even less of the TV than when he was on the floor. Great. He tried positioning himself to one side, but he only managed to place himself sideways on the ball. His view was then also sideways and made him dizzy as he gently swayed back and forth.

With a sigh he crawled completely under the ball and firmly planted his four hooks. He was now just a slightly oversized ball among a string of balls and would hardly be noticeable to Stegorski if he even glanced this way. Stegorski hadn't turned this lamp on and he thought it unlikely that the man would now, as he seemed to have taken the other side of the bed for his use, leaving Jared's side for his various possessions. The only problem was that everything was upside-down. He found this less annoying than the sideways view, though, and in a surprisingly short time he was enjoying the upside-down TV shows. He almost felt a camaraderie with Stegorski lying over there. But only almost, for he remembered the phone conversation, and the kitchen knife, and the reason why he was spying upside-down from a lampshade, while lying outside among garbage bags on a winter's night.

Too soon for his liking, Stegorski decided he'd had enough TV for the night and clicked it off. He watched as the giant took off his shirt. The man stepped in and out of view in the bathroom area just out of sight to the right as he prepared for bed. He wasn't sure he wanted to watch all these preparations, but decided that he'd better keep the visor active. And, good thing, because just after he finished shaving, Stegorski, apparently on a whim, picked up the box and pushed the button. The green LED remained dark, and he put it back on the dresser and continued his preparations.

He realized just how risky taking off the visor was. Stegorski finally turned off the bathroom lights and started to unbuckle his pants. He definitely didn't want to see this, and closed his eyes for a few moments. When he opened them, Stegorski's buttocks were directly in front of him. He almost lost his grip. He clenched his eyes closed again until he sensed that the light was gone. He opened his eyes to darkness. Stegorski had gone to bed.

Jared made himself ready for sleep as well. He slipped off the visor. The parking lot was unchanged. A light breeze had picked up again. Here and there he saw stray snowflakes float by. A small gust rattled a tin can over near the garbage bin, causing him to jump. He fished out the pocketknife that Stegorski had given him and lay it near his shoes next to his head. He found the flashlight and lay that there as well, completing his survival kit. He had a dilemma with the visor. He always slept on his stomach, but that wouldn't be possible with the visor on. He was considering whether he should forgo the visor for the night—whether he could count on waking up before Stegorski in the morning—when there was a loud thud at the far end of the lot. He tensed but couldn't see anything. He heard a door thud shut and then voices. He couldn't make out many words, but the tones had an emotional randomness of men that are drunk. The sweet, woodsy aroma of marijuana drifted by, familiar to him from bus rides home from football games. He caught enough words to make out that one of the men must be the night manager, for he was complaining about the motel owner. After some minutes he heard footsteps shuffling along the wall towards him. He saw the figure of a man stop just short of the alcove and turn towards the wall, unzipping his pants. He heard the swish of piss splashing against the wall as the man sighed with relief. He could smell the sour ammonia of the urine. Then the man looked straight down at him.

"Jay-sus kee-rist!" he bellowed. He staggered back, fumbling to zip up his pants. "Ya God-damn bums! Get the hell outta here!"

The man stepped over and he saw a foot swing back ready to kick. He twisted away just as the foot glanced across his back.

"Ev-ry time a' turn around ya bums are back!" the drunk yelled.

The woozy manager cocked his foot for another kick, but lost his balance and stepped back to catch himself.

Just then the other man yelled from the other door, "Buck! I think there's somebody at the desk!"

His attacker looked over at the friend then down at Jared. He muttered more curses and shuffled off towards the far door. He heard the door slam shut and then silence.

He was stunned. He was found out! His cave was violated. It was no longer his private haven. The stoned night manager would probably come back as soon as he was done with the customer. He clawed his way in a panic out of the sleeping bags and pulled on his shoes. He gathered together all his things and dumped them in the green garbage bag. Grabbing everything in his arms, he staggered out into the lot. Where to go? He headed for the chain fence and shoved his load, piece by piece, through the gap. He then crawled through and hid in the weeds, pulling his piles along with him.

He lay in the dry grass and dead milkweed stalks among the rain-flattened paper trash. The winter cold began its slow counter-attack. Reaction from the shock set in, and he began shivering uncontrollably again. The world truly could be a hard place sometimes.

Sure enough, after a while he saw the manager emerge and walk over to the alcove. He could see that the man was probably no more than twenty years old. He heard vague curses as the manager kicked around the boxes and trash bags, then trotted back inside out of the cold, hugging his arms to his sides against the cold.

He felt like crying. Why hadn't he just gone home? He could have gone with his mom to the hospital and visited Jack. When he thought of this lost opportunity and the impression it made, he gave in to his grief. He cried, and as he let the tears flow, he lost all control and was soon sobbing. He clenched his fists and beat the dry grass in anger at the injustice of it all. Why should he care if they didn't believe him about Tony's stabbing? It was their fault if they didn't. He should have just told them what he'd heard, and let them suffer the consequences of their own unwillingness to believe him. He should have listened to Russ.

After a while he cried himself dry, and he lay exhausted, with his forehead on the cold ground. He was still chilled, but the shivering had stopped. He picked his head up. The snowflakes had increased. They sped by like moths in full flight. He very much wanted to return to the cave. But more than that, he wanted to know for sure that the manager was not going to come out again. He couldn't know that, of course, and not being sure, he understood that he couldn't risk it. He resigned himself to the situation this chosen fate had handed him, and arranged his sleeping bags in the weeds. He took off his shoes and crawled inside the cloth bags. He pulled Russ's plastic garbage bag back to him and found a pack of cheese crackers. He munched these as the snowflakes darted by above him. The wind was cold against his nose and cheeks. He poured hot chocolate from the thermos. The warm, sweet liquid was like an elixir. It seemed to represent all that stood between him and the hard, mean world. This thermos, and its contents, stood for the care and love of his friend, and of his family: his mom, and dad, ... and Jack.

He closed up the thermos, shoved it back in the plastic bag, and picked up the visor. He knew what he had to do. He slipped it over his head and lay back. At least it blocked the wind some.

****

He woke to a cold wetness on his chin. He opened his eyes, but saw only darkness. He remembered that he was inside the visor. He lifted it off and was surprised to feel a cold wetness wherever he touched. Above and all around him was a dense flow of white, an infinite flock of panicked moths. The snow flurries had built to a small blizzard. He was already covered. A layer of soft snow lay across everything so that all was smooth curves.

Damn! He sat upright and snow fell in a small avalanche from him. He had no watch, but his inner clock told him that it had been hours since he'd drifted off to sleep. It must be well after midnight. Through the driving snow he saw the dark protection of the cave. *Screw it!* The manager wouldn't be coming out this late. And, anyway, he didn't care anymore. If the drunk did come, he'd just kick him back.

He gathered up his snow-covered piles, shoved them back under the fence and was soon back in the alcove. It seemed truly like his safe harbor now. He shook out the sleeping bags and arranged everything as before. He snuggled in and, as the warmth returned, he drifted off, back to sleep. He was almost content.

Chapter Forty-four

J ared woke and opened his eyes. Everything was upside-down. He remembered that he'd left the drone hanging from the lampshade. Stegorski was gone from the bed, but he could hear water running in the bathroom. The sounds of Stegorski's morning preparations must have awakened him.

He took off the visor and stretched. The storm had passed, and he could see that it was going to be a sunny day. He fished the sandwich out of the green plastic bag, but before eating it, he had one thing to take care of. He put the visor back on. He could hear the shower running. He'd given some thought to his next move. He'd decided to move closer to the phone on the far dresser in order to get the best recording of Stegorski incriminating himself.

First he had to get down from the lampshade, which meant that he had to get off of his mini-swing. After many minutes of frustrating effort he realized that this was not possible. His legs just didn't have enough articulation to work in such tight quarters. All he managed to do in his struggles was to lose more and more grip on the ball. In the end, he was hanging by just one claw from the ball. He wouldn't get tired, of course, and he could hang here forever, but he was going to be way too obvious when Stegorski eventually came out of the bathroom. He steeled himself and went into Scan mode. Among the reeling sweep of images he saw that he was hanging over the edge of the dresser. It was hard to tell by how much. He wasn't willing to make himself dizzy again to find out. He took a deep breath and simply let go.

The room spun slowly as he fell, and then moved too quickly to see anything as he hit the carpet and rolled. When his view stabilized again, the dresser was before him, tilted at a forty-five degree angle. He quickly worked his legs back out and turned around. Stegorski's shoe towered above him. It must have stopped his roll. He heard Stegorski rustling his clothes. He sounded quite near. He realized that he didn't know how long ago the sound of the shower had stopped. He tilted himself up on his front legs as far as he could reach and managed to just see over the toe of the shoe. Stegorski's pant-leg was inches away, on the other side! Stegorski must have stepped out of the bathroom just as he fell!

He scrambled up to the edge of the shoe. Turning left, he headed for the heel and, a dozen inches beyond that, safety under the bed. As he rounded the heel he saw off to his right that Stegorski was finishing tying his left shoe. In another second he'd reach over and lift the right shoe. The drone would be revealed in full view. He hesitated, not sure if he had time to make a dash for the bed. Too late! He saw Stegorski's hand reaching over.

He let his reflexes take over. He reached up and grabbed the edge of the shoe. He managed to pull himself up enough to hook his front legs into the cloth above the rubber soul just as Stegorski grabbed the shoe and shoved his foot in. The pant leg fell, but didn't reach all the way down to him. He could hear Stegorski tying the shoe laces. Should he drop off? Would Stegorski walk away without looking down? Would he crush the drone as he stepped away?

A sharp pain stabbed him in the side.

"You god-damn bum!" the familiar voice of the night manager said. "I told ya ta git outta here!"

The second kick caught him in the butt.

He yanked off the visor. The night manager was looming above him, bleary-eyed. The man seemed surprised when he saw his face. "You're a kid! Christ, what's the world comin' to!"

He waved him away. "Git outta here! Go on, now!"

His mind was in a swirl. He grabbed the visor. There was too much to carry.

"Go on—outta here!" the man was yelling.

He grabbed the cassette recorder and pocketknife, and made for the fence. An inch of fresh snow covered the ground, and as he ducked through the hole he slipped and fell, the visor flying off. He ran to retrieve it, then made it through the fence. He hurried into the Palm Reader's lot and stopped. He looked around. He watched the night manager carry the sleeping bags across the parking lot, and throw them into the trash bins. The man then got into his beat-up old car and drove away.

He waited a moment longer, and when no one else came out of the motel, he went back under the fence to the cave. It seemed so forlorn now with only the sandwich wrapper lying on the cold cement. He sat down on the slab of cardboard and pulled the visor over his head.

The drone must have remained where he'd left it. Above him were Stegorski's pant leg and the top of his shoe. He rotated the drone to the right, but the pant leg hid his view. He crawled forward along the top of the sole, just under the bottom of the pant cuff. He rounded the ankle and came to the shoelaces. The pant leg flapped back and forth above and in front of him. He crawled up and over the shoelace knot, then out across the dunes of a couple of shoelace bindings until he could finally see ahead of him.

Stegorski was standing next to the long dresser, facing the bathroom counter. He realized that he could see Stegorski in the large mirror above the counter. He was standing there with his shirt unbuttoned ... holding the tracking box! The agent pushed the button a couple of times, then put the box down on the dresser.

His heart felt as though it had risen into his throat. Stegorski had clearly been using the direction box while Jared had the visor off, fleeing from the night manager. He'd have seen the green LED lit with no indication of direction. His father had told Stegorski on the phone that this could mean the drone was nearby—within ten feet, in fact. Stegorski didn't seem to remember that, otherwise he'd be searching for the drone right now. But, he might remember at any moment. It was just a matter of time.

Stegorski walked over to the bed. Jared could hear him above, fumbling with the briefcase. His giant host just stood there. The agent was probably doing something, but he wasn't able to maneuver himself to look up to see what. He went into Scan mode for a second. In the spin of images he saw Stegorski holding something in his hand above him, but he couldn't make out what it was. Stegorski then took a couple of steps, and Jared could again see him in the mirror. He was inserting something in his ear. A thin cord hung from it and was connected to a small, black object that Stegorski held in his hand. Stegorski pressed a finger against his ear, obviously listening to something associated with the earpiece.

Jared's calf was cramping. He straightened his leg to relieve it. As he did so, he saw Stegorski turn his head slightly and press harder against his ear, as though he could hear him move. He purposely slid his heels across the cement. He saw Stegorski react again. The agent definitely seemed to hear him ... but how? Was he somehow able to tap into some hidden microphone built into the visor? He saw Stegorski glance around as though thinking, then pick up the direction tracking box. Jared lost the mirror view as Stegorski turned and headed for the door. He had a bad feeling about this.

Where was Russ? He'd expected him at the crack of dawn. He guessed that it must be at least 7:30 by now. His shoe-view showed him that Stegorski paused outside his door, and then walked along the outside walkway and down the covered stairs. It was difficult to follow, as his view swung up and down repetitively as Stegorski's foot walked along. At the bottom of the stairs, Stegorski turned and walked through another door. He could see that this was the small motel office. Stegorski's foot walked up to the counter, and he was staring at wood paneling a few inches in front of him. He heard Stegorski say, "Excuse me, but have you seen a young teenage boy around here?"

"I haven't," said a female voice, "but the night clerk said he kicked out a bum around back last night. He didn't say whether it was a boy, though. We sometimes get these homeless folks sleeping back there. I'd let them in peace, but the night clerk, he just hates the thought of them."

"Okay, thanks."

It was that simple.

He felt panic rising in him again. Stegorski's shoe showed him that the MI agent was walking around the far side of the building. He saw the trash bins ahead, and Stegorski walked over to them. He walked behind them, then back around to the front. He heard the lid lifted, then drop with a crash. If he were to take off his visor he knew he'd see Stegorski across the lot, and, conversely, Stegorski could see him if he happened to look this way.

He pushed himself behind the large boxes. As he did so Stegorski suddenly stopped. Once again, it seemed that the agent could hear him. He felt like a trapped animal. His heart pounded, thump by thump. He wondered if Stegorski could hear *that*.

He saw Stegorski walk back to the building, then along the backside, right towards him. As the alcove came nearer, in addition to the sound coming through the visor, he began to hear Stegorski's footsteps coming directly to his ears. And then he was looking, through the lenses of the drone, into the alcove. The view was steady; Stegorski was standing there looking in.

He suddenly realized that he could see the tip of his own shoe there in the dark corner. Carefully, slowly, he lifted it very slightly and pulled it back a few inches. He saw it disappear.

Stegorski just stood there. He'd have to be an utter fool not to look behind the boxes where he was hiding. Stegorski took a step forward just as he heard the chain fence rattle.

"Hey! You!" he heard Stegorski yell. "Hold it there!" The shoe view twisted as Stegorski took off after whomever was at the fence. At that second, without even thinking about it, he tapped his waldo fingers against the cement wall and the drone leapt from Stegorski's shoe.

He heard Stegorski's pounding feet running away. He ripped off the visor and scrambled out from behind the boxes. The snow was all trampled around the alcove from his, the motel manager's, and now Stegorski's feet. He didn't see the drone. It might have rolled and covered itself with snow. He looked around and stopped, afraid that he might step on it.

He put the visor back on. All he saw was gray. The drone must indeed be covered by snow. He squatted down and slowly waved his arms around. Nothing. He stood up, took a step in the direction of the fence where Stegorski had run, and repeated the process. Nothing again. When he stood up and took a second step he saw the view in the visor darken slightly. He must be standing over the drone. This time when he squatted down and waved his arms, he could see a flash of a shadow. He pulled off the visor and ran his hands lightly over the snow. He felt a slight bump. He grabbed a whole handful of snow and inside, like a plastic toy in a handful of Cracker-Jacks, he found the drone.

It seemed like weeks since he'd last held it, even though it hadn't even been a full day. He gently wiped off the snow. He took it back to the alcove, and used the waldo to curl the legs in tightly so that he could place the compact ball in his pocket. He heard footsteps. He picked up the visor and cassette recorder and stepped out from the alcove. Stegorski was coming back around the near corner!

He took off in the other direction. He heard Stegorski yell, then the pounding of the man's feet behind him.

He ran for his life. He couldn't tell whether Stegorski was gaining on him, but it sure didn't sound like he was gaining distance on the man, either. He rounded the corner and sprinted towards the street. Stegorski yelled for him to stop.

At the sidewalk, he turned right towards the cluster of fast food restaurants. He glanced back and saw that Stegorski had fallen back some. Although he could sprint faster than Stegorski for a short while, he knew that the adult could probably outlast him over distance. He had to lose Stegorski quickly. He took a sharp right into the Burger King parking area and ran to the back of the lot. Here, weeds and thick brush melted into a tangle of small, close-set trees beyond. He dove into the thicket. He saw Stegorski round into the lot behind him. The agent would have seen him. In any case, Stegorski could follow his footsteps in the new snow. He fought his way into the thicket and, not knowing what lay beyond, he turned left, keeping low and out of Stegorksi's view from the parking lot. He didn't want to be trapped by some hidden fence farther in. He slowed down and concentrated on being quiet and avoiding shaking the bushes. The snowfall helped by absorbing sound. At the same time, the tangle of bushes helped hide his footprints. He didn't hear the sound of Stegorski pursuing him from behind. It seemed that his pursuer had chosen not to try to navigate the thick brush.

He proceeded as quietly as he could. When he thought that he'd about reached the edge of the Burger King lot, he stopped underneath a large bush that formed a dry little cave. He listened. Nothing. Then, directly in front of him at the edge of the parking lot he heard the rustle of branches. Silence. Then the rustle again. Silence. Someone was making deliberate progress through the brush towards him. He peered through the maze of twigs and branches. There! He had a glimpse of Stegorski. There! Another glimpse! He could see that Stegorski was holding the tracking box in front of him.

Of course! How could he be so stupid! He'd been holding the visor under his arm. Stegorski was tracking the de-activated drone in his pocket!

He jumped up and began thrashing his way ahead, parallel to the parking lot.

"Ha! I got you, kid." Stegorski sounded like he was right next to him.

He guessed that he must be getting close to the edge of the Burger King property by now. He prayed there'd be no fence ahead of him.

There was. It was another chain-link fence, probably completely surrounding the property. He heard Stegorski crashing behind him. He tossed the visor and cassette recorder over the fence and scrambled up. His feet were wet and slippery, and they kept sliding off the wire. Stegorski seemed to be right on top of him. In total panic, he pulled himself up with his arms alone. When he got to the top he pushed his feet against a tree trunk and launched himself up and over. He fell heavily to the ground. There, a foot from his face was Stegorski's shoes on the other side of the fence.

He quickly stood up. Stegorski wasn't trying to climb over the fence. He probably knew that he was no match for it.

"Well, Jared Martin," Stegorski said looking him in the eye, "so we meet again. You lied at the police station, didn't you?"

He didn't say anything.

Stegorski pressed his face against the fence. "You stole valuable government property. You're going to jail. So's your dad."

He returned the gloating agent's stare. "You can't intimidate me," he said.

Stegorski grinned evilly. "You don't know who you're dealing with. Yes, I'm afraid that I can indeed intimidate you."

"Maybe with a kitchen knife?"

Stegorski's eyes opened wide in surprise. He grabbed the visor and recorder and took off towards the highway.

Behind him, he heard Stegorski say calmly, "You're dead, kid."

Jared had upped the ante. He hoped he wasn't just bluffing.

CHAPTER FORTY-FIVE

J ared burst from the brush and saw that he was now in the KFC parking lot next to the Burger King. He heard Stegorski's thrashing and saw him emerge from the thicket on the other side of the fence that ran right out to the sidewalk. Stegorski would have to go out all the way to the street before he could get to him. He had a handful of seconds.

He sprinted across the parking lot, away from the fence and Stegorski. On the other side of the lot was a wood rail fence which barely slowed him down. He was now in the McDonald's parking lot. The KFC building hid him from Stegorski. He looked around quickly. The McDonald's lot was full of breakfast customers' cars. The drive-through lane curved around the building, and the cars were lined up out to the highway. In the center of the lot was a square fence, which camouflaged a trash bin within. He ran over and found he could slide one of the large doors open enough to slip inside. He pulled the door shut behind him.

On the left side there was just enough room for him to slip in between the bin and the fence wall. Behind the bin there was more room, and he could squat among the sandwich wrappers which formed an unbroken floor. This time he remembered to slip on the visor. He should be invisible to Stegorski now.

He waited, and his breathing slowed after a few minutes. He stood up quietly. He was still hidden behind the trash bin. All he heard was the sound of idling engines waiting in the take-out line and, through the outdoor speaker, the voice of the attendant taking orders. It seemed strange. Here he was fighting for his life, and right outside was a pleasant-sounding girl welcoming drivers to McDonald's before taking their order, as if nothing in the world was wrong.

He took the drone from his pocket and held it in his right hand. With his left hand, he felt along the enclosure wall and found a crack where it met the other fence panel at the corner. Holding the drone between his thumb and finger, he inserted it into the crack. He could now view the parking lot. There, out on the sidewalk, stood Stegorski with his hand to his ear. He was listening again.

Jared heard the attendant say clearly, "Welcome to McDonald's. Can I take your order?" As she said that, he saw Stegorski look directly at the fenced garbage bin.

Stegorski had somehow heard her! How? Stegorski started walking towards him.

Fear gripped him. Trapped again! Try to make a dash? Stegorski would have him for sure. He was only a hundred feet away. He took off the visor and put the drone back in his pocket. No need to worry about that now. Seconds later, he heard Stegorski's footsteps outside.

"Come on, Jared," he said, "it's no use. I won't hurt you. Come out and let's talk."

He had heard those very words from Ahmed: *I won't hurt you.* They always seemed to be the last words he heard before he got hurt. Could he crawl under the bin? Not enough room. He heard Stegorski yank open one of the large doors. Jared ducked his head down and peered under the bin. He could see Stegorski following his own route, squeezing between the bin and the same wall. He stood up and backed to the far corner. There was grunting and scraping, and then Stegorski's head appeared around the side of the bin. He looked at him and grinned. "Well, hello. It looks like we have a trapped little rabbit."

Jared knew that if he tried to squeeze out on his own side he'd be slowed by the narrow space, and Stegorski would grab him before he made the exit. He had to draw him in farther. Jared stared at him. He put his hand in his pocket and took out the drone. He held it up for Stegorski to see. The agent's eyes widened. He lunged forward and Jared threw himself into the gap between the bin and the wall, shoving the drone back into his pocket. This gap was indeed smaller than the other side, and he became jammed. He had nothing to get a hold of to pull his way through. Stegorski's hand and arm appeared around the corner, groping to find him. Jared reached up and placed his hand against Stegorski's, palm-to-palm. As Stegorski reached in still farther to grab him, Jared pushed against him and popped through the gap. Stegorski tried to hang on to Jared's hand, but with a quick twist he was free. He dashed through the enclosure door and sprinted across the parking lot. He'd held on to the visor and cassette recorder, and he now carried one in each hand as he ran as fast as his legs could carry him.

He ran and didn't stop. Long distance advantage or not, Stegorski wasn't going to catch him this time. He ran past a garage, a real-estate business, and a gas station, before coming to a corner. He looked back, but Stegorski was no where in sight. He remembered that the drone was in his pocket. Stegorski had the direction tracker. The thought came that he could simply toss the drone away. Never. He could never do that. The agent seemed to have some way of listening to him, but whatever that was, he apparently couldn't use it to get a direction. Otherwise, he wouldn't have used the drone tracker back at the KFC. He had no choice. He slipped on the visor. He then took the drone out of his pocket and held it up. He could see fine once he turned it so that everything wasn't upside down. He pointed it back towards the McDonald's—still no Stegorski. He took off down a side street. He ran as fast as he could, holding the drone out in front of him. As he ran, his view swayed and shook. Several times he stumbled. Once he fell to the ground, but he never let go of the drone.

He came to another street crossing. He turned the drone back and forth. To the right were houses. To the left he could see old, one-story commercial buildings. He pointed the drone to the left and followed it. He passed a long line of commercial/industrial shops. Each comprised a bay in a long warehouse-type metal building. When he came to the end of this, he saw a driveway that ran behind the building. He looked back—still no sign of Stegorski. He dashed down this driveway and came out behind the building. Whereas the front of the building had normal-sized doors, here each bay had one or two large garage doors that lifted up, out of the way. He raced down along these. Most were half open and he could see various activities going on inside. Again, he had the strange sense of being disconnected from the normal world. Here were people going about their everyday business, while he raced along, running for his life. Several looked up at him as he sprinted by, holding something out in front of him with some sort of helmet covering his eyes. But they immediately went back about their business, as though they'd only seen a shadow of a boy.

Near the end of the building, he came across one bay that was dark. He stopped and looked back— still no Stegorski. He went up to it. A regular door to one side of the large garage entrance was locked, but there was a pane of glass missing in the folding garage door. He was able to squeeze through.

Inside, the only light was that which filtered through the filthy door windows. He walked into the bay. It looked like it was used just for storage. Large wooden crates and metal barrels lined the two sides. He came across a small pile of ashes on the floor. Apparently some homeless folks had found refuge in here at one time. It obviously wasn't visited often.

He needed a place to hide. Even if he'd given Stegorski the slip, he didn't want somebody else to find him and make him leave. The wooden crates were all nailed tightly shut. He tried the barrels. They were very large—larger than the type of barrel he was familiar with. Again, most were sealed, but he came across one that looked like the tabs along one side had been pried up. He gave the lid a shove and it moved a little. He looked around and found a stick. He was able to jam it into the crack between the lid and barrel side, but when he hauled up on the stick it snapped in two. The inner piece fell inside with a clang. That was good. It meant that the barrel was empty, or nearly so.

He needed something stronger to pry the lid open. He searched around, holding the drone out like an eyeball that he'd popped out of his socket. His foot kicked something and it clanged along the cement floor. It was a pipe—perfect! It wouldn't fit under the lid until he used another stick to leverage the crack open further. Once he slipped the pipe in, he pulled down on it until he lifted himself right off the floor and swung in the air. He gave a jerk and heard the satisfying sound of one of the tabs giving way. He yanked it again, and another gave way. He moved the pipe to one side, and was able to progress around the perimeter, popping tabs as he went. It was slow work, since he first had to hold the drone with one hand to see as he positioned everything. Then he'd put it in his pocket and swing blindly from the pipe. He dared not take off the visor for even a second. It was a great relief when he was finally able to lift the lid completely.

He held the drone over the edge of the barrel, but it was far too dark to see inside. He'd been working at the barrel for many minutes, making a lot of noise in the process. He worried that somebody would come by and discover him. He had to drag a box over to stand on in order to climb inside. It wasn't easy, since he had to hold the cassette recorder as well as the lid, which he wanted to place back over him once inside ... all the while working by feel with only occasional views through the tiny artificial eye peering out from his fingers.

He finally crawled inside and pulled the lid over him, letting complete darkness envelop him. It stunk! It smelled like ... he'd smelled this before. It burned his nose slightly. It was fertilizer! The barrel must have been used to transport it. He'd just have to get used to it. But there was something else as well ... something ... rotten. He hesitated, but decided he really needed to know. He squatted down and felt around the bottom of the barrel. There were loose granules of what he assumed was remnant fertilizer. His hand felt along and came to something furry and stiff. He jumped up and smelled his fingers. Definitely! A rat must have fallen inside and died there. He wiped his fingers on his pants. He then spit on his fingers and wiped them again, trying not to think about what he'd just touched.

CHAPTER FORTY-SIX

Jared waited in the pitch-dark barrel. His legs got tired, and he wanted to sit down. There was just enough room for him to huddle with his knees against his chest, but the knowledge of the dead rat prevented that. Instead, he squatted down on his haunches and he waited.

How long would he wait in here? He ran through the events of the last day. He remembered why he'd camped out at the motel in the first place. He hadn't even come close to his objective of getting evidence to prove that Stegorski had killed Tony. He hadn't gotten one minute of taped conversation. And, what about the agent's listening device? What was that all about? He wondered if perhaps there was some hidden microphone in the visor. No, he'd have known about it. What else could it be? He had planted the drone on both Ahmed and Stegorski—inadvertently both times, but, however it had happened, it had been planted. Had Stegorski managed something similar with him?

Then it came to him. The pocketknife! Of course! It was a bug. Stegorski would never give a kid a gift simply as a kind gesture. He decided to lift the lid and throw it as far as he could. But just then he heard a sound. It was a scratching off towards the back doors. He pushed up the barrel lid and held the drone up to peer out. There, by the back door, he could see the silhouette of a man through the garage door windows. He had something in his hands and it looked like he was prying at the doorknob. *Bang*! The door swung out and the man walked in.

"Jaaarrred!" Stegorski called.

He could have cried. He couldn't *believe* it. How did this guy *do* it? Even if he could listen to Jared, how did Stegorski find him now? He'd been so careful to not take off the visor. He'd thought Stegorski a Neanderthal half-wit, but he was proving to have magical powers of tracking. He realized he'd now got himself into a much worse situation than before. Here, in this abandoned warehouse, hidden from view, Stegorski would be free to do to him whatever he wanted. He fought the urge to climb from the barrel and attempt to flee. That's exactly what Stegorski would want.

"Come on Jared!" Stegorski's voice echoed through the dark, cavernous space. "I know you're in here. The game's finally up for you."

Through the drone, Jared followed him as the agent walked down between the rows of boxes and barrels.

"You like to hide, but I always find you, don't I?"

Stegorski walked back to the rear doors. He turned and pressed his hand to his ear and yelled, "ARE YOU AT THIS END?"

He then walked to the front door and yelled again. "OR, ARE YOU AT THIS END?"

He realized what Stegorski was doing. He was going to locate him by listening through his pocketknife bug, just as he and Russ themselves had done to find the drone in the park. He took the knife from his pocket. As he did so, he saw that Stegorski heard him.

"I can hear you moving, my little friend!"

Stegorski picked up a stick and started walking back, hitting it against the ground. Jared's mind raced. He fought his panic with all his might. He focused on the original goal. Don't scream. Stay focused. He took the recording adapter cord from his pocket and tried to plug one end into the visor. His hand shook, but he finally got it in. He then plugged the other end into the recorder. By feel, he started the recorder. He then took the knife and held it to his lips. He whispered into it, "You're a murderer, Stegorski!".

He heard the agent freeze. It must be very loud in his ear.

"Ah, Jared! You shouldn't make such dangerous accusations.

You know not of what you speak."

He could hear Stegorski walking along, getting closer.

"I saw you," he whispered. "I saw you stab Tony."

Stegorski stopped.

Would he buy his little lie? He continued: "I saw you through the drone before I went to the barn. You stabbed him. You *murdered* him."

"I think you're lying, little weasel." Stegorski's sarcastic play voice was developing an angry edge.

He remembered Stegorski's temper. Focus. "You used my mom's kitchen knife. You're a real bastard, Stegorski."

He held up the drone to see. Stegorski was standing only twenty feet away.

"A bastard?" Stegorski said, clearly getting angry. "A *bastard*? You don't know anything, you little prick. You have no idea what it takes to keep you and your families safe. We sacrifice everything for your security, and you thank us by treating us like bloodthirsty mercenaries."

"You're a coward, Stegorski. You murdered Tony while he was lying helpless on the ground. You *are* a bloodthirsty mercenary."

Stegorski threw the stick and it rattled noisily among the barrels. "Go to hell you little son-of-a-bitch!"

The MI agent picked up another stick and started banging it against one barrel after another. "I'm going to kill you too, and it won't be with any kitchen knife this time! I'm going to use my bare hands!"

Stegorski was two barrels away, then one, then he whacked Jared's with a deafening clang. He stopped. All was quiet. Calmly, Stegorski said, "Hello, Jared."

He pulled off the visor as the lid was thrown off, clattering away across the floor. He saw fingers bend over the edge of the barrel, and he was thrown headlong as Stegorski tipped it violently towards himself. As he fell forward, he felt the dead rat flop against his chest and face. Then Stegorski was dragging him from the barrel. The agent threw him to the floor and placed his foot on his arm. He cried out in pain.

"That's only the beginning, little weasel," Stegorski said.

Holding him down with his foot Stegorski picked up the visor and then the recorder. "So, our little detective thinks he's caught the big, bad man, eh?"

He yanked open the cassette door and pulled out the tape. He tossed the recorder aside and began pulling the tape from the cassette. He pulled it faster and faster, then threw it to the ground and stomped on it. His foot was back on Jared's arm before he could move.

"You're going to be sorry you ever stuck your nose into the government's business."

"*And* which *government is that?*"

It was a woman's voice. It was Sara's voice! He looked over towards the back doors. There stood a policeman, and next to him was Sara. She was wearing a visor!

She took it off and walked forward. "Handy things, these viewers. I see a future for them in the FBI. Take your foot off that boy, Stegorski!" He did so and Jared got up slowly.

"The drone!" Jared exclaimed.

Sara looked at him. She smiled. "Yes, your father got this visor to me this morning. I've been following you for the last half hour."

"How did you know?"

"Russell. He called last night, but I didn't get the message until early this morning."

He smiled. "He ratted me."

Sara laughed. "He saved your life!"

Stegorski took a step back. "Well, now that we've recovered the drone I guess we can all go."

"*We're* going to go," replied Sara, "but I'm afraid that you'll have to go to the police station. There's a matter of Tony's murder."

Stegorski gave her a cold, steely glare. "I don't think so. You don't have anything on me."

Sara tapped the visor in her hands. "You want to know one of the great things about these gadgets? They have built-in digital recorders. I recorded your entire conversation with Jared ... including your confession."

Jared looked at her quizzically, but didn't say anything.

"My business is not for you to judge," Stegorski said between tight lips.

Sara came close and looked him in the eye. "Oh no, brother. When it comes to murder, we make it our business."

Stegorski nodded slowly. "We'll see."

Sara leaned closer. "You really think you can beat this one?"

Stegorski leaned in even closer so that they were practically nose-to-nose. "I do. All in the line of business, lady. I'd do it again if I had to."

Sara immediately stepped back and turned to the policeman. "Think that'll do it, Fred?"

The officer nodded and stepped forward with his handcuffs."

Stegorski looked from Sara to the cop, puzzled.

Without taking her eyes from Stegorski she said, "Tell him, Jared."

He looked at Stegorski and grinned. "You mean that the visors don't *have* recording mechanisms?"

Sara nodded. "Jared knows his technology. He also knows when somebody's just made a second confession in front of three people."

The policeman reached for Stegorski's wrists, and when the agent refused to comply, he grabbed them roughly and snapped on the cuffs.

"In any case," Sara continued, "in court, a witnessed confession is a lot better than a digitally recorded one anyway. Defense attorneys have a field day with those." She nodded at the broken tape on the floor. "But we do indeed have a recording. Do you think that the material on that tape was destroyed simply because you pulled it out and stepped on it? You're so naïve, Stegorski. The magnetic imprint is still there."

She smiled at Jared, then turned to the policeman. "You know, I've been waiting a long time to say this: 'Take him away, officer.' "

CHAPTER FORTY-SEVEN

Jared sat in the back seat of his father's car as they drove to the hospital to see Jack. His mom sat next to his father, just like years ago, but now they were not heading off on a happy vacation together. These two people were no longer a couple. They were his parents. The three of them would always be that: a father, a mother, a son. But each of them also had their own individual lives to live, and his and his mom's now included Jack.

The interview at the police station had taken even longer than before. The same detective took his statements. He didn't think it had been executed according to strict procedure, since the detective kept calling in colleagues with, "Hey! You won't believe this one. Jared repeat what you just told me." When they were done, the detective shook his hand like before, but this time he glanced around and then pulled a metal star from his pocket. He handed it to him. "This was my rookie badge," he'd said. "It's been in my desk for twenty years. I figured there'd come a time when it'd be useful again. I'd like you to have it."

He looked at it, and then looked at the detective. He didn't even know this guy. The world could indeed be a pretty hard place, but it could be a pretty good place too.

****

His dad pulled into the hospital and found a parking space. As they were getting out of the car, Jared heard his mom ask his dad, "Are you sure it's okay taking off work today?"

"Sure," he replied, "nobody's going to be doing any work anyway. Might as well let them stand around and get all the gossiping out of their system. In any case, we'll have to wait for things to settle with our ... sponsors before setting a new course. I suspect they're awfully busy right now."

They walked a ways across the parking lot and his mom asked, "Do you think this Stegorski's an exception? You don't think these secret government types are really all this cold-blooded, do you?"

They walked on. He wasn't sure whether his dad was going to answer, but he finally said, "I hope he's the exception. For all our sakes I hope to God he is."

Inside, they took the elevator and stepped out into the competent bustle of the recovery ward; Jack had been moved from intensive care the day before. His mom pointed out the room to him and he entered first. This was quite a different Jack from two days ago. He was sitting up in bed smiling a goofy grin. His left shoulder was bandaged.

"Here's the intrepid Luke Skywalker! I hear you've had quite an impressive series of adventures."

Jared felt himself blushing. A jolly Jack took him by surprise. He didn't know what to say. His father came in and asked, "How do you feel, Jack?"

"I feel great! I won't be tossing a basketball for a while, but they say I'll be good as new by next season. In the meantime, these are pretty nice drugs they've got me on."

Jack looked again at Jared. "You all right?"

He nodded his head. He had so much to say, but didn't know where to start.

"They told me you risked your life to save Russ," Jack said.

He blushed deeper.

"And the story goes," his father said to Jack," that you risked yours to save Jared ... except that you came a lot closer to losing it."

Jack laughed. "And I might have actually been of some use if I were a better batter with a pipe. Baseball never was my sport."

"No!" Jared cried. He hadn't meant to say it so loudly.

They all looked at him. "I mean," he continued, "if you hadn't come in, I wouldn't have gotten away from Ahmed, and Sara wouldn't have been able to shoot him." He looked around at everybody. "Don't you see? Jack *did* save my life!"

Jack was smiling at him. "And if you hadn't held that little spy thing, Sara wouldn't have been able to shoot him. So *you* saved *my* life."

"Well," his mom joined in, "with all that's happened over the last three days, I don't think it would be too difficult to see that each of you saved each other's lives." She grinned and raised one of her eyebrows. "And isn't that the way it's supposed to be?"

"You too, mom," Jared said.

"Excuse me?"

"You helped too when you stood up to Mr. Stegorski at our house."

She gave him a puzzled look.

"Up 'till then I was totally intimidated by him. I wouldn't ever have imagined that he could have killed Tony. But when you put him in his place, I saw him in a totally different way. I don't know ... he was just a mean man then, instead of some important government agent."

He ran out of steam and stood looking at his feet. That may have been the largest consecutive number of words he'd ever spoken to his family.

No, there was one more thing. He took a deep breath. "Jack," he said looking up at his stepfather, "I'm really sorry I didn't come to see you yesterday. I ... I *wanted* to."

Jack grew solemn and gave him a hard stare. "You say you wanted to come, but as I hear it you were having fun camping out."

It took him a second to understand that Jack was joking. "Yeah, but the fish weren't biting."

Jack broke into a grin. "I don't know, you caught quite a whopper—a rare species: Stegorskius-Criminalus."

A nurse bustled in and said, "The circus has to hit the road, it's time for baby's bath."

They filed out, but at the doorway he turned back to Jack. "Thanks," he said and just stood there.

Jack smiled broadly at him. "My pleasure." He gave a nod. "See you tomorrow."

He nodded back and hurried away to catch up to his mom and dad.

T he lab was dark. A door opened and the banks of fluorescent lights burst to life. Ted walked in, followed by Sara.

"First," Sara said, "I want to thank you for seeing me on a Saturday."

"My pleasure," Ted replied. "I had to stop by anyway—I left the tickets on my desk."

He pulled a lab chair over for her and sat down himself. "The adventures of the last week haven't been enough for the boys. The three of us are going to a concert tonight. The band's name is Bad Rap. It's obviously supposed to be a play on words ... multiple plays, I guess. "Bad" as in "good," and "bad rap" as in "I've been framed." I suspect, though, that I'm going to find the band's name simply accurate."

She chuckled. "I'm afraid, Dr. Martin, you're probably right. I'm embarrassed to admit that I have a friend who listens to them, mostly when she's driving. She claims that if anybody bothers her, she just turns it up. Even when I can't understand the words, I find myself intimidated just by the tone."

"Yes, I've heard some of it. I tell myself there's no words there that the boys haven't already heard. Then the band manages to surprise me with one *I* haven't heard in twenty years. I'm getting old, Sara. In my youth I would've been arrested for playing music like that."

"How *are* Jared and Russell?"

"They're boys. A day or two after they're nearly killed, they're complaining that they need a new computer game because their lives are too boring. Jared wants his mom to leave the wall in his room torn open—he thinks it looks cool."

"Are they here?"

"I left them in my office with strict instructions that they're to remain there under all circumstances short of the building catching on fire, and then only when they see the flames. We're coming back in tomorrow. We're going to see if we can get Jared's CAT working. They haven't gotten remote surveillance out of their system yet."

"I'll stop by and say 'hi' before I go." She folded her hands on her lap. "Now ... why I wanted to see you—"

"I can guess. You're looking for information about Stegorski and the drone. I had a call from his office yesterday. They wanted to make sure I understood what my security clearance meant and what I could, and could not, discuss. They don't want me to talk to anybody in law enforcement without somebody from their office present. They specifically mentioned the FBI."

"I see." She got up to go. "Well, that was quick."

"Sara, sit down, please. I didn't say I wasn't going to talk to you. I don't need them to help me interpret my security obligations, and I don't believe they have any authority over a criminal murder investigation."

"Actually, they might. It's not specifically spelled out in the statutes, but there's plenty of precedence—"

"I'm sorry," Ted interrupted, holding his hand to his ear, "I have problems hearing sometimes when the words aren't making any sense."

She smiled and sat back down. "Actually, I'm also interested in finding out about Tony Stone as well."

"Tony? Sure, I knew Tony for about eight years. We worked together at another company before Stelltech."

"Did he ever express any ... radical views?"

"Radical? Like terrorist tendencies? No, not at all."

"Actually, I wasn't thinking nearly so extreme—

conservationist associations, maybe?"

"Ah yes, that's a different story. You know, I'd almost forgotten Tony's environmental bent. He was pretty involved in the early days. He volunteered to lobby for various environmental bills. He was active in Green Peace. I used to kid him by calling him that, in fact—'Mr. Green Peace.' After a while, though, he seemed to give up on it. I think he was soured by the illogic of Washington politics ... I think I'm beginning to see the connection here. Just because he abandoned the political process doesn't necessarily mean he'd given up his passions."

Sara gave no response other than making notes. "Can you remember the names of some of these organizations or associations?"

"Let's see, it was a long time ago, and I wasn't all that tuned in. I do remember that he belonged to the Sierra Club. Then there was Green Peace, of course. There were others, I don't remember if I ever actually knew them."

"How about recently?"

"Umm, no, not at all ... at least, not that I knew of. We didn't have that much social contact in the last few years though."

"How about Stegorski?"

Dr. Martin put his hands in his pockets and rocked back and forth on his heels. "Let's think about this a moment. Although I have no problem helping where I can, we have to understand that a good portion of our development funding comes via MI. Now, regardless of any non-disclosure agreements or possible violations of security policies, there's the more fundamental matter of business—punching the patron in the nose, if you see what I mean."

"I understand, Dr. Martin. I knew when I came that I wasn't likely to get much."

"No, Sara, you're still misunderstanding me. When I say 'let's think about this,' I mean just that. I need to figure out how I can help. Tony was my friend and it's pretty clear that Stegorski killed him. It's simply a matter of how justice can be best served."

Sara studied her hands folded in her lap. She then looked up at

Ted. "Unfortunately it's not simply a matter of justice. Any time the government is involved it's never simple."

"I know that from first-hand experience working with MI. Also, I never imagined that Stegorski killed Tony for personal reasons."

"Right."

Sara took her time deciding her next move. She took a deep breath. "Dr. Martin, my job is to ask questions and get as much information as possible. The procedure is clear that I'm not supposed to offer information in return unless clearly appropriate. I find myself, however, in a position where I need a lot more of your help than I can get by generating a series of questions. Because of the technical complexities and the ... political complications, I'm going to set policy aside. These are deep and dirty waters we're about to go swimming in, and I'd like to suggest that we work as a team. We'll have to trust each other and look out for each other's interests."

Ted nodded slowly. "I hope that both of our interests, although originating from different places, point in the same direction." He smiled. "When Jared was younger and had problems in elementary school with teachers or classmates, I'd always tell him to just do the right thing, that he'd always know what that was if he asked himself. And I warned him that the right thing wasn't always going to be the easiest or best for him."

Sara looked at him.

"So!" he said, "Shall we get started?"

Sara smiled back. "I'll begin by jumping right in the deep water. I'm sure you can guess that government agencies run into each other in the course of their work, FBI-with-the-CIA, CIA-with-MI, and, of course, FBI and MI. Although the FBI had its own share of intrigue and secret agendas in the fifties and sixties—the Hoover regime—in the last decades it's been pretty much the straight shooter. That's a big reason why I pursued a career here rather than with the CIA. I haven't had to compromise my personal values with the FBI.

"Now, inter-agency conflicts typically get resolved at upper levels of the organizations. It's not uncommon for some of the stickiest to reach the White House, or, at least the staff. I want to nail Stegorski. MI is already making moves to divorce itself. They're calling him a 'rogue agent'. He was removed from Special Forces for being too aggressive, a maverick—that sort of thing.

"The reality, of course, is that he most assuredly had the buy-in of somebody in his agency. Stegorski's fall is unfolding in the open. I didn't go out of my way to keep it under wraps. It's important to put Stegorski away, but there's bigger fish that I'd like to add to the frying pan ... or, at least to splatter with some hot grease so they'll think twice next time about their methods. This can't be done publicly, though. The whole thing would be clamped hard and nothing would come of it. I can try to force trouble up and back down the command chain, though. I'm just a junior agent, but I know my boss will back me.

"But I need leverage. There's obviously something in the technology here that's so important, MI was willing to silence people. I'm guessing there's something beyond just the drone itself. So, here we come to it: what can you tell me?"

Ted was watching her thoughtfully. "What I'm about to tell you could spell the demise of Stelltech." Before she could react he continued, "Have you thought it odd that the drone could operate for so long without a change of batteries?"

Sara considered. "I hadn't thought about it until now, but, yes, I can see that it was definitely like the bunny that keeps going and going. Have you developed a new type of battery?"

Ted looked at her a couple of seconds before answering. "We, Stelltech, didn't develop the drone's power source. It came from MI. I have no idea what company actually made it. What I *do* know is that it's not a battery, at least not a battery as we know it. You may already understand that a battery, whether it's alkaline or lithium or whatever, generates its power from chemical reactions. Once the chemicals are used up, you change the battery or undo the chemical reactions via a recharge. Other examples of power sources are solar and fuel cells. The former requires a strong source of light and a fairly large surface area, and the latter, like the chemical batteries, has a limited supply of fuel. There's one other type of power source that we've known about for a long time..."

Ted let her make a guess. "Wind? No, of course not for something this small. Uh ... gas?"

Ted didn't respond.

"No, again too small. Gee, nuclear? Obviously not ... I'm grasping at straws here."

Ted shook his head. "No, you got it."

"Gas?"

He shook his head.

"*Nuclear*? That's crazy! Nuclear reactors are the size of buildings ... or at least cars."

"Traditional ones, yes. But traditional nuclear reactors are like steam engines in comparison to this technology. You see, a traditional nuclear reactor is nothing more than a heat source. The heat given off by the controlled nuclear chain reaction turns water into steam, which then drives turbines that generate electricity. It's no easy task refining the nuclear fuel and precisely controlling the reaction, let alone building in the 99.99 percent safety mechanisms. But, fundamentally a nuclear reactor operates exactly the same as a steam engine, except that the heat comes from decaying atomic nuclei rather than burning coal. And, as such, there's a lot of support structures and inefficiency. Most of the nuclear energy is dumped into the atmosphere or rivers as waste heat.

"Now, there are nuclear power sources that bypass the complex turbines, like the ones used in deep space probes, but still, they're using the heat indirectly to generate electricity. Again, the process is relatively inefficient, producing electrical energy from just a small fraction of the total energy given off by the nuclear reaction."

Sara raised her eyebrows. "I'm guessing that someone has figured out how to generate electricity directly from the nuclear reaction?"

"Truthfully, I don't know the exact mechanism. They won't

tell me anything, of course, but I can make some obvious inferences. I don't think that they can actually get electrons moving—which is what electrical energy is—directly from the nuclear reaction, but the process that they *have* developed is at a molecular level. They're taking advantage of the same nano-technology that we used to create the articulated arms and legs of the drone. The result is a power source that is very small and very efficient. Sara, I've heard estimates that the drone's power source will last from between fourteen and twenty years."

Sara's eyebrows arched. "The uses of this...." Her voice trailed off.

"Yes," Ted continued, "cars that run for a year before requiring a power cell change, artificial hearts that can operate for a person's entire lifetime, ... and, of course, tiny robot drones that can 'keep going' almost indefinitely."

Sara nodded slowly. "But, of all the possibilities, the only one we get is the spy drone, and then only for the military, all for the sake of 'national security.' "

Ted folded his arms. "We're beginning to see Tony's connection."

"Yes, it's pretty clear. Let me ask you about something else, though: what do you know about JSAD?"

"Ah, yes, the thorn in Stegorski's side. You probably know that it stands for 'Joint Service Applications Development.' Their charter is supposed to be to coordinate technology development across the military branches. The integration of MI's nuclear cell power source with our mini-drone began before JSAD took on oversight of the whole development. Stegorski absolutely hated the situation. He was convinced they were going to completely blow the secrecy of the whole thing."

Sara nodded. "That falls into place then. Tony was trying to go public with this nuclear cell technology. He was willing to sacrifice his career, and maybe go to jail, in order to get this technology into the public's hands. But he knew that he really needed an example to be effective. He was waiting for an opportunity to steal the drone. But he also knew that he couldn't just walk out with it. Once he did have it, he'd need time to line up the media. Without this time he understood that MI would be able to bring the clamp down before he could get the word out. I think Tony must have accidentally observed Jared take the drone from the lab and realized that this was his opportunity. He made it look like the cleaning people threw it out in the trash. But then he had to get the drone from Jared. That's when he called Ahmed for help."

She gave Ted a knowing look. "Here's the kicker: I think Stegorski had already hooked Tony up with Ahmed."

"What!"

"Yes, it sounds incredible, but MI had been monitoring advocacy groups that try to dig out government secrets, and, as a consequence, discovered that Tony Stone had been making overtures. Stegorski's plan was to use Tony as what they call a blind agent. I think his original intention was to simply expose security risks and internally discredit JSAD. That way MI could pull out of the whole thing before JSAD could cause too much damage. I imagine that by connecting Tony with Ahmed, Stegorski thought that having a recognized terrorist involved would lend credence to the whole scheme.

"I imagine Stegorski was going to bring the hammer down as soon as he'd collected enough evidence on Tony. Unfortunately for him, Jared threw his whole plan into a spin. Against all odds, right under their noses, a child got away with the drone. Jared was a curve ball for both Stegorski and Tony. Stegorski, originally the puppet master, now found himself scrambling with everybody else to just keep up. On top of that, the whole thing was on the verge of blowing out into the public arena. I can guess that Stegorski was thinking that you and I were not immediate threats, and that Jared and Russell were just kids nobody would pay attention to. That left Jack and Tony. Stegorski was alone with Tony. It was easy to make his death appear to be at the hands of Ahmed. My best guess is that Stegorski would have made sure that Ahmed didn't survive long either if I hadn't already taken care of that. I'm not sure what he would've done about Jack. I'd like to believe that he'd have arranged a close watch to see if he was going to cause trouble. In any case, Jack may not have known enough to be a problem anyway."

Ted was frowning. "I find this hard to swallow. It sounds like the plot from a Tom Clancy book. I can't believe that MI would sanction murder."

Sara shrugged. "Directions to agents such as Stegorski aren't always very specific. I'm quite sure you'll never find instructions to kill civilians written down anywhere, but agents at that level understand how to read between the lines. Stegorski knew full well that he'd be left out on the line if he were found out. My task now is to yank on enough people up the line inside MI to make them think twice before implicitly allowing this sort of thing next time."

Ted sighed. "At least I won't regret the inevitable end to Stelltech's relationship with MI."

Sara grinned. "You never know what I might get out of Stegorski yet. He might tell me everything you have." She winked.

Ted looked at her, not understanding. He then nodded. "I see. You'll more or less put words into his mouth."

Sara only raised one eyebrow.

Ted grinned and shrugged. "Maybe they'll buy it."

Sara got up to leave.

Ted said, "There's a couple of questions about Stegorski's pursuit of Jared you might be able to help me with."

She sat back down. "Shoot."

"Jared tells me that Stegorski almost had him when he was hiding at the motel, but somebody came to the fence and distracted him. Was that you?"

"No, I was still on my way. That was Russell. When he called me, I told him very clearly to stay away. So, of course, he rushed over to try to help his friend."

Ted smiled. "The other mystery was how Stegorski was able to track Jared around like a blood-hound."

Sara nodded. "Stegorski had your drone tracking box, and, of course, he was able to use that when Jared wasn't wearing the visor. But mainly he used the bugged knife that he'd given to Jared. Stegorski could hear the McDonald's attendant when Jared was hiding behind the trash bin. Later he tracked Jared to the warehouse by simple proximity detection. Stegorski knew that he could only pick up the signal from the knife within a certain range—something like an eighth of a mile or so. He just drove around, and when he picked up the signal from the knife, he established a few perimeter points and found the commercial strip. He picked the actual warehouse bay by intuition, the same reasons that Jared had used. Then, by making sounds with a stick hitting the ground he used a kind of sonar to find Jared's barrel, except instead of picking up returning echoes, he listened directly through the bugged knife. Stegorski isn't really very bright with technology. These are all techniques he'd used in the Special Forces ... until he got booted."

Ted stood up. "Okay, thanks. We'd better be going, the boys must be getting pretty bored in my office by now."

He opened the door to the lab and held it for Sara. As she walked through he said, "Uh, Sara, would you like to have dinner some night?"

She smiled at him and nodded as the lab door closed.

She hadn't noticed the fly clinging to his belt at his back.

CHAPTER FORTY-NINE

In his dad's office, Jared pulled the visor off his head. As he did so he accidentally ripped the earphones plugged into the auxiliary jack from Russ's head as well.

"Ow!" Russ cried. "Watch it Martin! Are you daft?"

He ignored the complaint. "I can't believe this! Russ how did you get the drone?"

His friend sat, looking smug. "I can't divulge that."

He sometimes thought he really could strangle him. "Come on, Russ, tell me! Dad's going to be back any second."

Russ was sitting in his dad's chair and he put his feet up on the desk and leaned his head back against his intertwined fingers. "I went back to the warehouse Wednesday. I just wanted to see what it was like. Some Stelltech people were looking for the drone, but I don't think they were all that serious."

"Why not?"

"They poked around and used a rake, but they weren't willing to disturb a dead rat."

"The same rat that was in the barrel with me?"

"Right. They never moved it—it stunk pretty bad."

"You mean the drone was *under* the rat?"

Russ grinned.

They heard footsteps coming down the hall.

Jared shook his head. "Oh Russ," he grinned, "why do I have the distinct feeling we're not done with our little friend yet?"

****

After a few minutes the lights automatically shut off and the Stelltech lab was empty once again—very empty.